Tr

Matthew Law studied Fine Art at Central St Martins and Creative Writing at the University of East Anglia. An established screenwriter (as Matthew Law McGuchan), his work has been commissioned by companies including Gold Circle, Element Films, Warp X, Channel 4, BBC2 and the UK Film Council. Two of his scripts have been produced as feature films, 2003's *LD 50 Lethal Dose* and 2012's *Truth or Dare*. TRIGGER POINT is his first novel, part of an ongoing collaboration with Pure Grass Films that also includes web episodes and a full-length feature film adaptation. Matthew lives in Ipswich, Suffolk with his wife, Maria, and two sons, Joseph and Patrick.

Pure Grass Films (www.puregrassfilms.com) is an award-winning production company based in London. Pure Grass have created and launched a range of successful digital entertainment properties such as Beyond the Rave (MySpace's first digital series outside the US) and Kirill (MSN's first drama series in the UK, which won a Webby and was nominated for a Digital Emmy). The company are currently developing a range of feature film and television properties, including a modern adaptation of *Oliver Twist* called *Twist*. Pure Grass conceived the original idea for TRIGGER POINT, and partnered with Matthew Law to develop the novel, web series and an upcoming feature film. The company is run by CEO Ben Grass, and Chairman Christophe Charlier (also the Chairman of the Brooklyn Nets NBA Basketball team).

MATTHEW LAW

Trigger Point

HODDER

First published in Great Britain in 2013 by Hodder & Stoughton
An Hachette UK Company

1

Copyright © Pure Grass Films 2013

A CIP catalogue record for this title is available from the British Library.

B-format ISBN 978 1 444 72683 1
eBook ISBN 978 1 444 72687 9

Printed and bound by CPI Group (UK) Ltd, Croydon, CR0 4YY

Hodder & Stoughton policy is to use papers that are natural,
renewable and recyclable products and made from wood grown in
sustainable forests. The logging and manufacturing processes are expected
to conform to the environmental regulations of the country of origin.

Hodder & Stoughton Ltd
338 Euston Road
London NW1 3BH

www.hodder.co.uk

Trigger Point

Prologue

Between punches, Guy MacMillan thought of magnolias. A fine example had overshadowed his childhood garden in Winterville, Georgia. It bloomed early; by April its knotted boughs were sagging under the weight of cream-coloured blossom. As spring headed into summer, his young sister would demand he throw his football into the branches, hard as he could, while she lay on the lawn beneath and the thick, pink-edged petals showered down. Now, as he knelt in the dust of Safed Koh, the swish of his captors' robes became the rush of wind about the ball; the crack of knuckles into his ribs became the sound of branches snapping. Forty years on from Winterville, war-hardened correspondent Guy MacMillan was facing death at the hands of Islamist insurgents – but under the darkness of his sackcloth hood, petals fell.

Not that it was ever truly dark in this particular corner of northwest Pakistan. Clouds were rare, and even on a moonless night, the stars were impossibly bright. The days were bathed in a fierce, dry light that seeped into every pore, ubiquitous as the dust. Even the shadows seemed filled with it. MacMillan had been held hostage for months now, in the crumbling ruins of a mountain fortress that dated back to the Mughal era. He'd lost count of the individual days – though he'd promised himself he wouldn't. Yet still the sunlight and the stars amazed him.

A heavy blow knocked him to the ground, accompanied by a flurry of insults in the local Pashtun dialect, of which he understood a little. Face down, he tasted blood, stinging his chapped lips, high notes to the deep bass throb of discomfort radiating from his torso. Pain played endless music within him, sometimes the sharp orchestral stabs of fractured bones, more often the whining dissonance of hunger and thirst. But never silence. Beyond the brutalisation of his flesh, the simplistic 'good cop, bad cop' routines of his captors had softened him up thoroughly. After a string of beatings, it was impossible not to feel gratitude at the small kindnesses of food or blankets, even though bitter experience told him he had no friends here. The predictability of it all only made the anticipation worse. There was no hope for MacMillan; only endurance until the inevitable end. And so he reached back into his past, wandered there, seeking distraction as much as self-knowledge. The magnolia, the moon landing, teenage activism, the *Washington Post*, the Berlin Wall, petals falling . . .

Footsteps on the flagstones brought him round. Dread sparked, as he replayed the details of his latest beating: had the guards seemed more on edge than usual? They'd hardly started before they'd knocked him down and cursed his name: why were they stopping so soon? Had there been a change of plan? A hundred smaller questions swarmed in moments to form the one big question that overrode all others: *Is this my time to die?*

He had never believed in God, not even as a headstrong child in Winterville, certainly not as a frequent witness to the thuggery meted out in the name of religion by fanatics the world over. And yet as the footsteps came to a stop just inches away from his face, the words spilled like tears from his trembling mouth: *Our father, who art in Heaven, hallow'd be thy name—*

'Your God does not see into these mountains, Mister MacMillan'. The hood came off, leaving him blinking and half-blind. Massoud Ahmed stood before him: in his late thirties, he projected calm authority. His eyes showed keen intelligence; his beard was clipped and tidy, as ever. If it wasn't for the traditional robes of the feudal warlord, he could have been mistaken for a college lecturer. He sank to his haunches in front of the journalist, who shuffled back until he was pressed against the wall. Ahmed wanted eye contact; MacMillan offered it reluctantly.

'You pray for this ordeal to end, yes?'

MacMillan said nothing.

'I assure you, it will end soon.'

What did that mean? They'd had this kind of exchange before, Ahmed sharing softly voiced intimations of a grand design in motion while his own mind spun with pain and fear. MacMillan understood the insurgent leader's political purpose, but he still hadn't grasped why he chose to share these quiet, oddly close moments with his hostage. Was it compassion at play? He doubted it. He had written more than one report dissecting Ahmed and his kind, exposing the posturing, turf wars and criminal self-interest that lay behind so many supposedly 'holy' missions. More likely Ahmed took a subtle pleasure in his dominance; or worse, it was the simple savouring of the kill, drawn out over months of anticipation.

The hurried approach of a guard broke the spell. A hasty exchange took place, and MacMillan did his best to translate the words in his head. Something, or someone, had arrived in Peshawar. Russians? Ahmed was issuing orders; two guards departed swiftly.

Russians in Peshawar? Ahmed's was one of a number of factions in the region vying to earn itself a place on the world's front pages, and with international nerve-endings deadened to the impact of suicide bombing, more spectacular means of drawing attention were being sought. Could there be a connection between Ahmed's ambitions and this mysterious shred of news?

MacMillan could hear the sounds of activity spreading through the compound: footsteps, voices, vehicles firing up. Whatever the Russians were bringing, its significance was known to everyone in the fortress. Ahmed turned back to face his prisoner. His gaze glittered.

'Extraordinary times lie ahead, my friend. Extraordinary times.' The rebel smiled, exhilaration held in check as he straightened up and walked from the dusty cell, leaving a solitary, stony-faced guard on duty. MacMillan closed his eyes and sank back, cold sweat breaking out as a thought gripped hold of him, nauseating in its quiet certainty: he would not see Winterville again.

One

It didn't feel like lying any more, Tom Wisher reflected. After four months undercover – 126 days, to be precise – he was, as Blake had predicted, eating, sleeping and shitting the mercenary life. He recalled the fictional past of his alias, Jim Thompson, more often than he thought of his own. He drank contraband liquor when Graff and his crew drank, shared the hookah when they smoked. He had visited Peshawar's brothels on occasion, and enjoyed his time there – well, 'Thompson' enjoyed it, and was considered a good customer. Watching at a remove within himself, Wisher was not sorry to relieve the build-up of sexual tension that was natural in any twenty-seven-year-old male. But his knowledge that some of these girls would be underage, most would have been trafficked, all would certainly have been intimidated, bullied or raped to ensure their submission, brought with it a burden of guilt that he struggled to process.

At least the lying was easy. His CIA training had covered various role-play scenarios, and his memory was superb, refined by out-of-hours study in a bid to top his fellow cadets at Camp Peary. After 126 days, posing as army-deserter-turned-freebooter, Jim Thompson was a walk in the park: what elevated Wisher's pulse right now, tightening his chest and adding a sheen of perspiration to his palms, was the concealed surveillance technology he wore.

His wristwatch contained a pinhead camera and microphone; a wireless transmitter was built into the padded back of a holster-style money belt that he wore under his shirt. A single thin wire ran to the MP3 player that served as a disguised power supply. Wearing a surveillance device in such close quarters was one hell of a risk; its discovery would be proof positive of his duplicity. If he were exposed, he would certainly have to kill the men who had become his comrades-in-arms these past months, or be killed himself. Mercy was not in their DNA.

Wisher sat with Graff and his colleagues, Turturro and Singh, in the dingy recesses of a Peshawar street café, doing what they did most often of all: wait. He'd grown accustomed to the buzz of thick, sweet Pakistani coffee and the fragrant shisha fumes that coiled inside his lungs. The tobacco had brought down his fitness levels, but he was confident he could still run four hundred metres in fifty seconds, or kick himself an exit through the café's cinder-block walls, should the need arise. He was younger than his fellow mercenaries, clean-shaven and light on his feet – but he was stronger than he looked, and he knew how to focus that strength.

The gigs, when they came, were for hired muscle, standing guard or riding shotgun for the various black-market ops in play around the Pakistan–Afghanistan border. Wisher had dealt arms, delivered drugs, roughed up debtors. He hadn't had to take a life yet, but he would, if called upon, whatever the blow to his private moral compass. Rescuing Guy MacMillan meant that much.

It was not merely the fact that MacMillan was an American citizen held prisoner by foreign nationals. The veteran journalist was a symbol of the democratic principles that legitimised US foreign policy in territories like

Afghanistan; thus his kidnap was also symbolic, a middle finger flipped defiantly towards the West. And the apologist broadcasts he had been forced to make since his capture, though clearly the words of a broken man, were an embarrassment.

Beyond all that, there were personal reasons: an agenda that Wisher had kept secret from his superiors at CIA headquarters in Langley. The young agent had fought hard to get this assignment, his first in the field, and he wasn't about to let nerves screw it up. Feigning lassitude, he reached across to the chessboard, his hand slow and steady as he brought a second knight into play. Across the board from him, Turturro frowned. Wisher's wasn't the smartest of moves, truth be told; but then Turturro wasn't the smartest of players.

Graff passed the hookah pipe over the low table and Wisher inhaled deeply from it. Graff liked him, he knew. Turturro was a hard worker but lacked imagination; Singh was getting old, and had a tendency to moan. Wisher as 'Thompson' was disciplined and good with weapons, keen to stay busy and kept his thoughts to himself. Wisher speculated that Graff saw a younger version of himself in Thompson: a talented infantryman who could have risen through the ranks, if the dice had rolled differently.

Wisher played his alias as having an unspoken trauma at the heart of his story, that had tipped the scales from duty to desertion. One vodka-soaked evening, Graff had confessed something similar: German by birth, he'd been the gunner on a UN armoured patrol vehicle during the Bosnian War of the early 1990s, and had taken point on a patrol into the disputed eastern territories of that fractured state. Heading off road, he'd run into a ditch that turned out to be a mass grave, dismembered women and children in the main. Graff lost his faith in humanity after that. He finished his tour but skipped the flight home, taking up instead with a band of Serb smugglers running ordnance through Turkey to fuel the endless Afghan unrest. His only loyalty now was to himself.

Since that drunken night there'd been an expectation from Graff that 'Thompson' would reveal the events that triggered his own unauthorised exit from Camp Leatherneck, the US Marine base in Helmand Province. Wisher had been prevaricating between a number of back stories, uncertain as to which would best cement Graff's trust in him. If this latest gig panned out as he hoped, however, he wouldn't need to decide.

The grizzled squad leader's eyes were fixed firmly on the open doorway that led to the sun-bleached street outside. The clients were overdue, but that was not unusual given the poor state of Pakistan's transport network. Wisher knew they were Russian; Graff had also mentioned Safed Koh in passing – an indiscretion that had prompted the surveillance device. The Agency's best intel pointed to the bleak north western mountain range as the most likely hiding place for MacMillan. A delivery run into this terrain gave Wisher a good shot at getting close to his objective. He might not get another such chance for weeks – and the consensus at CIA headquarters in Langley was that the clock was ticking towards MacMillan's execution.

The Russians arrived, and Wisher snapped into focus. Three burly Caucasians in pale suits and Ray-Ban shades, blocking the light as they strode into the narrow café – they may as well have had 'mafioso' tattooed on their foreheads. Not that it bothered these men: they had no need to dissemble in a city that thrived on intrigue. Two had briefcases handcuffed to their wrists; they flanked the lead courier, a pace behind him.

The point man introduced himself as Sergei, his cohorts as Victor and Fyodor. Graff named his crew in return. The briefcases were set down; Wisher noted how the couriers' wrist-veins were distended beneath the handcuffs – those cases were *heavy*. Certainly it was not cash inside; more likely it was gold, a secure currency in troubled times – though why such a consignment should be heading into the wilderness of Safed Koh was far from obvious.

The Russians joined the mercenaries at the low table. Stony glances all round; Fyodor straightened his jacket, pulling it down tight so the shape of the handgun beneath was visible, then glowering at Wisher to check his point had been made. Wisher glanced away dismissively. These meetings were expected to be tense.

Sergei flattened a crumpled computer print-out on to the tabletop: a map, with several handwritten annotations. His accent was thick when he spoke:

'You will drive us here, stand guard while we make the trade, then return us to Peshawar.'

'If the price is right.' Graff liked to keep it simple.

Victor fished an envelope from his pocket, slid it across the table. As Graff counted the cash inside, Wisher tilted his wrist to get a clear shot of the map, risking a casual glance himself. The destination was circled, a note scrawled in Cyrillic beside it: МАСОД АМЭД. Wisher had taken a course in basic Russian at college, already thinking about a career in the Secret Service. His knowledge of the language was sufficient to sound out the words in his head: Massoud Ahmed.

Wisher's pulse jumped significantly. He'd hit the jackpot. In a hotel room just a few miles away, Bill Blake would see the words relayed on to his laptop screen and would alert the chain of command. Ahmed had

MacMillan, this was certain, but his location had been impossible to pin down amid the wilderness of Safed Koh – and now Wisher was being hired to deliver Russian bullion to his doorstep!

Strict protocol dictated that he should stay undercover and gather intelligence for a military manoeuvre on the insurgent stronghold. But the pressing nature of the threat to MacMillan meant Wisher had the authority to seize the moment, should it arise. The mercenaries and their paymasters wouldn't set off till first light. Blake was tracking them via satellite: all Wisher needed was a well-timed diversion – a fly-by, or some rocket fire – and he could do the rest. He could get MacMillan out.

As Wisher's mind raced, so Graff slipped the envelope inside his own jacket, grunting approval at the fee. Sergei leant close to address him, supposedly with discretion, though his voice was more of a stage whisper.

'Florescu is taking a personal interest in this transaction. A successful outcome would be very beneficial – for all of us.'

Graff scowled. The words sounded almost like a threat.

'We wouldn't want to disappoint Mister Florescu.'

Sergei shot the grizzled mercenary a sour look – then offered a dry smile at the sarcasm. The tension ebbed, albeit only slightly.

Mercs and Russians would stay close now until the set-off at 0500, a chance to smoke and swap stories, getting the measure of each other before sharing a day's drive into one of the world's most hostile territories. Wisher would use the time to find his 'centre' and hunker down close to it – not his physical centre of balance, his spiritual centre, though this wasn't a word he would use himself. Combat wasn't sport for him, it was the expression of his will. The outcome of tomorrow's events would hinge on his ability to call upon his body's resources. Every sense, every sinew, had to be on full alert.

His cellphone buzzed in his pocket, three times on silent, then stopped, a coded message from Blake: *Make contact.*

'You play?' Fyodor was indicating the chessboard, laid out in mid-match.

Wisher nodded. 'Sure.'

'I give you game,' continued the Russian. Wisher glanced at Turturro, who shrugged. Fyodor started rearranging the pieces. There was a gleam in his eyes; he clearly fancied his chances.

'I make you white,' he grinned. Wisher smiled back; he had no problem with taking the man's money off him.

In his breast pocket, his cellphone buzzed again, three times on silent, then it stopped.

Make contact . . .

TWO

'This is risky.'

Wisher hadn't wanted to take the call, hadn't wanted to draw attention his way while the atmosphere was so charged. But Blake had been persistent; then Fyodor had received a call of his own, and Wisher had used the break in play to slip outside.

Down the line, Blake cut straight to the chase. 'There's been a change of plan. We want the delivery to go through. We can't risk trying to reach the hostage.'

'What?' Wisher could hardly make sense of the words. How could the rescue of an American hostage be less important than some kind of black-market money deal?

'I know how much you've invested in this, Tom, believe me. But this comes from the top.'

Wisher glanced round, partly to check for eavesdroppers, but also to snatch a moment away from the catastrophe that was starting to unfold.

'What happens to MacMillan?'

'We can't help him right now.'

The statement lodged itself in Wisher's mind, rancid and indigestible. Blake was undoubtedly speaking the truth. Yet he also had at least some notion of Wisher's personal stake in the mission. He'd been at the briefing that spring as the designated point of contact for the deep-cover operation in Peshawar. He knew the city well from his own tour in the early nineties and had run seminars for the Agency's trainees during his stateside sojourns. Wisher had connected well with him even then: his gruff, no-bullshit manner stood in contrast to some of the other senior officers, who could seem cerebral and disengaged. Blake was a bit rough around the edges, his still-powerful physique starting to thicken round the middle, but he was the real deal.

He was smart, too. He'd picked up on something at the briefing, an over-zealous edge to Wisher's attitude that his pen-pushing section chief, John Morgan, had failed to register. He'd collared the young agent in the corridor afterwards:

'MacMillan was in the Gulf in ninety-one, right?'

Wisher had tried his best to shrug the observation off, but Blake had pursued the line:

'Same time as your father. So there's history there.'

It was true. USAF Flight Captain Frank Wisher had flown Tornadoes out of Saudi Arabia during the first Gulf War. He'd been shot down behind enemy lines, taken prisoner when his chute got tangled in pylons south of Baghdad. He'd died out there, executed by officers of Saddam Hussein's imperial guard. This was in the public record. Less well known was the fact that Guy MacMillan had been the last US citizen to see Frank Wisher alive.

The memories were private. Wisher was rattled, but he kept guard of them.

'I want this mission, sir.'

'I hear you.' Blake could have chosen to push the point. Instead he put his hands on Wisher's shoulders and fixed him with a hard but not unfriendly stare: 'Head first, heart second. That's all I'm saying.' Wisher nodded, surprised and relieved to be off the hook. Blake had already made a start towards the canteen before he thought to dig further into his intentions:

'Bill— '

'It stays with me, buddy.' A glance back from Blake, and he was gone through the swing doors. Those few casual words had earned him Wisher's respect – and his trust. Until a few moments ago, he would have taken a bullet for the man. But now, this . . .

Blake was still talking down the line, something about Tom keeping the wire on, making sure he made a thorough sweep of Ahmed's base, they'd get another crack at extracting MacMillan. Wisher wasn't taking it in. He was remembering the war correspondent's visit to the family's overseas billet at RAF Woodbridge in Suffolk, in the days that followed the announcement of his father's death. They weren't the only US Air Force family stationed in the east of England during the Cold War and the Gulf War that followed – but they were one of the few to receive such bleak news.

Wisher had been seven years old at the time; his sister Rachel only four. MacMillan must have been pushing forty; the child in Wisher recalled his appearance as somewhat scary, unshaven and with deep, tired eyes. But his voice was warm and articulate – comforting to the young siblings. He'd sat with them on the bare lawn outside the barracks, shared with them a story about his own childhood, playing with his sister under a magnolia tree. He'd told the boy Wisher that sisters were precious, and it was a brother's duty to watch out for them. Then he'd explained that their father had died protecting something that was precious to all of them.

Later, Wisher had slipped away from the TV to listen at the door as MacMillan told his mother about the desperate effort to negotiate her husband's release, and their brief meeting in a Baghdad jail. The correspondent took her hands gently in his own as he passed on Frank

Wisher's declaration of love to her and their children; the reason for his visit, this last request of a condemned man. Stood behind the crack of the door, the boy had trembled as emotion surged through him. Twenty years on, those same feelings welled up again inside the man.

'Are we cool, Tom?' Blake's voice, tinny down the phone, cut through the stillness. Wisher narrowed his eyes.

'Sure, we're cool.'

Wisher hung up. In a hotel room nearby, Bill Blake slipped off his headset and frowned at his laptop screen, which showed a grainy image of the back alley where Wisher stood. The spycam point-of-view reeled as the undercover agent headed back indoors. Blake pushed his chair away from the desk and let his gaze drift out through the shutters and across the rooftops of night-time Peshawar, his mind racing in frantic calculation.

In the crumbling fortress of Safed Koh, Guy MacMillan was the centre of attention for a small band of insurgents, who seemed to find great amusement in forcing him to adopt the Murgha stress position. Gun barrels and bayonet tips prodded him until he was bent over with his arms between his legs, holding on to his ears. Once a popular classroom punishment, it was humiliating in the extreme – not to mention agonisingly painful after a few minutes.

This particular session lasted for more than an hour. When it was over, and MacMillan was alone once more in the darkness of his cell, he stared up through the high window at the constellations far above. In his mind's eye, he drew lines between the stars to create the shimmering outlines of men and beasts, locked in their eternal dance against the pale band of the Milky Way – and not for the first time since his incarceration, he wept.

Three

'Fuck.'

Turturro cursed as the pickup truck hit a pothole, scattering a handful of rounds across the floor. Fyodor picked up one of the bullets and examined it.

'Hollow point,' he observed. 'Make a big hole, yes?'

Turturro nodded. 'They're NATO rounds. I drill them out myself.' He grinned. 'It's sort of a hobby.'

Fyodor pulled a massive handgun from inside his jacket, thumbed a bullet from the magazine to show Turturro.

'Armour-piercing – from Belgium. Copper jacket, steel core. Very nasty.'

Turturro whistled, impressed. Fyodor's lips peeled back in a smile, revealing huge, discoloured teeth. He liked guns.

Behind the wheel in the driver's cab, Wisher scanned the bleak terrain that stretched out on all sides. Forty miles southwest of Peshawar, the going was slow along a rugged track winding into the Safed Koh range. They'd left greenery some distance behind; the ground was bare and rocky, crumpled and gouged with ravines for much of its extent – plenty of cover, Wisher noted, should cover be required. Singh drove the pickup truck that rattled ahead of him, with Sergei and Victor as his passengers; in the back, Graff stood behind his beloved Browning M2 machine gun, which was tripod-mounted to provide 360 degrees of targeting opportunities.

Wisher was tooled up himself, with an ex-service Glock in a shoulder holster and an M16 assault rifle wedged into custom straps on the driver's door, not to mention a pair of M67 grenades in a webbing pouch on his belt. He still wore the watch containing the hidden camera; Blake would be trailing at a distance, keeping to the limit of the device's range. Wisher's orders were clear: scope out Ahmed's base, map the layout, estimate head-count and armaments. Don't move on the hostage; don't jeopardise the delivery. Head first, heart second. Don't question the chain of command. Don't speculate about the sleek, heavy briefcases the Russians carried, a delivery of such significance that 127 days of field work could be over-ridden, with likely fatal consequences for MacMillan. Backup was no longer in place; the only option was to stay 'on mission'. Head first, heart second.

The pickup mounted a rise up ahead and dipped briefly out of sight. Wisher shifted down from second to first gear and gunned up the short slope. As he crested the rise, the fortress came into view. A huge, ramshackle structure built from cement and local stone, it must have made quite an impression in centuries gone by. The outer wall measured around sixty metres along its side, though it was breached in several places. The battlements were topped with razor wire behind which guards paced, rifles at the ready.

The vehicles drove through the main gate and into a cratered forecourt littered with slabs of fallen masonry, daubed with militant slogans. The main building was two stories high, with towers at each corner and a central keep that rose to the level of the outer wall. It had suffered significant damage over the years and the structure was precarious in places. But it remained imposing.

Wisher's eyes darted round. He quickly counted

fourteen hostiles, of which three were boys; there were bound to be more within the main fortress. Efforts had been made to keep the size and nature of the base hidden from satellite eyes; vehicles were covered by tarpaulins and dressed down with dust and stones; supplies and weapons were stacked in doorways and alcoves. Only a battered Nissan was parked in plain sight – and that particular car was so rusty, it could pass for derelict.

Graff raised his hand and the two vehicles drew to a halt in the centre of the forecourt. The mercs and Russian couriers disembarked cautiously; Graff stayed in the pickup, his grip tight on the handles of the M2. Wisher took a deep swig from his canteen, then slung his rifle and stepped out to join the others.

A band of insurgents stood waiting, bearded men in grimy desert robes, fingers on triggers, instinctively distrustful of the infidels in their midst. Graff called down from his post:

'Let's keep this nice and friendly.'

A trim figure stepped forward, dressed in black, a sign of status: Massoud Ahmed himself. Wisher drew in a long slow breath. He hadn't smoked since the previous afternoon. His lungs felt clean, the mountain air was crisp and energizing. It was important to stay hydrated: other than that, all he needed right now was oxygen. He visualised himself as a furnace, filled with smouldering coals that lit up as he drew the air across them. A crucible tipped, and rivulets of molten metal sped down the channels of his veins, awakening limbs and senses. As he stepped from the cover of the pickup and into the sights of a dozen rebel gunmen, he had to hold back a grin. He knew it was adrenaline, but it felt like . . . *joy*. He was in the zone. He could do anything.

'Singh, point left. Thompson, top left. Turturro, top right.'

The mercenaries fanned out across the forecourt as the Russians stepped up to Ahmed and his men, briefcases in hand. Wisher was within twenty yards of the main keep. A guard stood inside its deep-set entranceway, observing the exchange in the main courtyard; the only windows were fifteen feet above ground level. *If I had a hostage,* Wisher thought, *that's where I'd keep him.*

He continued his sweep, veering closer to the keep itself. Two camouflaged vehicles were parked head to toe in the shade of its high wall, providing a straight line of cover to the entranceway. *Head first . . .*

An order was barked in Pashtun and the guard in the entrance snapped to attention, running out into the courtyard. Wisher glanced back toward the centre; a trestle table was being set up with lab kit spread out on it, and one of the insurgents was pulling on protective gloves. If the delivery was gold bullion, they would want to test it for purity.

The thought was gone almost as soon as it had arrived. The keep was now unguarded. All eyes were on the scene unfolding in the forecourt. He had a window.

Heart second . . .

Wisher darted, low and quiet. He knew Blake could follow his actions via the spycam; he could only hope that his handler would understand his motivations and back him up. A quick glance as he passed showed him keys in the ignition of one of the parked cars. Within seconds he was inside the fortress. Barely pausing, he pushed forward down a dim corridor, rifle trained, eyes adjusting as he scanned a doorway to his left. Stacks of rifles were stored in the side room; rocket-propelled grenades in boxes, cases of ammunition. A second storeroom held more of the same. Ahmed must be trading weapons; no way he needed all this kit.

Corner turn to the right – straight into a guard. The man raised his gun, startled, clumsy; Wisher snapped out his rifle butt. The guard's nose broke open like a ripe tomato, blood spattering as he keeled backwards. A second blow to the head made sure he would stay down. Wisher stepped over him, hardly breaking his stride.

The corridor opened out into a central room. There were no doors as such in this ancient section of the building, just archways leading off on either side, any of which could hide an attacker. Wisher stepped quickly from post to post, aware that he was exposed. But there was no turning back. He pressed his eye to the rifle sight, kept his back to the wall where he could. One doorway at a time – sound carried from the forecourt, Ahmed's clipped English, Sergei's bullish monotone, as the testing proceeded – Wisher crept onwards, willing his own movements to silence.

The figure knelt in a shaft of sunlight. Beneath the sacking hood, a head twitched at the sound of footsteps approaching. The voice was filled with fear, battling to maintain dignity:

'I'm an American citizen. Please, think about what you're doing— '

Wisher fished a small, stubby syringe from a webbing pocket, pushed it through MacMillan's ragged shirt sleeve, into his upper arm. The older man gasped, recoiling too slow from the needle and the certain oblivion it bore:

'Please, God, no— !'

Wisher took hold of the sacking hood, pulled it away – and felt his childhood surge back to him. It was the sight of Guy MacMillan, blinking up at him. The news of his father's death had been brought by this thin ghost of a man. In this moment of recognition, it seemed like all he knew about himself came from that sad encounter. Emotion exploded but was contained, like a bomb test deep underground. The dazed instant passed and Wisher snapped back into focus:

'It's a satellite tag. We can't lose you now.'

The habit of fear fell away from MacMillan as he stared with something approaching wonder at the intense young man crouched beside him, untying his bonds.

'Is it just you?'

There wasn't a comfortable answer to that question. Wisher pulled the ropes free and helped MacMillan to his feet. Faint in the distance, a cellphone rang; Wisher barely registered the sound.

'There's cover north of the fortress. Stay low, don't try to outrun them. Just keep out of sight.'

'What about you?'

'I'll make sure they're looking the other way.'

He'd spotted a roll of firing cable in amongst the cache of weapons that he could wire to the detonator caps he kept dry in a watertight pouch. His only concern now was making sure he didn't end up twenty yards above the ground and disintegrating along with the rest of the fortress and its occupants.

'I know you. How do I know you?'

MacMillan's eyes, though bloodshot, had regained their keenness. His mind, unfolding from its dark corner, had resumed its journalistic habits, sorting memories, making connections. There was something about this particular young mercenary . . .

'You knew my father.' The words emerged unbidden, uttered before Wisher could clamp his mouth shut. MacMillan seemed to shed ten years in a moment as information converted into revelation:

'You're Frank Wisher's boy.'

Smoke and flame coiled up the subterranean shaft of memory; Wisher choked them back.

'I know you fought to get him back. Risked your own life. Thank you for that.'

'Wish I could have brought his body home.'

MacMillan sought out his rescuer's eyes. He seemed to want to say more.

The moment passed quickly. Instead, he offered a handshake.

'I'll see you soon.'

The two men went their separate ways: MacMillan toward the rear of the fortress, where a crumbled wall offered his best chance of escaping undetected; Wisher retracing his steps to the cache of ordnance. He kept it sharp, attention focused outwards and ahead, visualising each turn before he took it, snapping round corners in a crouch, back to the wall, assault rifle levelled. Pure action, pure agency, but behind that, deep within the clockwork of his mind, something had fallen into place. A thread had been drawn from the past through to now. A lever under permanent strain had shifted some inches towards balance. Wisher had defied orders, but he had done right by his father's memory, and he was proud of that fact.

One more turn to the exit corridor. The ordnance was stored in two rooms to the left, he could see it clearly in his mind's eye. But there were footsteps approaching, three men, instinct told him. He needed time to set the charges, and a confrontation now could lose him those precious undisturbed moments. Oozing like a shadow, he slipped back into a doorway.

Cold metal pressed into the back of his neck. Cold and sharp, a blade breaking the skin. A bayonet.

A voice was barking at him. He couldn't make out the words. It was like a wind tunnel, the silent rush of adrenaline that stripped all detail from his perceptions apart from that cold metal tip and warm blood seeping from under it. He raised his arms, slowly, because he knew that was how he was meant to seem. In fractions of a second bone and muscle would snap to his command, pivoting him fast enough to beat the trigger finger hanging in the void behind him.

But there were three more of them. In front of him, guns raised and trained. They'd come looking for him and they'd found him. His eyes darted, seeking the best exit window. But their eyes were bright too. Fire coursed through them like it did through him. One had taken hold of his rifle – he had to let it go. He couldn't dodge four bullets; the best he could hope for was to take one or two of his enemies down with him. His mind darted, recalling the distant sound of a cellphone.

Had they been tipped off?

Four

Where the hell is Thompson?

Graff's poise was slipping from him; his by-the-numbers handover was starting to fall apart. It had started off smoothly enough, both sides strung out but playing by the rules. The Russians had been stone-faced but compliant as Massoud's team inspected the merchandise. He'd assumed gold – he'd handled a 'good delivery' bar one time, post-Gulf War contraband passing through Yusekova: two of those bars in a briefcase would get very heavy, very quickly. But this delivery was another sort of metal, dull grey slabs nested in foam rubber. They could have been roof slates, but there was something grim about their presence. Graff knew straight away that these slabs mattered; it was evident in the hushed reverence of the insurgents, the nervousness of the Russians. Glancing round, he saw that all eyes were on the trestle tables set up in the fortress's battered courtyard. Guards on the battlements had drifted from their posts to look down as the testing progressed, two dozen men and boys, watching in silence. A drop of sweat raced a crooked line down the gnarls of Graff's spine.

A scraping of the metal was dropped into a test tube. The soft fizz of a chemical reaction. A few words in Pashtun between Ahmed and his scientist, a man of dust and robes like the others. It seemed the merchandise had met with approval. Quiet excitement had rippled through

24

the gathered insurgents, a hush fell – then, incongruously, a cellphone rang.

Ahmed frowned. One of his youngest followers ran out across the square, holding out the phone for him to answer. This was all wrong. The timing could not be coincidence. This was when Graff's eyes had flicked between his men and realised he was one down.

Where the *hell* was Thompson?

Ahmed stepped back from the table, pocketing the phone. He issued quiet orders to his lieutenant, who beckoned two armed men and jogged towards the entrance to the inner keep. Looks shot between Graff, Singh and Turturro, then back to the three Russians. The couriers could sense the coming stand-off and were backing towards each other.

Fyodor was first to draw his handgun, drawing the sights of a dozen rifles to him in the process. The Russians were too close to Ahmed for the comfort of his followers. Sergei and Victor were quick to back up their comrade, their own guns jutting out, a necessary posture with the balance of firepower weighted so far against them.

Now Ahmed's lieutenant was emerging from the keep – with *Thompson* as his hostage. Two men flanking, a fourth, broken-nosed, driving the young mercenary forward with his bayonet. Thompson had been stripped of his weapons and equipment; his face was blank and still, as if his mind were drawn back to some inner place. It made no sense. Again the courtyard fell silent, as Ahmed stepped up to Thompson and ripped open his shirt. The money belt fastened there seemed innocent enough – until Ahmed unbuckled it, revealing the wire that trailed from it, then tore it apart to reveal the hidden circuitry within . . .

Fucking CIA. No wonder Thompson was so sharp, so

skilled, such a damn good fit with Graff and his team. Bile rose but Graff swallowed it back. Thirty seconds earlier this man had been his friend. Right now, he'd happily stake him out and take a hammer to him, working his way in from the hands and feet, making sure that every inch of bone was broken along the way.

Ahmed nodded to his lieutenant and Graff smiled grimly. Game on. He bore down on the handles of the M2, swinging it into play. Killing was a savage pleasure for lost souls. A sharp retort echoed off the fortress walls. Graff made to press the trigger – but his fingers were not on the handles. He was falling away from the gun. A plume of blood was dancing from his chest, like a flame, almost. Gunfire was breaking out all around him but the sound was slowed to a growl. The blue cloudless sky burnt out to white as Graff fell back, away from the gunfight, away from the fortress, into that ditch in Bosnia. Fear surged: once he had looked upon a vision of hell, had he now been cast down into it? But as he hit the ground, and death took hold, pain and sensation flew away from him, along with the fear. The cold, sad bodies that he visualised beneath him could feel nothing, not any more. He took comfort in the fact, becoming nothing himself.

Five

Wisher saw the bullet lance through Graff, watched helplessly as the gun battle kicked off. He knew his mercenary comrades were done for: the insurgents massively outnumbered them, and held all the points of vantage around the fortress. The Russians, armed only with handguns, were picked off swiftly; Singh and Turturro's assault rifles meant they brought a few down with them as they fell. Wisher would gladly have run out into the hail of bullets and taken his chances, anything rather than endure the sickness coiling in his gut. But he was held firm by the men either side of him, and the captor at his back knew how to hold a bayonet. The blade stayed embedded in his skin, literally wedged in the gaps of his vertebrae, poised to twist, like a key resting in a lock. This was the guard whose nose he'd smashed open, but who he'd neglected to kill. The pain must be excruciating, but his hands were steady on his rifle. *He's got balls*, Wisher reflected, pointlessly.

Blake would have watched it all, of course, up until the point at which the wire was ripped away. He'd have seen and heard Wisher's entry into the fortress and the encounter with MacMillan. No doubt here, no grey area: Wisher had deliberately disobeyed orders; his actions had led to this bloodbath. Blake had links to American military bases in the region. It was possible that fighter planes had already been scrambled and were en route to launch a strike against Ahmed's stronghold. Possible, but unlikely. Wisher's fate would be presumed sealed. A rescue mission would only draw attention to the botched assignment. He was on his own.

It was little consolation that Graff would certainly have turned his gun on Wisher, and rightly so, had he lived a few moments longer. Singh was the last of them to die, shot through and through but still moving feebly on the ground. As his executioner stepped over his body, Singh craned his neck, and his eyes found Wisher's. An accusing glare burned from the grizzled merc – then a bullet in the temple laid him to rest.

Ahmed emerged from cover, walked out into the courtyard. The leader's authority over his men was palpable, Wisher felt it in the stance of his captors, the slightest lessening of their focus on him. As Ahmed walked among the living and the dead, Wisher observed his thin wrists, the gaunt frame of the ascetic. He could kill Ahmed with one blow, but he needed his guards to reconfigure and offer him a launch window for action. He readied himself, sending out his perceptions along his limbs, checking . . .

'Is this the man you seek?'

Ahmed was in front of him, not too close. He was looking at Wisher, but glancing past him too. Wisher tried to turn and was constrained. Instead he had to wait for long, long moments, dread taking firm hold of him again as two insurgents walked forward from the fortress and into his field of view. Guy MacMillan hung between them, shattered and offering little resistance as they dragged him across the dust to sprawl at Ahmed's feet.

Wisher tried to look away, to present some kind of show of disinterest, but he was too slow, he'd let his true feelings shape his face with fear and desperation. He locked eyes with Ahmed, let him see the stone wall he'd built in his mind. The rebel leader smiled. Compressed within his false humility was the arrogance of dogmatism: the enemies of 'truth' had been denied; justice was about to be meted out. Ahmed took the ornamental dagger from his waistband. Without ceremony, he took hold of the wisps of MacMillan's hair, pulled the old man's head back and slit open his throat.

Wisher saw the skin part in the wake of the blade. He saw momentary dots of red on the pale flesh thus exposed, individual arteries and veins caught in mid-flow, then quickly voiding their load. He closed his mind to it. During training he had killed a pig, slit its throat just like Ahmed had done. It was an exercise in desensitisation: feel the warm body that you clutch hold of, feel the hot gush of blood over your knife hand, the quiver of life departing. Understand that this organism you bear down upon depends entirely on a physical infrastructure to deliver vitality to its thinking brain. Not a person you are killing, just a body, to be stopped or not. Just a dead pig on the ground.

Ahmed wiped his dagger on MacMillan's clothing, slipped it back into his belt as he straightened. Also on his belt was a leather cellphone holster. Wisher's mind darted: the phone call . . .

'We should talk.' The *conceit* of the man, offering Wisher a pat on the back, as if he were inviting him into the drawing room for a cigar. Wisher's captors twisted his arms to turn him as Ahmed passed, heading back into the fortress. The bayonet blade momentarily lost contact with his neck—

Wisher tripped forward, like he was stumbling, and gained several foot-pounds of leverage in the process. He dropped his right shoulder down, fast, unexpected, and twisted his right arm free. His eyes were tracking the dagger in Ahmed's belt as he fell – as he seemed to fall. He bent his right leg to the haunch, his hand shot out and he had hold of the dagger. He pushed up with the right leg, pulled down with the left arm, tipping his second captor. In just a few dizzying moments, the tables had been turned. He now had the dagger at Ahmed's neck, the insurgent's thin body pulled off balance and held close as a shield.

The air was thick with Pashtun. Exclamations, curses, screamed orders – and Wisher's own voice, barking hoarsely, ordering the rebels to stay clear. He had Ahmed in an arm lock and was backing towards the parked car, half scrambling, kicking up dust, keeping his movements jerky, anything to obscure the line of sight to the back of his head. The insurgents were circling, their numbers increasing as word spread around the fortress.

Wisher opened the passenger door and shoved Ahmed through into the driver's seat. Dagger pressed to his neck, he reached across him to turn the ignition key. The engine started, smooth-running for such a battered car. Eyes flicking round, he found a well-worn first-generation Glock pistol under the dash. He snatched the gun and pushed it into Ahmed's belly, keeping the dagger in place on his throat, scrunching himself down in his seat as insurgents started to gather round the car, guns poised and looking for an angle. Two ways now for Ahmed to die. Wisher's eyes found the rebel captain's:

'Drive.'

No doubting his intent. Beaded with sweat, Ahmed slammed the car into gear and reversed away from the parking spot, out into the courtyard. His men were forced to scatter, bewildered, leaderless.

'Go!' Wisher pressed gun and knife into his hostage.

Ahmed pushed his foot to the floor and the car surged ahead, out of the fortress, on to the dirt road that led away into the mountains.

Ahmed's men were running after the car, firing rounds, only now thinking about shooting out the car's tyres. A stray bullet pinged through the rear windshield but didn't find flesh and bone. Fifty yards clear now, seventy-five . . . Wisher shifted up in his seat, risked a glance back at the fortress. Another vehicle was at the gate, Graff's pickup, commandeered and in pursuit.

'What do you believe in, my friend?'

Ahmed was talking to him. He pushed the dagger up into the soft underside of the insurgent's jaw, forcing him to tilt his head.

'Just drive the car.'

'You have no faith. Only death awaits you. But I will live forever. This day will be remembered in song.'

'Right. You keep telling yourself that.'

Wisher took Ahmed's cellphone from its belt holster. He needed to call in, to try to explain, while he still had the chance. As he pushed a button to activate the device, he glanced back. A figure was standing in the back of the pickup. Fire flashed at his shoulder and a rocket-propelled grenade arced toward them, trailing smoke . . .

Wisher grabbed hold of the steering wheel, sending the car off the road. The missile clipped the rear of the vehicle and exploded – but Wisher was already diving clear, rolling down an incline, scattered rocks bruising his arms and ribcage as he tumbled. The car hit a boulder and burst into flames. A vital diversion, and Wisher knew it. Ignoring the build-up of pain in his battered body, he snaked across the ground, a lizard in the dust, pistol in one hand, cellphone pushed into a back pocket. He made it to a narrow ravine, worked his way down it. He was now at the base of a ridge that blocked the line of sight from the road. The land opened up beyond, a cracked and rocky plain extending into the haze. It would take Ahmed's men time to inspect the car wreck and discover their quarry's corpse was not inside. It was a vital opportunity for Wisher to gain distance on his enemies. He ran, flat out, without looking back.

After fifteen minutes he slowed his pace, settling into a jog. With no food and water, he was only too aware of his limited physical resources. Regret threatened to overwhelm him. He tried to rationalise: MacMillan's fate was inevitable: without Wisher's efforts to rescue him, he would have been executed. Everything that he had observed about Ahmed and his men pointed to the fact. It was awful indeed to have given the old man hope, then seen it dashed. But maybe it was better that he had been there to witness his death. Better than dreadful isolation. Better that he has made the connection, that MacMillan had known that his memory was honoured, had known for sure that he had mattered.

Still it burned Wisher to his core. He had tried and he had failed. He had sacrificed the mission, sacrificed his career – and sacrificed MacMillan, in the end. His thoughts circled back on themselves. There had been an opportunity, he had taken it. What choice had he, really? Ahmed accused him of having no faith but that was not true. He had believed in himself, and in what he was capable of. This was the faith that guided him. He had followed it as blindly as the insurgents followed theirs.

Head first, heart second. Blake had the measure of him, even back at that first briefing, and had tried to warn him against losing perspective. If only he had known himself better.

Time passed, measured in the juddering beats of

Wisher's feet upon the barren land. It was the best part of an hour before he stumbled to a halt, exhausted and dehydrated. The fortress was now some distance behind – but Peshawar was still many miles to the north. He would need water soon. His only real option was to head down towards the Indus Highway, which led back to the city. The trading route was a world away from the wilderness of the mountains. Hard currency would count for more than politics or religion; he had dollars sewn into a fold of trouser fabric, with luck he could negotiate a ride. Or there was the river itself, slower but perhaps less conspicuous once he had found a berth. And if a bribe didn't do the trick, he still had the handgun.

A cellphone rang softly. Ahmed's phone, forgotten in Wisher's pocket. The ringtone stirred a memory: he had heard it before, while he was in the fortress, freeing MacMillan. He fished it out of his pocket, stared at it. It rang again. He put it to his ear, pressed to receive the call. An American grated:

'Massoud? What the fuck's going on?'

The voice was instantly familiar to Wisher. Despite the pounding sun and the dry earth, his insides turned to ice.

Bill Blake.

Six

There are too many people.

It was a simple idea but a powerful one, and once it took hold, it was hard as hell to shake off. Blake could still remember a teenage epiphany that had made sense of the bitterness that seemed to permanently sour his thoughts, despite his success at school, the admiration he garnered on the football pitch, the girls who swooned at his naturally brooding presence.

Too many people, and, in particular, too many idiots.

The scion of a wealthy Boston family, Blake had felt like a stranger among them, moody and cynical despite his privileged upbringing, bored to his core by their liberal leanings, his mother's desperate worthiness, his father's lip service to good causes. He found respite from his stifling home life in the discipline of martial arts, though he was turned off by the escalation in mystical mumbo-jumbo that accompanied his rise through the belts. Instead he took to hiking in the rugged peaks of New Hampshire's White Mountains, and kinship with the hunters and woodsmen he met there, who shared his urge for solitude, who understood without being told how to leave a person enough space to draw breath and see the stars once in a while.

On his eighteenth birthday, Blake purchased a Remington 700 rifle with telescopic sights and headed off into the wilds with a pup tent and three days of supplies, intent on shooting a black bear. Instead he broke his leg in three places and spent thirty-six hours trapped in a ravine, licking rainwater off the rocks, before a rescue crew tracked him down. The incident led to a long-term weakening of the injured limb. It also meant that Blake ended up heading towards college to study politics and law, though his motivation was principally to alleviate boredom during his long recuperation, rather than any desire to better himself.

There are too many people. He had wheeled the argument out on more than one occasion during his college years, to neutralise the supposed freethinkers who swarmed like flies around the political sciences. Their endless parade of solutions to the world's ills seemed like the chattering of monkeys to his jaundiced ears. The world didn't need dolphins or rainforests or renewable energy. It needed a plague. It needed the Black Death.

In short bursts, Blake could be charming company, quick-witted and perceptive. But he wasn't interested in caring. Life was a game to be played. There were prizes – sex, money, status – and ways to win them. Not all the ways were deemed socially acceptable, but then social acceptance wasn't a prize he was interested in.

His relationships inevitably ended in hostility, and he learned to avoid offering the illusion of commitment. Somewhat to his surprise, he found there were some women who were cut from a similar cloth, who considered themselves emotionally self-sufficient and sought sex not love; and he soon figured out the bars they frequented. It was through one such liaison that his CIA career began. One hell of a fuck too, with a European secret-service courier en route to Washington. They'd both left bruises on each other; in the small hours she'd told him, boasting somewhat, of a spy she once screwed over, a suave Englishman who'd tried to access her padlocked attaché case via her inner thighs, only to find himself on the streets of Vienna at three a.m. with no money, no papers and no clothes. Blake had grinned at the anecdote, but in another part of his mind, gears were whirring. Could she have outsmarted him if he'd been that spy? Finally, he'd found a game that seemed worth playing.

Intelligence work proved a perfect fit with Blake's combination of roguish exterior and dark, scheming inner world. He trusted no one, which made betrayal irrelevant. His loyalty was to the game. As a field agent he had been ruthlessly efficient at playing one side against the other, earning his spurs as a special-forces liaison in the build-up to the Gulf War. As a handler, he found it easy to impress novice agents with his straight-talking, shoot-from-the-hip routine. These were his chessmen, some more powerful than others, none that were above being sacrificed. Always he was on lookout for that darker mindset, agents who signalled that they might be drawn into the shadow side of the game. But he had yet to spot a protégé among the rank and file.

The CIA, like all big organisations, had more than one structure within it. Although steeped in subterfuge, the main part of it was 'accountable', meaning its workings could be revealed, however reluctantly, with sufficient scrutiny. Blake had a presence in this hierarchy: the seasoned field agent turned handler, tough but fair, wily but risk-averse. This was not where his real work was done, however. That was off the record, under the radar. Not against the law, exactly; beyond it. He reported in secret to Lawrence Kincaid, the CIA's current deputy director. It was with Kincaid alone that he pursued the deep game that he found so satisfying.

Acting on Kincaid's orders, Blake had made overtures to Arkady Florescu, an arms dealer and self-appointed warlord operating out of Transnistria. This was in 2008, though in fact Blake and Florescu had first crossed paths during Operation MIAS, back in '92, buying back Stinger missiles from the mujahideen in the wake of Soviet withdrawal from Afghanistan.

Florescu was a ruthless thug, but he was also carrying some highly specialised stock – and was willing to do business with the CIA. Blake built the relationship skilfully, passing on contacts, organising a weapons buy-back at an inflated price, gaining the arms dealer's trust.

Among Florescu's clients were several Islamist groups active in the Afghanistan–Pakistan border territory. These groups were Blake's true target. Kincaid had a covert strategy for the region and he was looking for local insurgents to implement it. Massoud Ahmed fitted the bill perfectly: elusive, educated, utterly committed to jihad, he was ready to raise his game. Via Florescu's network, Blake made sure Ahmed was aware of the full list of available 'merchandise' – and just how it could be exploited to maximum effect. As he hoped, Ahmed saw the potential of Florescu's unique contraband, and negotiations began on price.

Everything was falling into place. Blake found it both thrilling and terrifying – a hell of a buzz both ways. In his own way, he was making history.

Then Ahmed abducted Guy MacMillan and went into hiding, and things started to get more complicated. It was pure grandstanding on the part of the insurgent, who was no doubt emboldened by thoughts of the 'shining path' to come, but it drew attention at exactly the wrong time. CIA section chief John Morgan was on the brink of retirement and looking to go out on a high note.

He pushed through the deep-cover mission to locate and rescue MacMillan, with fresh meat Tom Wisher as the point man. All of a sudden, there was a car crash waiting to happen.

If Blake told Florescu about the CIA plan to extract MacMillan, Florescu would accuse him of trying to scupper a lucrative deal. And Blake obviously couldn't alert John Morgan's team to the hidden agenda he was running on Kincaid's private orders. That was one secret he intended to take to his grave. He could only hope the two trajectories would fail to collide.

Luck was not on his side. Florescu's delivery boys found their way to the same mercenary team infiltrated by Tom Wisher – and Blake found himself facing a massive conflict of interest.

After the call to Wisher, the night before the drive to Safed Koh, Blake had started to make contingency plans. The young agent's barely concealed anger could easily tip him towards insubordination. Blake recognised the warning signs, plus he knew Wisher had that holier-than-thou thing going on. But as he stared through his apartment window, out across the jumbled rooftops of Peshawar, he also saw an opportunity to turn the situation to his advantage. By the time morning came, and Wisher was driving up the potholed road into the Safed Koh range, Blake was virtually willing him to go off-mission.

He had followed Graff's vehicles partway along their route, then parked up on an outcrop, around twenty miles from the mountain fortress. The wristwatch surveillance device gave him audio and visual contact via his laptop, though the camera angle was often less than ideal, concealed as the lens was within Wisher's wrist watch.

He watched the drive into Ahmed's lair, staying with Wisher as he fanned out under Graff's orders. He'd already seen the entrance to the inner keep, felt Wisher's temptation. His own heart had started to pound

Then Wisher had made his run for MacMillan, and rich satisfaction glowed through Blake. He'd read the situation to a tee. Now it was just a case of timing. It was Florescu's policy to provide all his clients with cellphones through which they could be contacted directly. At Blake's insistence, he now had the number of Ahmed's phone. He waited until agent and hostage were face to face – Christ, MacMillan looked rough! – then a simple call was all it took. There were a few heart-stopping seconds when it looked like Wisher might actually slip the net, but the young man's principles came back to bite him: a guard who should have been dead became the man who brought him to heel. To be fair, if Wisher had survived, he would have learnt that lesson. But Blake had made it clear to Ahmed that Wisher's survival was not to be an option under any circumstances.

Contact via the wristwatch spycam was terminated within seconds of Wisher's emergence back into the daylight. Blake had expected that. It was why he had instructed Ahmed to confirm delivery of the contraband – and the elimination of Wisher. When this response had not been forthcoming, he'd made an angry call to the insurgent leader, but got dead air instead, then some babbling, moronic lackey he could hardly understand, hanging up on him. It wasn't satisfactory, but Blake had urgent business to attend to, getting his house in order before Ahmed's jihadists made their move to stun the world – by which point he intended to be several thousand miles away.

He packed up his remote surveillance kit and headed

back to the city. In the quiet of his rented apartment, he got back online and hacked his way into the small hours, deleting and rewriting digital history to his advantage and Wisher's eternal detriment. By dawn he was nearly done: bleary and over-caffeinated, he pushed himself away from his desk, ground the heels of his palms into his bloodshot eyes. The final move was a call to John Morgan at Langley. It was evening on the East Coast, but the veteran agency man was still at his desk, anxiously awaiting news of the situation. Morgan was 'account-able', a man who claimed to prize integrity above all else; to Blake's perceptions, a man supremely gifted in the art of self-deception. The bid to rescue MacMillan had been conceived in Morgan's office, an act of incontrovertible virtue, despite its covert nature. The kind of operation the CIA liked people to know they were engaged in, defending American citizens, containing radicalism, protecting the innocent.

And now Blake was having to break it to Morgan that his poster boy, Tom Wisher, had gone loco. At least that was how Blake intended to spin the events of the past twenty-four hours. The way he told it to Morgan, Wisher had deliberately severed contact shortly after gaining access to Ahmed's stronghold. Blake had spent hours trying to re-establish the link, hoping against hope that it was some kind of spycam malfunction. But it seemed like Wisher was deliberately hiding his actions. Could it be connected to the mysterious delivery from the Russian couriers?

'What's your assessment, Bill?' There was genuine concern in Morgan's voice. The seed had been planted: was Tom Wisher a double agent? Blake offered a mild defence of the young agent:

'I know Tom. He's a good kid.'

'That's what we all thought.' Such an easy steer. Now to link Morgan with the false data trail he had constructed overnight.

'Maybe I can track his phone records, get a fix on him— '

That was when Blake heard the click of a trigger being cocked, and he looked round to see Tom Wisher at the door to his hotel room, pointing a gun at him. He kept his voice level—

'I'll call you later.'

—switched off the phone and turned to face the agent he thought was dead, and whom he was in the process of incriminating for the delivery to Massoud Ahmed, of two slabs of dull grey metal with the capacity to reshape the war on terror for decades to come.

Wisher was grimy and haggard, eyes sunk back in their sockets with tiredness. His gun hand trembled, adrenaline and fatigue joining forces to make him wired and unpredictable. Blake readied himself for action. The thought flashed through his mind:

This should be interesting.

Seven

'Why d'you do it, Tom?'

'Why did *I* do it?' Wisher was incredulous. Did Blake know that he knew? He'd had the sense to dissemble when he heard Blake's voice on Ahmed's cellphone, barking in pidgin English like some distracted foot soldier. He couldn't yet tell if Blake had seen through the ruse. But then, he had very little confidence right now that he could read Blake at all.

'You had your orders. Leave the hostage. All eyes on the delivery.' Blake's bemusement seemed real enough. Almost without noticing, the two men were starting to circle. The room was wide enough for them to keep their distance, sparsely furnished: bed, desk, easy chair. A ceiling fan rattled overhead. Dawn pushed grey light through the balcony doors. Wisher had the gun, but he was worn through – as tired as he had ever been. He didn't want to play games, but he needed to know more. Why had Blake betrayed him?

'Who's paying you? Ahmed? The Russians?'

The question had gnawed at him through the long uncomfortable hours of his journey back into Peshawar, hiding in the back of a farmer's rickety truck packed tight with gaunt, bleating goats. Blake just shook his head, like a weary parent digging deep to placate a bothersome child.

'This is the real work, kid. This is the chess game.

Tough calls have to be made. But I'm glad you made it back, truly I am.'

'Bullshit.'

The two men locked stares. For a moment it seemed like the older agent was on the point of surging forward, but instead he sagged, sitting down on the end of the bed.

'We're losing this war, Tom. People are tired of the fight, our own goddamn government is trying to make peace left, right and centre . . .'

'Which is a good thing, right?'

'Christ you're naïve!' Blake was back on his feet again, pacing. Wisher kept the handgun lined up, tracking him as he crossed the room. But Blake seemed more concerned with communicating his point than with the weapon aimed at him.

'Conflict is our business. It's how we impose our will on the world. People bleat on about oil being the subtext for the Gulf War, like that was a bad thing. What the hell do they think their cars run on? Why the hell do they think we're in Afghanistan?'

'Not to break the law—'

Blake snorted with contempt. Wisher knew he was being clumsy. He didn't want to argue, he wanted to hit out.

'I don't mean that.'

'You mean justice.'

'I mean right and wrong! I mean not killing innocent people, acting with integrity—'

'Again, very naïve. We're fighting against romantics who don't even care about their own lives, let alone their people's. We can't reason with them. We have to pick our own cause and stick to it.'

'And what's your cause?'

'American interests. That's my fucking cause. Is that

okay with you?' It was so blunt, so simple. Wisher's mind was starting to swim – he hardly knew what he was thinking any more. He kept the handgun aimed, but he was losing concentration. Blake was still talking:

'This is the crossroads. East meets west right here. The world's great resource reserves are next door, Iran, Turkmenistan. We need a pretext to maintain and increase our presence here. A localised nuclear detonation in Peshawar will do just fine.'

Wisher's face went blank. He knew he must look like a moron. Certainly Blake's smug expression said as much.

'What did you think was in those cases? Gold?'

Uranium. Weapons grade, ex-Russian military. Of course.

'They're making a *bomb*?'

'It's simple enough in principle: slam two sub-critical masses together and you get fission.' He mimed the action with his fists, warming to this theme. 'Tricky in practice, especially when you're not massively smart. Chances are the damn thing will fizzle out, but that still works for us. Terrorists make their own nuke. The war on terror is justified. Troop numbers go up, infrastructure deals are negotiated and enforced. Roads are repaired, towns are rebuilt, by American companies. The national interest is served.'

Blake had taken on a manic edge. Wisher felt his own nerves hum in response. It was like they were in some kind of down-the-rabbit-hole dream world. Logic had become unhinged, the corners of the room were bending inwards, fish-eyed. Wisher clung desperately to common sense:

'Thousands could die. Tens of thousands. Have you thought about that?'

Blake merely smiled: inward-directed, a private joke.

'You think that's funny?'

'Did you know smiling is a modified fear reflex?' The agent's eyes were two hard stones. 'Maybe I'm just scared.'

Keeping his gun hand true, Wisher took the cellphone from his pocket and threw it down on the bed.

'It's Ahmed's.'

Blake kept smiling, but his eyes narrowed.

'I know you called him.'

Wisher had hoped for a moment of triumph, but Blake just shrugged:

'So?'

'Head office can check the log. They'll see that you're in bed with terrorists. Let them decide if that's in America's interests.'

Wisher was trembling again. He was worn through: he needed to force the showdown but couldn't seem to wrap it up. Was he going to have to kill in cold blood? Blake rubbed his stubbled chin – and shot Wisher a crafty look.

'I haven't just been sitting here, you know. I've been tinkering. Cutting and pasting, a number here, an ID there. It's amazing what you can accomplish with a laptop and a few security codes.'

'What's your point, Bill?'

'You called Ahmed. Not me. You. That's what the records will show.'

'You're insane.' Wisher spat out the words, but he couldn't deflect Blake's growing confidence.

'You're the bad apple, Tom. I just wish I'd spotted it sooner.'

Just a joke to Blake. No, not a joke: a game. Smugness practically oozed out of him. Wisher cocked the trigger.

'Shooting me will only prove the point, of course.'

'Guess I'll have to live with that.' Bravado from Wisher; but truthfully, he was at a loss. He thought John Morgan would believe his side of the story, if he could argue his point face to face ... but if Blake were dead? Could a data trail really be so totally reinvented? Blake would say anything to get inside his head right now.

Wisher thought of his father, his sister. He thought of MacMillan, blood pumping from his neck, the scattered bodies of the mercs and the rebels they'd killed. He'd seen death up close and personal in the last twenty-four hours – but he'd never killed before. Drawing on his training, he tried to wipe his mind of conscience and concern, to visualise himself as something cold and hard, unyielding, metal, stone, ice, a black hole—

A knock at the door. It opened, unbidden, and a maid stepped through.

'Mister Blake—'

All of a sudden Blake was in motion, surging towards Wisher, a bulldozer driving into the younger man's centre of balance. The handgun went off, a reflex as Blake slammed into him. The maid screamed, far off at the periphery of Wisher's attention. His breath had been driven out of him, Blake had his gun hand pushed up high, agonising torque upon his wrist as his grip was forced to loosen. Blake jabbed at his face, hoping to stun him, he knew. He soaked up the blow, angled his own elbow inwards. Blake's flank was exposed; Wisher let the gun fall – a momentary lure for Blake's attention – and put everything he had into the triangle of his arm, jabbing its apex into Blake's ribs. Bone cracked. Wisher rolled out of the grapple.

Blake dived for the gun, his face creased with pain. Wisher came down on top of him, elbow first again, into the back of his neck. Not enough force to break it, but his senses would be disoriented at least. Arm lock, twisting round on the floor, his foot flicking out to kick the gun away from reach—

He had the advantage. Blake was stronger in terms of muscle mass, though heavy set and out of shape; Wisher was younger, his reflexes sharpened by recent combat. Death was in his mind's eye, firing up his instincts in a way that just couldn't happen behind a desk, or the wheel of a car. Exhaustion fell away from him as he bore down.

Blake's knee smashed into his shoulder, unexpected suppleness providing a new avenue of attack. The big man reared up like an angry bear, throwing Wisher across the room, hurling him into the rickety chair where Blake had sat at his laptop. Blake continued his attack, hoping to catch Wisher unprepared, but the young agent had a weapon now, a splintered chair leg. He turned as Blake homed in on him, swinging the jagged shard of wood. It connected with Blake's cheek, ripping the flesh open, scattering droplets of blood.

Blake roared, stumbling back. Wisher leapt to his feet. The heat of battle had swept aside the shackles of his conscience. He knew he could finish Blake. He *wanted* to. And he had the means: the gun he had brought from Safed Koh, back in his hands . . .

The apartment door slammed open once more. Two police officers were on the threshold, summoned from the street below. They barked orders, unholstering their side arms. The maid cowered behind them. Wisher registered their presence and snapped out of combat mode, head spinning. Across the room, Blake had his balance back and was focused on him despite his injury. Two cops in the doorway. Two guns, aiming his way.

Don't think. Act.

Wisher ran for the balcony doors, which were standing open, curtains shifting in a morning breeze. Three strides took him there. The first bullet was fired, chipping splinters from the frame. Wisher grabbed the rail and vaulted. Air rushed around him—

There was a pitched roof ten feet below. He hit the tiles, slid down the incline. The two policemen were at the balcony. Bullets flew – but so did Wisher, fast off the roof, catching hold of the last lip to take the edge off his speed as he tumbled into the narrow alleyway below. He crashed into a side wall, grabbed for a window ledge with his free hand. The jolt tugged at his arm joints, but his grip was good enough to bring him to a stop. He braced his legs against the alley wall and made quick work of the remaining fifteen feet to street level.

He had escaped, for now. But he had work to do.

Eight

'Who's Rendlesham91?'

Stuart called out from the main room of the studio flat. Rachel Wisher didn't hear him; she was in the shower. She'd hardly slept last night: she and Stuart had only met a few weeks ago, only got it together in the last few days, so there was a *lot* of sex to be explored. She smiled as she remembered, the tingle of water over her skin triggering sense memories of their shared intimacy. She was serious by nature, reluctant to get bogged down by romance. She'd had one proper boyfriend, her partner from the age of seventeen to twenty-one. She was twenty-four now, and with only a handful of one-night stands to show for the past three years, until Stuart.

Not that she hadn't had offers. She was a good-looking young woman, slender and fair. Her strong features were rarely augmented with make-up, unless it was for work. Presently, she was pursuing a doctorate in political science at Cambridge while she developed her career as a journalist and correspondent, which increasingly involved appearing on camera, either for the blogosphere or – on two occasions so far – for the mainstream media. Her contemporaries in academia looked down their noses at her ambitions, but she didn't care. She had opinions and she wanted them to be heard.

That's why she was showering now, instead of lounging in Saturday morning post-coital bliss. She had to interview the MP for Huntingdon at noon and she needed to get her head together. It was for the radio, which was fortunate given her current eye-bag situation. Stuart had long-term potential but she was going to have to rein in the pre-match sex. It was what boxers did, after all.

Stuart pulled back the shower curtain. He was rangy, bearded, kind-eyed and pretty damn horny for a physicist. Well read, too, good company out of bed as well as in it.

'Hey!' She grinned with mock outrage, but she turned away from him, too. Ridiculous really, given the amount of time they'd spent exploring each other's bodies in the last twenty-four hours. But she liked having her own space. Privacy was the issue, not prudishness. Stuart didn't seem to pick up on her concerns, however – he was too interested in admiring her shapely backside.

'Your laptop's beeping. Incoming Skype. Very persistent.'

'Did you see who it was?' She was always online; it came with the journalist's territory. But it meant you had to get used to ignoring people.

'Rendlesham91.'

Rachel turned off the shower, suddenly in a hurry. Naked and dripping wet, she ran through into the living room, where her laptop was chirping on her bedside table. Stuart followed, amused by her nudity, baffled by her urgency.

'Do you want a towel or something?'

'Ta.' Rachel fished in her bedside drawer for earphones. She didn't want to broadcast this particular call. The laptop continued to chime as she fiddled the minijack into its socket. Stuart sat down beside her, draping her dressing gown over her shoulders.

'Who's Rendlesham91?'

'My brother.'

Now Stuart was really confused. She hadn't told him about Tom. Not because she didn't think about him often – she did – but because they were on such different paths, herself an outspoken liberal, him the very antithesis: a CIA man. When it had become clear he was committed to his career path, she had considered wheeling out the standard 'works in the oil business slash stock market slash international sales' line to cover for him, but if felt wrong, an invitation to slip-ups and a lie besides, something she was fiercely against.

In her view, the bulk of the world's problems stemmed from the absolute and entrenched dishonesty of politicians. Not only did everyone in politics lie all the time, it was reaching a point where it was virtually expected of them, by the press and the public at large. As a political commentator, pointing out these persistent falsehoods was frustratingly inadequate; she was playing a role like the rest of them, preaching to a small and diminishing congregation. Nothing changed, and Rachel believed in change. She craved it. Was it too much to dream of a society based on truth?

Always there had been honesty between her and Tom. They'd been through so much, the death of their father and their mother's gradual decline. They both needed that clarity at least in one small corner of their lives. And yet his trade was diametrically opposed to hers. He dealt in violence and deception; even as a means to an end, she considered both profoundly unethical.

She knew everything he did; she knew too much, but the honesty they shared demanded it. They'd always been so different: he was the boy who couldn't sit still, she was the girl who hid in books. So close, yet so far apart. Geographically, once she'd moved to England to study;

philosophically, the distance seemed to be increasing. And yet here he was, the prodigal sibling, knocking on her laptop screen . . .

She took the call.

A video link, not Tom's usual mode. *Something up?* she thought in passing. She straightened her dressing gown, the link connected, she saw her brother – and she knew something was.

'It's good to see you, Rach.'

He looked terrible. Dirty, dressed in rags, pale and drawn: he must have lost ten pounds since she'd last seen him, and he'd been a whippet to start with. He appeared to be in some sort of tatty internet café – she could make out other booths behind him, tariff notices in Arabic script on the walls of his cubicle.

'Where are you? And what are you wearing? You look like an old woman!'

'It's a long story . . .'

Image quality was poor: low-resolution and scratched by static, refreshing just a couple of times each second. It was enough for Rachel to see clearly that Tom was in trouble. And yet she knew he would know that – and he was still making the call.

'It's been too long, bro. It's been months.' *Don't nag him.* 'We need a system, code words or something. Proper spy style.' She offered a smile: Tom didn't return it.

'Rachel, listen. There's something I have to do, but I needed to talk to you first.'

Deadly serious.

'One second, Tom.' Rachel turned to Stuart, who had pulled on trousers and a T-shirt, and was now loitering in the background, flicking through *New Scientist* and trying not to look in her direction.

'I need privacy, Stu. Sorry.'

'I'll take a shower.' No drama, no wounded look: just an understanding nod as he ambled from the room. He had just gone up considerably in Rachel's estimation.

She turned back to her laptop.

'Okay, I'm all yours.'

Tom took a moment before he continued. And when he did speak, his voice was halting and heavy, like he was forcing the words out.

'People are going to come looking for me. They're going to seek you out. They're going to say things about me.'

Rachel felt a vaguely nauseous feeling start to build. She'd tried to talk Tom out of joining the agency, back when they were still arguing the point. She'd seen the prospect of moral compromise lying in wait for him, had known even then that he would have to cross the line at some point, the job demanded it. He'd have to do wrong, to do right . . .

'What is it? What's happened?'

'Don't believe them. Don't trust *anyone*.'

'Jesus, you're scaring me.' She wasn't exaggerating. He had confided in her, last time they'd met, that he was going undercover. At first she'd worried about the personal danger he would be facing. But in the weeks that followed, she'd started to reflect on the danger *he* posed. The West was desperate for results in the region, as desperate as the revolutionaries they were trying to undermine.

'The ones it seems safe to trust are the worst of all. Seriously. Don't talk to anyone. I'll contact you when I can.'

'Oh Tom . . .' He was always the bright star, the fastest, the smartest. The bravest. To see him twisted with paranoia like this sickened her to her core. His voice stumbled:

'I shouldn't have made this call, but we haven't spoken for so long. I needed you to know . . .'

He was choking up, his emotions right at the surface.
'I tried to do the right thing, Rach. I really did.'

He seemed ready to break down. On instinct Rachel reached out to the screen, touched the small square of pixels that was conjuring up her stricken brother's image.

'Go to the police, Tom. Trust the law. There are good people in the system, they'll fight your corner—'

His face was closing down. He couldn't allow himself to hear her advice: it wasn't compatible with his situation. They both knew it. His sign-off was swift, matter-of-fact:

'Take care. Switch on the old phone. Love you.'

End call. His face was gone, leaving a small, glitching rectangle on screen.

Rachel leaned back from the laptop. The old phone was her first mobile, a pay-as-you-go Nokia dating back to 2000, with changeable covers and the Snake game preinstalled. She'd gone on contract within months and it had been consigned to her dressing-table drawer. With no paper or digital trail to either of them, the SIM was untraceable. It was their last line of communication.

Stuart emerged from the shower room, towel wrapped round his waist, hair slicked back. She glanced round, her face stern, emotion held in check, as was her habit. He frowned.

'Everything okay?'

Nine

Contacting Rachel was a probably a mistake, Wisher realised. As he broke the link, his mind raced ahead to view the consequences of this particular action. The call could be traced, of course, they would know that Rachel had spent several minutes online to an internet café in back-street Peshawar. It wouldn't take a rocket scientist to deduce she'd been in touch with her rogue agent brother. They'd need to know everything about the exchange – the British authorities initially, with CIA intervention certain to follow, up to and including rendition.

And yet he'd made the call. It had been necessary because there was a substantial chance he would not survive this day. The truth was Rachel's most prized possession; he'd judged she would value it higher than her personal safety and acted accordingly. Later, if there was a later, he would have the chance to reflect on this decision and how much of his motivation was selfish, the need for a witness, for validation. But not now.

He got to his feet, keeping his head down, and made his way out of the internet café. He was clearly Caucasian, despite the soiled coat and turban he had purchased from the farmers who drove him into Peshawar. The city's impoverished residents were curious, not directly hostile so far, but news of his presence would soon spread to those who were. He needed to make his move.

He headed out into a market street. It had been less than thirty minutes since the confrontation with Bill Blake. Wisher knew his way around the back alleys of Peshawar; he had become familiar with the city while in Graff's employ, particularly its black-market access points, essential for cheap liquor and mercenary supplies.

Blake had let it slip that Peshawar was the location of a home-made nuclear bomb, built by followers of Massoud Ahmed, with a payload of contraband uranium from the stores of Arkady Florescu. For the device to work, the metal would have be weapons-grade, highly enriched with the U_{235} isotope. The Agency knew of several black-market sources that had claimed access to stockpiles of Soviet-era HEU. Now they could add Florescu to the list.

Even if the bomb chassis had been prepared in advance, the uranium elements would need to be worked into a suitable shape for detonation, meaning the insurgents would require a base somewhere in the city. Wisher had planned to stay in hiding until he had tracked down its location, but here luck had dealt him a decent hand at last: he had spotted a certain broken-nosed insurgent from the fortress in Safed Koh, promoted in the wake of Massoud Ahmed's demise, and now driving a contingent of comrades into the heart of the city's warehouse district. He'd tailed their vehicle on foot – the pick-up barely got above walking speed, negotiating the cluttered streets – and discovered its destination, a barricaded courtyard with a nervous young guard conspicuous at its entrance.

Now that Wisher had spoken to his sister, he was free from personal obligation. Turning himself in was not an option. Blake would have closed down that avenue; no way would he get a fair hearing. He was already positioned as the double agent who procured uranium for terrorists. And there was no time. The bomb's inner mechanism would have been prepared in advance. This would be his only chance to intervene.

Head down, pushing against the morning crowd that jostled him, Wisher unwrapped a half-finished portion of baklava and forced himself to eat the remainder. He had no appetite, but he would need sugar in his bloodstream.

A few minutes' walk took him to the edge of the market district. He quickly spied what he was looking for: a police officer, engaged in stern conversation with two shifty traders hawking western sportswear from a hand-drawn cart.

Wisher had the run mapped out in his head. Around half a mile, mainly alleyways, impossible to pick up speed by car, too many obstacles. Pursuit would be on foot, leaving time and opportunity for a force to gather.

He stepped out into the middle of the street. A van that was rattling past honked at him. The police officer glanced up. Wisher took the handgun from inside his coat, aimed it above the police officer's head. He fired, twice – and the chase was on.

The officer pulled his own pistol, but Wisher was already running from the scene. He paced himself, making sure his pursuer didn't lose sight of him. This particular policeman was no athlete but he had a radio and he was using it. Backup would be quick to arrive, especially with the authorities on the lookout for a fair-skinned rogue agent.

The officer shouted out to passers-by, breathlessly ordering them to intercept his quarry. But the impover-ished denizens of these back alleys were no friends of the police and Wisher moved unheeded. Out on to a main street – sirens wailing, brakes complaining – he didn't stop to look. Another alley. More voices behind him now. Step up the pace.

The narrow exit lay up ahead, twenty yards away, ten yards. A police car screeched to a halt, blocking the way. Wisher barely broke his stride, bounding up on to the roof of the vehicle, thin metal denting under his back as he rolled across it and was gone, landing on his feet and sprinting off. A bullet struck fragments from the brickwork to one side: a warning shot. Passers-by dropped low at the sound, then carried on about their business. They'd heard gunfire enough times before.

More sirens. Wisher could see the courtyard entrance up ahead. The young guard was stepping back through the smaller door set into the truck-high wooden gates, clearly troubled by the sense of an escalating alert in the surrounding streets. Someone's son, thought Wisher. Someone's brother, someone's father too, possibly. Shit.

He was at the courtyard gate, heart pumping, breath rasping. Looking back down the narrow roadway, he could see the first of the police officers just running into view. There were three or four now, maybe thirty seconds behind him; sirens wailed, vehicles en route to back them up.

He knocked hard on the inner door. Flattened himself out against the gate, away from the door itself, handgun at the ready. Seconds ticked by, pursuers gaining ground. Wisher heard a heavy bolt slide. The door creaked open, a gun barrel poked out.

Wisher grabbed hold of the barrel and pulled with all his strength. The gun discharged; its bearer, the young guard, stumbled into view, eyes wide with alarm.

Wisher shot him. Bullet to the forehead. Red spouted from the neat hole as the young man fell back into the courtyard.

Wisher still had hold of the rifle: a Type 56 Chinese AK-47 copy. He spun it in his hands, flicked the selector to full automatic and barged through the door, stepping over the fallen guard.

High walls on all sides. A small tank truck in the centre of the courtyard, its back end cut open to reveal a rail mechanism inside, prepared in advance for a uranium payload. Hostiles everywhere, above, around. A wave of reaction racing out from the dead body at his feet, voices raised, hands reaching for guns. Wisher squeezed the trigger and the assault rifle sprayed out bullets. Two, three men down as he ran for cover among a row of columns to one side of the space, supporting an overhanging storey.

A bullet tore a hole in the shabby coat he wore, burning as it grazed his upper arm. He hunkered down behind a barrel, picked off another insurgent who had poked his head out of a nearby doorway into the building at his back. Half a dozen guns were firing now, plaster and brick dust showering him, getting in his eyes.

New voices joined the cacophony: police officers, discharging their side arms, trying to impose order, receiving a hail of hot metal in return. Sirens howled as reinforcements pulled up outside; panic flew like sparks between the ragged band defending their home-made atomic device.

Wisher darted to the nearby doorway. One of the men he had shot moments earlier was slumped there, bleeding out from a neck wound. His eyes met Wisher's at the moment of his death: the living orbs seemed to harden to glass at Wisher's glance.

A well-aimed round knocked brick shards from a pillar, just inches away. Wisher dropped to the ground, drove himself into the gloomy corridor with his elbows. The assault rifle was empty and discarded; he had two rounds left in the handgun. He lifted himself from the cracked tiles, enervated but ready to sprint. Gunfire and voices echoed from outside. A door creaked open beside him; he dropped back on to one knee as he spun, pistol thrust forward –

and found himself level with a goat, skittish in the doorway, its weird, alien eyes offering a vacant stare. Sound penetrated from the outside, police presence massing and the terrorist plot in disarray, as he had hoped. He glanced down the corridor. Daylight burned thin lines around the edge of a door leading back out on to the street.

Time to run.

Ten

The television news showed a succession of images from the courtyard in Peshawar: the tank truck, with a tangle of wires and struts showing inside it; insurgents on their knees, hands behind their heads; dead bodies on the ground, covered with sheets.

A British newsreader intoned:

'The American secret service is tonight claiming a landmark victory in the war against terrorism in northern Pakistan – but a spokesman for the Central Intelligence Agency also issued a stark warning of the escalating risks posed by radicalism.'

The newsfeed cut to a press conference, where John Morgan, CIA Section Chief and spokesperson, was making a statement to reporters:

'I can confirm that police in Peshawar, working in conjunction with undercover intelligence officers, today took possession of an improvised atomic device . . .'

Questions bombarded Morgan: *Was the bomb live? Was it radioactive? Was anyone hurt?* He remained unflustered, reading from a list of prepared responses, his demeanour restrained: he was a senior civil servant, after all.

'We're still examining the device and it is not clear yet whether it was fully operational. But I can confirm that nuclear materials were retrieved of sufficient critical mass, when brought together, to have triggered a nuclear explosion in excess of the blast that levelled Hiroshima.'

Do you know who was behind the bomb? Have the bomb-ers been arrested? Can you clarify the bombers' intentions?

His voice remained steady, but Morgan was no longer looking at the documents he held. Instead he glared at the assembled journalists:

'The *intention* seems perfectly clear. These terrorists were intent on causing a massive and indiscriminate loss of life. Thank God America was there to stop them.'

The TV broadcast was being watched in a boardroom, within the CIA's headquarters in Langley, Virginia. Deputy Director Lawrence Kincaid nodded to his personal assistant, Dale Peavey, who held the remote control. Peavey muted the volume.

John Morgan, grey haired, weary eyed, jowls begin-ning to sag from his jaw line, glanced across the conference table at Kincaid. Morgan thought of himself as the back-room type, but he'd been increasingly pushed to the fore in public-relations situations, a trustworthy, avuncular figure to represent an increasingly fractured intelligence community.

The Deputy Director was looking straight at him, his expression hawkish, his prematurely bald head rising above thick brows and glinting under the lights.

'You went off script there, John.'

'Caught a wave, sir.' Morgan kept it light.

'I liked it. Patriotic. Good job.'

'Thank you sir.' Morgan felt ashamed of his brown-nosing, but he'd learned the hard way that it was the best approach where his superior was concerned. Kincaid was ruthlessly ambitious. Still in his forties, he'd been promoted above Morgan in the wake of 9/11, out of the Clandestine Service and into the upper tiers of manage-ment. On the surface he was sleek and dedicated, yet there was a tacit understanding that he was prepared to do what it took to get results.

As legislation regulating the intelligence community had loosened over the decade following the destruction of the Twin Towers, Morgan had found himself margin- alised within his department. He still devised and organised missions, working within the parameters of the organisation's ethical guidelines, but his authority had been diminished.

Morgan was still trying to piece together exactly what had happened in Peshawar. When he'd been informed of Tom Wisher's apparent defection – information that brought with it the certain demise of Guy MacMillan – cold sweat had broken out on his palms at the thought of breaking the news to Kincaid. The deputy director had a knack for humiliating him; Morgan knew he was a butt for canteen jokes among the younger operatives, and it burnt him to his core.

The next hours had brought baffling and contradict- ory reports. Tom Wisher had attacked and injured his handler, Bill Blake, having revealed himself to be a double agent working in collusion with a known insurgent, Massoud Ahmed. He had fled into the backstreets of Peshawar, with local police officers in pursuit. This chase had led the authorities to the terrorists' city stronghold – and straight to a goddamned nuclear weapon, cobbled together out of building supplies and duct tape in the back of a tank truck, with sixty kilos of weapons-grade Russian uranium nestled at its heart.

As the news started to break via the international media channels, Bill Blake was on the line from Peshawar, filling in the gaps. Wisher had attempted to silence him because he knew about the uranium: he'd seen evidence on the spycam feed from Ahmed's mountain fortress, before Wisher had deliberately severed the connection. Blake had been on the point of disclosing his suspicions to Morgan when Wisher had entered his apartment with the intention of killing him. The younger agent had been overconfident, but Blake had managed to hold him at bay till the police arrived. Wisher had escaped and run back to the bomb-builders, presumably to warn them that the game was up.

Morgan had organised the mission to locate and extract MacMillan. It had been his baby; he was on the cusp of retirement and was determined to end his middling career with a notable success. He'd hand-picked Tom Wisher as the best of the best, a new recruit bringing flair and energy to a gruelling infiltration operation. He had high hopes.

By any sane estimation, the mission had failed utterly to achieve its objectives. Morgan's lead agent had gone haywire, the hostage had been executed, a gun battle had left a pile of corpses in the mountains of northwest Pakistan. And yet that same mission was now being hailed as the espionage success of the decade!

Early reports had suggested that Wisher had been the first to fire a gunshot in Peshawar, alerting the police and leading them to the rebel hideout. Blake explained that he had been tailing Wisher, despite his injuries, and it was *he* who had fired the warning shot. Bill Blake, the rookies' favourite, was the action man of the moment. Who'd have thought it? Not Morgan, for one: Blake, like so many of his colleagues, showed little instinct for heroism and an impressive knack for getting others to do the dirty work.

Blake was sat across from Morgan right now, hot off the plane after a fourteen-hour flight from the subcontinent, bruised and exhausted. The dressing taped to his cheek was spotted with blood. Thirteen stitches, apparently. Morgan imagined Blake sat by a campfire, biting down on a hunting knife while a sawbones splashed whisky on the wound. Just like a real cowboy.

It was thirty-six hours since the showdown in Peshawar. Ahmed's men were dead or in custody; Guy MacMillan's body had been located by an aerial reconnaissance team and flown to a US base in Afghanistan. The renowned correspondent had been executed, throat cut, on his knees in the mountain dirt. Tom Wisher was still missing.

According to Blake, Tom Wisher had betrayed his country and colluded with terrorists who were plotting to murder thousands of innocent civilians – then led the police to his hideout? Even allowing for the confusion surrounding the events in Pakistan, this didn't add up to Morgan.

He couldn't believe Wisher was some kind of conspirator. The lad had stood out among his fellow trainees as strong, smart and committed. Morgan had interviewed him face-to-face several times as part of the selection process for the mission to rescue MacMillan, and he'd been nothing other than impressed by his passion and perception.

And yet Blake seemed one hundred per cent certain of Wisher's treachery – and Kincaid seemed only too ready to concur. Morgan was itching to challenge their conclusions, but his instincts told him to hold back. Let them say what they had to say. He'd listen, for now.

Kincaid flicked through a dossier on Wisher, training reports, evaluations, medical records, personal documents.

'So John, I'm guessing you had a line on Wisher from the start, right? Smart move. Damn smart. His sister's a radical, you know? Father killed in action. Bit of a loner at Camp Peary. Just the type to develop some kind of fucked-up antisocial world view. This operation has bagged us a bad apple and a grade A insurgent in one swoop. Good work.'

Kincaid offered a snake-like stare. What the hell was Morgan supposed to say? Kincaid was offering him the opportunity to take credit for the situation – but at the expense of tarring Wisher as a traitor. Could he sense Morgan's reluctance?

'It was a team effort, sir. Bill did a hell of a job out there. I don't think either of us realised quite how far the rot had set in.'

'I had my suspicions,' Blake glowered. He didn't seem too happy to be sharing the limelight.

'Sometimes you have to roll the dice, I guess. Right, Bill?' Morgan tried to keep the sourness out of his expression. The case against Wisher was far from proven, whatever Blake and Kincaid might appear to think.

'Didn't see you as a gambling man, sir.' This was Peavey piping up. Morgan disliked Blake and feared Kincaid, but Peavey he despised. There was something repellent about the young executive. Something asexual and oily. He couldn't seem to open his mouth without expressing disdain, as if Morgan and his ilk, the backbone of the agency, were specimens of an inferior species. He had a high forehead, wide-spaced eyes, thin lips: if aliens landed on Earth and took on human form, they would look a lot like Peavey.

'A safe pair of hands, Dale. That's John Morgan for you. A team player. Rock-solid, proud of his reputation. And rightly so, in my opinion. You'd do well to watch how he works.'

Kincaid smiled at Morgan. Actually *smiled*. Now Morgan knew for sure that something was up. He'd long suspected that Kincaid had been playing a deep game, deeper and darker than Morgan was comfortable even thinking about.

Codes of ethics might be regarded as luxuries by the military industrial complex – the global merging of business, strategic and political interests that shaped policy behind the scenes in many nation states – and yet they were actually the whole point in a democracy. They were the reason the West was allowed to regard itself as the 'good guy'. We had principles.

And yet Morgan accepted that such manoeuvrings might be unavoidable at Kincaid's level; indeed, they could conceivably be necessary. And so Morgan looked away. He'd found his niche, he'd had a few successes, he could tell himself he'd made a difference.

But what about Tom Wisher? Morgan had seen something special in the young agent. Something that only came along once in a generation. It wasn't his passion for the job: all the young agents had passion of one kind or another. They'd fought to get a place on the training programmes, they considered themselves the best of the best. No, it was more than that, it was a certain honesty, an instinct for justice. The CIA tended to attract mavericks and cynics nowadays. There were a lot of good liars rising through its ranks. Maybe it was just the wishful thinking of an old man, but Wisher had seemed to Morgan to be a breed apart. To wheel out an old-fashioned word, he seemed *honourable*.

Morgan thought of his retirement package, less than a year away. He thought of the bottle of Californian Pinot Noir waiting for him at home. Most of all, he dreaded the prospect of locking horns with Kincaid. It wouldn't take much to trigger the deputy director's wrath. There were many reasons not to stick his head above the parapet at this juncture. And yet . . . his gut told him Tom Wisher was being hung out to dry.

'We need to keep our eyes on the big picture, sir. Someone is supplying nuclear materials to the region. We need to trace the supply line back to its source, strike at the heart of the operation.'

Nothing too controversial, just a move to refocus the discussion away from Wisher. Still, it was enough to freeze the room. Blake fired a look at Kincaid, who jabbed his finger at the file on Wisher, spread out in front of him.

'I agree. And the key to that problem is right here.'

Kincaid gathered up the dossier and handed it to Peavey.

'Circulate this via the global network. I'm setting an operational priority, effective immediately: find Tom Wisher.'

Morgan nodded. Eyes down, good dog. But within the privacy of his mind, he grinned defiantly. *Game on.*

Eleven

On bad days, he feels like a disembodied brain. Over the last few years, and more specifically since his diagnosis, he has become a creature of information rather than flesh. He has no home, very little property. He moves constantly, accompanied by his small team. Waking hours are spent almost entirely online, between screens, observing, eavesdropping, collating, deducing. He hardly sleeps, and when he does it is fitfully, his mind still adrift in the sea of intelligence. He isn't convinced that Tevis, his data analyst, sleeps at all.

He does have a body, of course, albeit a secretly stricken one. He is a man, he does eat, and excrete, he does talk, and laugh (although he can't remember the last time). Mostly, he observes, and reflects on what he learns.

When Tom Wisher wears a wire, he knows. When Wisher locates Guy MacMillan, he is watching. When Blake and Wisher fight, he is listening via the hotel's courtesy phone, and he can see via the camera on Blake's laptop. CCTV cover in Peshawar is patchy, but he is ready when Wisher contacts his sister via the internet. Police radios and in-car video-cameras mean he can follow officers as they chase Wisher to the insurgents' hideout, and the nuclear device is discovered. While the world's law enforcement agencies hunt in vain for America's most wanted man, he knows the young agent is currently stowed away on a container vessel bound for England.

This is not down to random chance. International security

is his trade, the intelligence community his obsession. He exists on its margins, invisible and untraceable. He heads a network of agents who are off the grid, like himself, who are free to act without reference to international law or hidden corporate agendas. He foresees a role for Tom Wisher in his organisation – which has no title, no headquarters, no infrastructure apart from himself, the disembodied brain, within which the dream of a life is unfolding. At least that's how it seems, sometimes.

If you met him, you would find him more than a little intimidating, with a deep rasp of a voice and a scarred, strangely shapeless face, its features broken and remade more than once. In truth, he is afraid. The world is in the grip of a conspiracy that seeks to perpetuate global conflict while extending its control over the world's diminishing resources. International law drifts over this conspiracy like fog over a battlefield, obscuring grim reality with the illusion of justice and accountability. Its tentacles reach into every country, every government. Within the CIA, it thrives.

A very rich and powerful individual revealed this truth to him many years ago, and he was faced with a choice – to look away, or to face the real enemy, at the cost of leaving everything he knew behind. And so it was that he was reborn outside of society, a lonely warrior, guarding the guards, policing the police, fighting the conspiracy, with deadly force as his modus operandi.

Like his organisation, the conspiracy has no name: he calls it the Consortium, because he has to call it something.

He calls himself Galloway, and he is watching.

Twelve

Metal clanked against metal, painfully loud as it resonated through the container. *They weren't designed for holding people*, thought Wisher, hunkered down in the dark with a dozen other wretched stowaways.

Motors hummed outside as the crane lifted and swung its load. Wisher braced himself against the cold, corrugated walls that had been his home for the past sixteen days. He was hungry and thirsty, penniless and filthy. But he was alive and he was free. The past long days had given him ample time to reflect on these latter two points, and he'd discovered that they meant a lot. It had taken all his skill and ingenuity to evade capture in the wake of Peshawar, to find a route to Karachi and secure illegal passage on a container ship bound for England – for Felixstowe, no less, just a few miles from his childhood billet at RAF Woodbridge.

He felt remorse about the men he had killed. He tried to think of it as context-specific: there was a greater good being served, a statistical weight in favour of his actions. A few lives had been spent – gambled, effectively – on the premise of many, many lives to be saved. Life, human life, remained the unit of value, untarnished by cruelty and corruption. Worth fighting for.

In the darkest moments, he drifted among childhood memories. Of the father who had died when he was seven, and who was so seldom there beforehand, he had just a few fragments: the rush of happiness at being lifted up and embraced, his fingers exploring the stubble on his father's chin and the soft, almost waxy skin of his ears. The smell of aftershave drifting up from his collar . . .

But could he remember his face, or his voice? Not really. He had two photographs: a military portrait from 1986, the year he was born, which showed a handsome, serious young man; and a family snap, of himself aged around three, being lifted up by a smiling man in a summer shirt. He had long ago combined the two images to form an idealised parent, handsome, brave, loving, loyal. Just two photos. His mother had destroyed the rest.

Thoughts of his mother brought sadness that he had long since learned to hold in check. He could recall her stoic expression in the years after her husband's death, but looking back now, he could see how she was broken inside, and her decline was already in progress. As he pushed into his teenage years, so she had retreated, her boundary gradually being beaten back by whatever forces were laying siege within her. At a certain point both siblings became aware that their mother no longer went outside; the walls of their house were her safe perimeter. Within months, it was the walls of her bedroom; within days of that particular falling back, the four edges of the marital bed became her limits; at the end, it was just the hard bone of her skull that remained, her last keep as despair ransacked her. And soon, that too had been overrun and she was no more.

Now Wisher was boxed in too, scanned and stacked with a thousand other containers, a mountain of boxes powering across the ocean. As the minutes gathered slowly into hours, then shuffled wearily forward into days, he stared into the gloom, reflecting. After so much training, then months undercover, he had been born

again under fire. Remade, like tempered steel. A keen
blade, yet without a hand to wield him. When he had
fired that first shot, at the doorway to the courtyard in
Peshawar, it was as if he himself had been fired from the
gun. He had become the projectile, resolute and deadly.
In the darkness and odour of the container, he was without purpose. What was he *for*?

The answer had come to him more than once. He had
met it with reason at first, defusing its tangle of motivations one strand at a time. Then he had tried to ignore it,
to bury it, to detonate it underground. But as his mind
idled, it forced itself into view again, endlessly resur-
rected, a zombie shuffling towards him, dead-eyed and
moaning. An idea born of darkness, that he knew would
kill him, but that he could not drive away.

Revenge.

Revenge on Bill Blake. Blake the betrayer. Blake the
traitor. There were times during the last few days when it
had felt to Wisher like he desired revenge more than food
or water. No, more than that, it *was* food, it *was* water. It
was sunlight and oxygen. It was everything he needed. If
he could kill Blake, if he could feel the man's life blood
slipping between his own fingers, it would complete him.

Wisher knew that his obsession was toxic, but he had
nothing else to cling to. He had tried to focus on the
bigger picture, to analyse what he knew about the
conspiracy that had delivered nuclear materials into
terrorist hands, to analyse Blake's role dispassionately.
But it was no use. Through the long, dark hours of the
voyage to England, revenge had become his friend, his
firelight, the secret glow he warmed himself upon.

The floor beneath him juddered, then was still. The
container had been set down, presumably on the back of
a lorry. Outside, there was the rattle of chains falling

away. A flashlight flicked on, the last of several, and this one at the end of its battery life. Its wan illumination revealed Wisher's fellow travellers: a sorry crew, scarecrows all, including himself, nestled in ratty blankets, their postures determined by the buckets of human waste that repelled them, that they hunched away from in far corners that weren't far enough away.

There had been little conversation during the journey. There were no happy stories to share; hope was a rare commodity among them, rarer even than flashlight batteries, and had to be jealousy guarded.

The minutes stretched out, and tension built among the stowaways. Their disembarkation was planned at a distance from the port, and required their container to be driven out without a customs check, which a hefty bribe was intended to facilitate. But now there were voices approaching.

Wisher's gut tightened. This wasn't right.

More conversation, heated, and just inches away, audible through metal. He couldn't make out the words, but he could judge the tone. He braced for action. Locking bars scraped and clanked. The container's end door opened . . .

The daylight was like an explosion, a blinding, bleaching rush of energy. Wisher couldn't help but gasp; among his fellow stowaways, there were some who staggered at the force of it.

There were half-a-dozen figures, silhouettes at first, occluding the light, rays seeming to shoot through them. Pupils tightened and the figures, briefly magical, resolved themselves into the burly shapes of customs officials, agitated and wielding batons, anxious to assert their authority at the discovery of a cache of bewildered illegal immigrants.

'Everybody out! Come on, move it!'

Wisher hung his head and joined the shuffling queue. He was the only Caucasian among the stowaways, but stubble and general grime mitigated the visual impact of his pallid skin. He drew some attention, but he wasn't the centre of it; a good sign, it meant this wasn't about him. Yet.

Indeed, it was another stowaway who was taking the heat, a wiry man with pock-marked cheeks who was crumbling under the pressure of the arrest, babbling and clutching at his captors. A welcome distraction as Wisher and the others filed out on to the tarmac, hands behind their heads, lining up to be searched. Wisher scoped his surroundings: early morning sunshine still bleached out the view, but his eyes were rapidly adjusting.

He was standing in a lorry park, at the foot of a veritable mountain range of containers. Tarmac on three sides, cluttered with trucks, most with bare flatbeds, some loaded with freight and ready to exit the port. A substantial customs building lay to his right, with a control room on its upper floor, large windows looking out over the landscape of the port.

The stowaways were organised with their backs to the container mountain, ready to be searched in order. Wisher's gaze was drawn to the wire mesh fences that surrounded the tarmac. A manned gate lay no more than fifty yards from the tips of his army boots. A laden lorry trundled towards it.

'Do you speak English?'

The customs officer was searching his eyes. A man of around fifty years old, overweight, he looked tired, nearing the end of his shift, perhaps. But he projected common decency.

Wisher shrugged:

'No English.'

He had an identity prepared: Goran, a Russian sailor fallen on hard times and stranded in Karachi, trying to reach an uncle in the UK. He consciously modelled his accent and body language on the couriers he had accompanied to Ahmed's fortress, what seemed like a lifetime ago.

A second officer was photographing the stowaways, three more stood guard. The senior among them addressed the group as a whole:

'Everyone please stay calm. You've entered the country illegally and you will be detained. But we'll make sure you are fed and you have beds to sleep on tonight.'

He mimed as he spoke, communicating the basics, eat, sleep, safe. Tension ebbed within the group as the stowaways started to understand that they were going to be treated with respect, at the very least.

Across the yard, the waiting lorry was being waved through the gate.

A hand alighted on Wisher's shoulder, steering him towards the waiting photographer. The customs officer mimed:

'We need to take your picture. Take ... your ... picture.'

His finger pushed down on an imaginary shutter button. Wisher nodded, keeping his eyes down. The guard paused, hand to his ear, listening to an incoming call on his Bluetooth earpiece. He shot a look upwards, Wisher followed the direction of the glance, and saw that its object was the high window of the control booth. Behind the glass, a colleague of the guard was talking animatedly on the phone while pointing down into the lorry park, a computer printout in his hand. Pointing at Wisher.

Wisher looked at the guard, who looked back at him.

All traces of tiredness had been swept away from the older man. He offered a smile, clumsily casual. Wisher's own eyes were crisp and clear as the morning air. For a fraction of a second there existed a strange camaraderie between them, two men both suddenly aware that a window of rare opportunity had just opened in front of them.

The guard didn't even see the hand that flashed towards him. The blow to his windpipe was cruel, but Wisher needed him to stay down. Instantly, he was running for the gate. The other officers' responses trailed by a second or two, equating to ten or fifteen yards of distance. Wisher was fast, opening up the gap. He'd hardly eaten or drunk in days, he was running on adrenaline, on fumes, a loping scarecrow. But he was running.

The gate officer stepped out to block his path, a rugby player by the look of him, his face already registering grim satisfaction at the tackle he was about to make. Only in the split-second before impact did his expression shift, as Wisher left the ground, a human projectile, focusing his momentum to the point of his elbow, audibly snapping the big man's ribs as he slammed into and over him.

A forward roll brought him back upright with barely a break in his stride. He was through the gates. Civilisation lay a couple of hundred yards ahead, the first in several rows of dingy terraced houses. Behind him, car doors were slamming. A motorbike revved into life. Perfect.

Wisher didn't need to look back. Sound told him everything he needed to know, here on this bare strip of land between the port fence and the town. He could hear the motorbike roar as it rapidly closed the gap on him. He ran on the tarmac, beside the double yellow line, but his eye was on the pavement. The kerb was recently repaired, a good six inches high. Lamp-posts at regular intervals. Timing was crucial.

The motorbike was close, maybe just a dozen yards behind. Wisher imagined the rider had his baton raised, hoping to bring his quarry down and become the evening's pub hero. At the last possible moment, Wisher sidestepped up the kerb, angling towards the grassy ground that lay on the far side of the pavement. The rider slowed to take the kerb – he had to – but Wisher's move was a feint. He grabbed hold of the lamp-post to jolt himself to a stop and the motorbike gunned past him, unsteady after hopping on to the pavement. Wisher chased the bike as the rider attempted a sharp turn, all but stopping in the process. A fierce assault on the hapless rider, blows to his midriff knocking the breath from him, then the man was down and the motorbike was his.

The other port vehicles were level with him now, but the motorbike was better suited to this kind of pursuit, through a working seaside town of alleys and scrubby playgrounds, easy cut-throughs for two wheels. Tyres spun on grass and dirt, and Wisher was away.

Five miles brought him to the marshy edge of the River Deben. Police sirens had been wailing by the time he left Felixstowe: he was confident that no one had followed his back-street route out of town, but he didn't want to risk riding the motorbike along any of the more major roads heading away from the coast, towards Woodbridge or Ipswich.

The Deben was often busy with yachts, but there was enough clear water this morning for him to swim its few dozen yards without being observed. There was a small motorboat moored under a hang of willow, offering the possibility of sustenance and dry clothes. But Wisher decided against it. It was only a couple of miles to his rendezvous; no sense in risking that the owner was still on board. Instead he lurched through mud to the far bank, then kept low along the field edges, past crops of potatoes and rapeseed. Pigs looked up from their sheds of galvanised metal at the scrawny figure making his way along their hedgerow, mud-encrusted like themselves.

Fields gave way to the edge of the Rendlesham Forest – Wisher's childhood playground. Moving at a light jog, he felt quickly at home among its long rows of Scots and Corsican pine. The woodland had been substantially destroyed by the storm of 1987 and subsequently replanted in rows, producing eerie, church-like corridors between the tree trunks.

He raced down one such row, recapturing some spark of innocence, despite his desperate situation. A bolt across open heath took him to the perimeter fence of the old air base, now abandoned and falling into disrepair, dandelion and buddleia sprouting along its concrete seams. He followed the fence for a quarter of a mile, until she came into view.

She was a hundred yards away, standing in plain sight down a long chalk forest track. He'd picked this spot so that he could observe from a distance, make sure that it was safe for them to meet. She'd brought someone with her, despite his clear instructions. Wisher should have been angry, but instead he smiled. Rachel had always been pathologically reluctant to do what she was told.

Wisher suspected the border guards wouldn't have had full information about who he was and what he stood accused of. The Agency would no doubt have been watching Rachel, but she was smart and she knew not to show up unless she was confident she had shaken off any tail. Right now he needed food and shelter. A day or two's rest and the world would start to make sense again.

He stepped clear of the foliage that obscured him, and waved.

'There he is!'

Rachel squeezed Stuart's arm. It had been sixteen days since the old pay-as-you-go had beeped, a text from Tom detailing his movements. She'd insisted on meeting him, on helping any way she could. Because he was family, obviously – but also because global politics was her life-blood, and she had a strong hunch that Tom was right at the centre of the extraordinary events that had recently unfolded in Peshawar.

She'd needed Stuart's help dodging the secret-service goons who were tracking her in Cambridge, but she was happy he was here. She wanted him to meet Tom. Despite their diametrically opposed views, she was fiercely proud of him. And now, perhaps, circumstances were forcing him over to her side of the fence. No way would Tom have tried to detonate a nuclear weapon. But if he'd tried to disarm it, why wasn't he a national hero?

Rachel believed in conspiracy. She believed in the influence of the military-industrial complex. She believed that the CIA were the puppets of corrupt government and corporate greed, whether they knew it or not. As she waited for Tom, her pulse fluttered at the prospect of being proved correct.

Tom started down the forest track towards them, grinning. She had an urge to run towards him but held it in check. They were siblings, not lovers, for Christ's sake!

If she had run ahead, she would have had a better view as the white van burst into life and surged out from hiding. She might have remembered more detail about the masked operatives revealed by the vehicle's sliding door, seen more clearly the guns they levelled at her brother. There was no crack of a bullet being fired: merely a muffled whoosh as a rifle discharged its load into Tom's back, slamming him forward.

Then Stuart was on top of her, blocking the view as he pushed her to the ground in a desperate, instinctive bid to protect her. She struggled against him – she wanted to see. But her only angle was from the chalk of the roadway, watching from the corner of her eye as the masked men lifted Tom's limp body into the van and drove swiftly away.

Thirteen

Don't believe them. Don't trust anyone.

Tom Wisher's words echoed through Rachel's mind as she sat across the bare desk from the CIA thug flown in to shake her down. She was in a police interview room, somewhere in the bowels of the Cambridgeshire Constabulary's Parkside headquarters. She wasn't under arrest, it had been made clear to her, though the pack of police vehicles parked outside her building when she returned from Suffolk might have suggested otherwise. Her help was being sought on a matter of national security. That was how they put it.

She'd been at the police station since lunchtime, now several hours ago. It seemed the flight from America had been delayed. To their credit, the local bobbies had kept her supplied with tea and biscuits. Now the man from the Agency was here at last, and the interview could begin.

'I'm Bill Blake. I work with your brother.'

He wasn't tall but he was broad, his torso square as a breeze block. He was carrying a little extra weight but he still looked pretty damn powerful. He had taken a beating recently: his face was bruised, with a dressing taped to one cheek. But his suit was well-tailored, and when he smiled – as he offered a handshake – it was unexpectedly appealing: roguish, charming, layered with knowing irony. Despite herself, she was rather drawn to him. Not that she had any intention of showing it.

'He hasn't mentioned you.'

'So you've talked with him?' Blake seemed genuinely concerned, anxious for news of a missing colleague.

The ones it seems safe to trust are worst of all.

Rachel shrugged.

'Not recently.'

The past twenty-four hours had been tough enough for Rachel; Stuart, poor Stuart, had been tested to breaking point. First, by the traumatic and violent abduction of her brother. Then by her steadfast refusal to allow him to contact the police – a pointless gesture considering the force they found waiting for them outside her digs. And yet he was still on the scene, waiting for her right now in reception. She was grateful for that.

'You know he's in England, right?'

'Really?'

If working in the blogosphere had taught Rachel anything, it was that information was the ultimate commodity. Once shared, it was worthless. It was imperative to spend it wisely.

Rachel had some grade-one, high-quality information in her possession. She'd seen her brother, whom she knew to be a CIA agent, abducted from an undisclosed, supposedly untraceable location. She'd seen him shot – but not killed. The more she replayed the scene in her mind, the more convinced she had become of this. A gun fired, but there was no retort. Tom was shot in the back, at close range, but there was no exit wound, no blood spray.

Tranquilliser dart, that was her conclusion. Which implied rendition: abduction by the secret service to a black site in central Europe or northern Africa, where interrogation could proceed out of sight, invisible and untraceable. The thought of her brother facing such a fate filled her with dread – it was her own worst nightmare for herself, that her journalism might trigger such a response from the governments and corporations she was committed to exposing.

And yet here she was, brought in for questioning by a supposed colleague of Tom's. If it was rendition, if the CIA or some cell within it had snatched Tom away in order to beat the truth out of him, why were they so anxious to talk to her?

She hadn't seen the movie *Marathon Man*, but Stuart had. It seemed perfectly plausible to him that the CIA would question her to find out if she knew what they already knew. Perhaps Tom was already in CIA custody, and this interview was for appearance's sake? That didn't add up either. If the CIA had known where Tom was going to be, they'd have known that she was going to be there too. How else could they have been waiting there at the location, except through intercepting their communications?

She had information. Now was the time to listen, not to talk. Blake was watching her keenly, weighing his next statement.

'I'm going to cut to the chase, Rachel. We've been watching you. We've been tapping your phone, tracking your internet use.'

'That doesn't surprise me.' The frankness did, however. Again, it was hard not to feel some sort of connection to Blake.

'We know you made contact with an internet café in Peshawar eighteen days ago. Our people were following you yesterday evening, you went to some trouble to evade them.'

'Not as much trouble as you might expect.'

She was trying to wind him up, get him to reveal his

hand. But it seemed that all he had to offer was sincerity. More than anything, Blake seemed concerned about *her.* That was where his tone pointed. *You're in over your head, kid.*

'This isn't a joke, Rachel. This is serious. Damn serious.'

'I never said it wasn't.'

'A container ship from Pakistan arrived at Felixstowe port yesterday. A man matching your brother's description escaped from custody. You were off the radar at around the same time. I don't believe in coincidence.'

'Stranger things have happened.'

She was faltering. Her flippancy felt pathetic even to her. A nuclear weapon had been discovered, a terrorist device, and Tom was somehow connected. Her trust in him was absolute – but if he was working for the CIA, who had claimed responsibility for intercepting and neutralising the threat, why were they pressuring her? Why wasn't Tom back at Langley, being debriefed? And who the hell *had* snatched him from Rendlesham Forest?

'Rachel. Look at me. Did you meet your brother yesterday?'

Blake leaned across the table. His rugged but kind face offered sympathy and support, but demanded sincerity in return.

The ones it seems safe to trust . . .

'Tom is a good person. I'm sure of it. Whatever it is you think he's done, you must be wrong.'

'People have died, Rachel. More will die, unless we can find him. Those are the facts.'

Rachel fought to hold her nerve.

'Died of what exactly?'

'You must know I can't be specific.'

'You want *me* to be specific . . .'

'We want the same thing. We want to save lives. That includes your brother's.'

Blake's eyes were locked with hers. Did he already know about Tom's abduction?

'He's a wanted man, Rachel – and not just by the West. The Pakistani secret service has put a price on his head. The Russians are interested. We're talking trained professionals here, who want to know what he knows. We can't help him while he's off the grid.'

She was in *so* far over her head. She'd felt so many conflicting emotions over the past few hours, exhilaration, anger, suspicion, defiance, but she'd never felt properly, completely afraid until now. Fear gripped her from all sides: fear for Tom, fear for the world and the vulnerable people within it; more than that, there was fear for her own future, her life, the loss of the career that was also her passion. All that she was seemed to hinge on this moment – and damn him if Blake didn't know it.

'Did you see Tom? Did he make contact with you?'

He had moved closer, looming, exerting subtle pressure with his physical presence; mentally he was already upon her, wrapping around her head like a sentient fog, slipping under her eyelids, testing the edges of her corneas, the clear jelly at the centre, looking for a way inside her head. His voice was soft, persuasive:

'What is it? What do you know?'

A knock at the door, a creak of the handle as it swung open. Blake barked without taking his eyes from Rachel's:

'Go away.'

But the moment had passed, the spell he had woven in Rachel's mind blew away like smoke from a snuffed candle, leaving a fleeting impression of his true nature: a snake.

'Sir— '

Blake seemed to shrink back into his own eyes as he turned towards the interloper, a constable, ready to tear a strip off him. But the young officer persisted.

'Sir, they've found a body.'

Blake stood across the mortuary slab from Rachel. He was stock-still, but she sensed he would rather be pacing. He flicked through various biometric measurements, fingerprints, dental records, DNA profile, all pulled from the CIA's secure servers. The data matched. The body on the slab was Tom Wisher. And it was clear to Rachel that Blake wasn't happy about it.

The corpse was certainly of a white male, of the right age and build, but it had been massively burned, including – conveniently – the face. One arm remained intact, one pallid hand that protruded from beneath the coverings.

It *could* be Tom . . . but the scenario of its discovery didn't chime with what Rachel had seen in Rendlesham. The body had been pulled from a car wreck in the vicinity of the forest, close to Orford Road, a long stretch running through open heath that was often empty of traffic. Time of death was estimated as being between six and eight a.m. the previous morning, several hours *before* she had seen Tom being abducted. There were signs of an impact but also evidence suggesting the vehicle had been torched. The police were treating the death as suspicious, but not the identity of the victim.

'I'm sorry for your loss.'

Blake placed a hand on her shoulder; his concern sounded forced, and she remained rigid beneath his touch. In their earlier encounter, he had revealed himself as a deceiver, a manipulator. She had seen it in his eyes, unmasked in the moment of anger as his mental pursuit of her had been interrupted. Tom's warning had been specifically about him, she felt sure now.

She made herself take hold of the cold, dead hand and examine it, turning it in her own. Then she got to her feet and left the room, avoiding eye contact. A small moment of theatre, probably not that convincing, but it would have to do. Blake had no reason to focus on her now, which would infuriate him. She had a secret, he had seen it in her eyes and had come perilously close to drawing it out of her.

She didn't know whether Tom was alive. She desperately hoped he was. But she knew for sure that he was a good man, and that Bill Blake was not. And so she had chosen to dissemble, in the hope that it would add to the distance between her brother and his pursuers. And by doing so, she had made an enemy of a very dangerous individual.

Whatever happened next, she had become part of it.

Fourteen

'My name is Galloway', said the scarred stranger as he poured the soup, 'and I want to offer you a job.'

It wasn't what Wisher expected to hear. He had stirred from unconsciousness twenty minutes earlier, to find himself lying on a camp bed, beside a tall, broken window, in a semi-derelict mansion. The high ceiling was decorated with cracked plaster mouldings; bare electrical wire coiled down from the central rose.

A lean black man was seated at the foot of his bed, on guard duty. He'd introduced himself as Jago. He was dressed in a polo neck, scuffed leather jacket, black denim trousers, combat boots; functional, hard-wearing garments. He moved and spoke with precision, a fighting man, but he'd been civil and done his best to answer Wisher's questions.

He informed Wisher they were in Poland, near the border with Belarus. They'd drugged him as a matter of exigency; the authorities were too close for comfort. They had no intention of harming or interrogating him. They were on his side.

Wisher had sat up with exaggerated slowness, as if still groggy from the sedatives he'd been dosed with. As Jago leant in to assist Wisher had gone for him, a supple turn to pull the man closer as he jabbed up with his fist . . .

Jago parried the blow, taking hold of Wisher's wrist and sinking low, using Wisher's own momentum against him. Wisher clutched at his adversary, aiming to regain balance and block a counter-attack; but Jago ducked under him and pulled him in a roll off the bed, twisting his arm to near breaking point as he flipped him.

Wisher found himself face down on the cold floor with his arm bent double and Jago's knee in the small of his back.

The grip had been released slowly. Jago stood back and allowed Wisher to get to his feet. He made no comment, but he looked distinctly unimpressed. He gestured for Wisher to precede him out of the room, perfectly courteous – but Wisher knew now that this enigmatic agent was a match for him.

He was also painfully aware of his wretched condition. Even without the benefit of a mirror, he could feel the beard stubble on his chin and examine his grimy hands and feet, dirt worked under the nails despite his efforts at personal hygiene during the long journey from Karachi. He didn't want to think about body odour.

A basin of water was provided for him, and a safety razor. His travelling clothes were binned in favour of disposable overalls, a better option for now. Hunger and thirst were starting to clamour for Wisher's attention but he needed to get himself back into some sort of present-able state, too. Jago didn't question his priorities, watching patiently from the sidelines as Wisher quickly stripped and freshened up.

Together they walked through the decaying mansion, past walls of peeling paper, streaked with damp and crusted with mould. A long gallery room led along the front of the building, its floor entirely covered with broken glass that crunched like fresh snow under their feet. Dilapidated shutters revealed a view out on to an overgrown patio and unkempt gardens beyond.

A mobile command centre had been set up in what was once the mansion's ballroom. Computer terminals sat on fold-out tables, with leads snaking towards them. A cluster of dish antennae stood by the window. There were refreshments on a side table: crackers, coffee – and soup, simmering. The smell hit Wisher like a physical force, pulling at his insides. True hunger. He hadn't eaten properly for days, hadn't eaten *at all* for twenty-four hours. Thirst was an issue too, but his hunger was overwhelming.

There were two men in front of the screens. One was Asian, wearing a black tracksuit and audio headset, gaunt, with lank hair in need of trimming. He barely looked up as they approached. His glasses reflected the screens that absorbed his attention.

The other was dressed in army fatigues, wearing a discreet headset with a pin mike curving round one cheek. Even from the back, he seemed imperious, like a rogue general. When he turned towards Wisher, his strange, brutalised face matched his physical presence. There was little expression in the scarred flesh, but a clear sense of pain endured. The force of his personality projected like a blade, cutting through the crap, cutting to the chase.

He saw that Wisher was hungry, of course, and reached for the soup even as he introduced himself. Instead of a handshake, he handed Wisher a tin mug – and an unexpected opportunity.

Wisher blew on to a spoonful of broth, swallowed it. Beef and vegetable, well salted and vivid with herbs. A wave of pleasure spread as the food made its way into him. His situation was extraordinary, bizarre even, but all that mattered to Wisher right now was this blissful sustenance.

His host watched him while he ate.

'Good, isn't it.' A statement, not a question.

'Very.'

'More?'

Wisher returned the mug, which was promptly refilled. Sense was returning, and he began to analyse his situation. These people were like him, he knew that much already. They swam in the same sea, all spies together. And however they'd manage to track him, they were clearly better at it than his own people.

They'd snatched him out of Suffolk, brought him to this crumbling ruin, because they wanted to keep him off the radar. But they seemed to be as good as Jago's word on the subject of his personal safety. Hard though it was to believe, given the trouble they must have gone to, they simply seemed to want to talk to him, to make him this mysterious offer of employment.

Wisher swallowed down another mouthful of food, wiped his mouth with his sleeve cuff.

'Okay. I'm listening.'

Galloway turned to his computer screen and opened a folder of images. He clicked on a thumbnail and it expanded to fill the screen.

'Recognise him?'

Wisher studied the image for a moment. It showed a swarthy, slightly overweight man in a tight-fitting military jacket, mirrored shades resting on his close-cropped hair, a dated fashion statement. The armed bodyguards either side gave an indication of the subject's diminutive stature, and his status as a senior criminal operator.

'Florescu?'

It was an educated guess: Wisher could think of half-a-dozen candidates that might have matched the photograph, but some half-buried scrap of memory had shunted this particular crook to the top of his mental list. Galloway nodded confirmation:

'That's right. Arkady Florescu.'

The memory tumbled into the light. The smoky bar in Peshawar. The first encounter with the Russian couriers. An exchange between Graff and Sergei during which Florescu's name was mentioned.

And just a few moments later, Wisher's cellphone had buzzed three times, the contact signal from Bill Blake . . . Meaning the mention of Florescu could have been the trigger.

So Florescu was Blake's paymaster?

Wisher refocused. The revelation had left him a little dazed and Galloway was watching him closely. Wisher sensed the veteran spy had followed his thought process, had intended him to draw the very conclusion he had just drawn.

'I want you to kill him.'

There it was, laid out in plain English.

'Florescu?'

'Yes.'

The job title had been revealed. Assassin.

They want me to kill.

'Why?'

'Because he controls access to a stockpile of contraband uranium. Because he has begun to sell this nuclear material to the highest bidder. Because he needs to be stopped, and yet no one seems prepared to stop him.'

'He's at the top of a dozen "most wanted" lists.'

'But he is *not being stopped*. He's being tolerated. Indulged, even. His location is common knowledge. So are his crimes. But he's supplying a demand. Market forces are keeping him safe.'

Like Blake had said: *Conflict is our business.* The picture snapped into sharper focus.

'And you think killing him will make a difference?'

Galloway paused; Wisher felt like he'd hit a nerve.

'That's a complicated question, about which I have thought long and hard. But in summary, yes I do.'

Wisher set his cup down. He was in a house he didn't recognise, in a country he had never visited, with people he had never met before. And yet it was familiarity that gripped him. Blake's betrayal had smashed meaning and purpose from his world. In the days and weeks that followed, survival had been his focus – the primal need to live and to be free. But now, in just a few short sentences, this stranger called Galloway has conjured up structure, organised Wisher's thoughts, galvanised his intellect.

He had offered Wisher a *mission.*

'Why me?'

'Because you can. You proved it in Peshawar. And because you want to.'

Wisher shot Galloway what he hoped was a scornful look at the older man's presumption, his arrogance. But when he met his cold grey eyes, the gambit evaporated, revealed as churlish and quickly discarded, as it deserved to be.

It wasn't arrogance that Galloway presented. It was knowledge. He continued:

'I'm not looking for a butcher. I'm looking for someone who gives a damn. You've got the skills and you've got a conscience, too. You're a rare species, believe me.'

Wisher had a dizzying sense of connection. He knew he was strung out and disoriented. He knew that Galloway's discourse was a strategy as much as it was a revelation. But the truth it contained was undeniable. Exhilarating, this feeling of being known and understood so thoroughly. Strangely flattering, too, to be held in such unequivocal regard.

Wisher recalled a childhood theme park visit, not long after the family had moved back to New York State in the wake of his father's death. He had pestered his mother relentlessly to be allowed on the rollercoaster, even though he barely met the height requirement and would have to ride it alone. His sister had looked on enviously as his mother strapped him in, seated between strangers. As the car had started to climb away from the safety of the ground, a delicious mix of sensations had gripped him: fear of the experience to come; absolute determination to go for it despite the fear; certainty that this determination proved something good about him.

The recollection took hold of him now. He was at the foot of the Behemoth and looking forward to the ride.

'Any questions?'

If there was wit in Galloway's query, it was bone dry. Questions were *all* Wisher had. He picked one at random from the pile:

'Is Galloway your real name?'

'That's not a question. That's making conversation, and we don't have time for that. Ask me a real question.'

Again, the thrilling clarity of thought. Wisher took a moment to consider more carefully what his priorities were.

'What about my sister?'

Galloway cracked a thin smile. It seemed sour at first, a fresh scar twisting over his harsh features. But his eyes revealed a different emotion – compassion – and his voice was sober when he spoke:

'We've wiped you out, Tom. We've erased you.'

Wisher frowned. It was Jago who continued the explanation:

'We had a corpse to stand in for you. Car crash victim. Burned the face off, switched the database biometrics. You've been identified. You're being buried tomorrow.'

'So Rachel thinks I'm dead.'

'That depends on how smart she is.'

'She's very smart.'

'Then possibly not. What she's been told doesn't fit with what she saw in Suffolk. And you told her not to trust anyone, which was good advice. But the rest of the world, including the intelligence community, believes you're deceased. Even Bill Blake.'

Just hearing the name made Wisher flinch.

'He'd connected various threads of the conspiracy to you. When you led the police to the Peshawar device, you tied the knot. There was no way out for you.'

Blake's frame had been perfectly executed; but still it rankled Wisher that his own fate had been taken out of his hands.

'I could have tried to explain. I could have told my side of the story. '

Galloway shook his head.

'You'd have been shot on sight, and the world would have cheered.'

Deep down, Wisher knew it. It was why he had chosen to run.

'To answer your original question, Rachel is safe, but only as long as you remain under the radar. We can try to get word to her, but I can't make any promises.'

You're dead. Please kill someone for us. And by the way, you can never see your sister again.

'What happens if I walk out the door right now?'

'You won't.'

Certainty, rigid and unyielding, stared across at him. It was like talking to a hammer.

'Fuck.'

A jolt of frustration went through Wisher. He turned away and paced, fingers kneading his brows. A chair scraped as Galloway got to his feet.

'I've followed you, Tom Wisher. I've watched you for months. I know you. Right now you don't want world peace, you want Blake's head in a box. I know that. But you've got to rise above it. There's too much at stake.'

Get out of my head!

Wisher closed his eyes. Galloway was right behind him now.

'You are what you are, son. A fighter. A warrior. There's no longer a place for you out there, thanks to Blake. But with me you can make a difference.'

'By killing people.'

Wisher turned to meet the older man's glare head on. He'd wanted a reaction: he got withering contempt.

'What do you want to shoot at? Rocks? Trees? Tin cans? You're not a boy any more.'

The words stung, but at least they had cleared away the last shreds of ambiguity. It was just the two of them now, face to face. He spoke quietly, plainly:

'What exactly do you want from me, Mister Galloway?'

'I want you to believe in yourself. Let me do the rest.'

Wisher looked round. Jago and the Asian were watching him. He realised they had both faced the same decision he was facing now. And, as had no doubt been the case for them also, there had only been one real option from the moment the formidable Galloway had set his sights on them.

And so Wisher nodded, and it began.

Fifteen

Her name was Jeanette Franklin. She was twenty-six years old, five feet two inches tall, with bottle-bottom glasses, a pageboy fringe and excess hair on her top lip. And right now she was John Morgan's only ally.

She'd been at her desk when he clocked on at eight that morning. She'd barely looked up from her screen since. He'd noted her diligence but hadn't had much expectation of results. She was new to the data analysis team and the feeling around the office was that she wouldn't make the cut. Hence her assignment to the soon-to-be-retiring Morgan as his personal assistant in the hunt for Tom Wisher – a hunt that had rapidly run out of steam with the discovery of the young agent's charred body in England.

Kincaid had been quick to order the section's eyes back on to the Afghan–Pakistan border, in a concerted effort to establish whether another nuclear plot was hatching in the region. Morgan paid lip-service to the new priority, but privately he was pursuing a different agenda. At the debriefing with Blake and Kincaid, it was apparent that they were keen to focus on the manhunt, not the nuclear materials themselves. As a result, Morgan had decided this was precisely where he should concentrate his attention.

The thing was, Morgan didn't buy Tom Wisher as a traitor, not for a moment. His death had pained him deeply; not just for the waste of a young life, but because a reputation that was barely in the process of being formed was now forever tarnished.

Trails of evidence could always be faked; character was a slightly more durable parameter, a matter of judgement as much as empirical fact. Morgan had judged Wisher's character as sound, and he stood by that assessment.

Jeanette messaged at around six-thirty p.m. as he was preparing to leave the office. Last time he'd checked, she was working her way through the several hundred hours of CCTV footage culled from Peshawar's patchy surveillance network, trying to piece together Wisher's movements in the days leading up to the Safed Koh sortie, but with instructions to flag up anything else of relevance, which pretty much ruled out the use of the agency's latest pattern-recognition algorithms, given that Morgan wasn't exactly sure what he was looking for. All in all, it was a pretty thankless task.

Welcome to the rest of your life, he thought wearily, as he made his way into the side office where she worked alone.

'This is central Peshawar, two days before the blast.'

Morgan squinted at the screen. Leaning over Jeanette's shoulder, he noted that she smelled of lavender, like an old woman.

The monitor showed video footage of a crowded market street. The image refreshed once per second. Jeanette froze the frame, selected an individual from the centre of the crowd and pulled out a grainy close-up. She filtered and sharpened the image until it was recognisable: a Caucasian man in a suit. Morgan could discern now that there were two similarly dressed men either side of the centre figure.

'Who is he?'

'He's called Sergei Rachov.'

Morgan nodded vaguely. The name meant nothing to him. An on-screen database cascaded through a vast deck of mugshots until it found the match and pulled out a rap sheet. Russian extraction, spells in prison, organised crime links, standard issue Eastern Bloc thug . . . Jeanette's hand continued to twitch the mouse.

'He's listed as a known associate of this man.'

Another mugshot, this time a familiar face:

'Arkady Florescu.'

Morgan named him; Jeanette continued, her words mirroring her superior's train of thought, heading to the same conclusion:

'He operates out of Transnistria, trading contraband raided from former Soviet strongholds. Everything from medical supplies to hand grenades to— '

'Weapons grade uranium.'

Morgan finished the sentence for her. Then he stared at the screen for a while, long enough for Jeanette to shoot him a concerned look. He felt her gaze, and smiled at her. There was more to this girl than her colleagues had realised.

'Did you get anything on the associates?'

Jeanette flicked through a folder of screen grabs.

'This is the best shot.'

The still showed Sergei in the lead with his two associates flanking him, partly obscured by the crowd – but it was clear that both were holding briefcases. Sufficient transportation space for two subcritical masses of weapons-grade uranium, enriched with a high proportion of the fissile U_{235} isotope, whose atoms had a nasty habit of spitting out neutrons. Below the threshold mass of fifty-two kilograms, these stray neutrons dissipated as mild radiation. Above the threshold mass, they started colliding with their neighbouring atoms, smashing them apart to release their stored energy while knocking free more neutrons in the process. Now you had a chain reaction, a nuclear reaction, the devastating power of the atom unleashed. If you had two HEU components of, say, thirty kilos apiece, all you had to do was bring them together in a snug fit and – in theory at least – you had an atomic bomb. The CIA had feared such a threat since the fall of the Iron Curtain and the pilfering of the Soviet Union's vast nuclear stockpiles. Thankfully, the catastrophe had been averted . . . this time.

'Will you burn this on to a disc for me, Jeanette? Stills, rap sheets, the relevant CCTV clip. The whole lot.'

'That's against protocol, sir.'

The agency was very strict about information, particularly when it involved moving data outside of its rigorously guarded intranet.

'Will you do it anyway?'

'Sir.'

'And thank you. Your work has been of immense value. I'll make sure the powers that be are notified to that effect.'

The young data analyst blushed. Morgan was pleased for her; for himself, the emotions were much deeper, fiercer – and darker too. He was about to take the plunge.

It took just under three minutes, from the time Morgan sent the email to the knock on his office door. Kincaid himself, not bothering to wait for the okay before entering.

'Florescu's men in Peshawar. Interesting.'

'Thank you, sir.'

Morgan didn't elaborate. He knew he had acted against

Kincaid's directive, focusing on the supply line instead of the terrorist client base. And that wasn't the half of it.

'Have you circulated this yet?'

Deep breath ...

'I met the Moldovan ambassador in Washington last year, as you know. He's been looking for an excuse to mobilise against Florescu. This seemed like the perfect opportunity.'

'You've informed him.'

'Sir.'

Yes, sir, that's right, I took it upon myself to send a clear signal that the Moldovan government would receive international support for a prompt military incursion into disputed territory. That's because I want to stop terrorists making atom bombs, sir, even if you don't seem to ...

For a moment, Kincaid's expression was uncharacteristically blank. Then he smiled. Morgan had the mental image of a scab cracking open and weeping pus.

'Good work, John.'

And that was that. Morgan felt like punching his fist in the air. Was it possible that he just actually scored a point?

At the door, Kincaid turned to face him.

'May I add my personal condolences over the death of Tom Wisher. I know he was a protégé of yours. It must have hurt. Especially because of his betrayal.'

Twist the knife, why don't you?

'Thank you sir. Appreciate it.'

'He's about the same age as your boy, isn't he?'

Suddenly, it seemed to Morgan that the air had turned cold, cold enough to shrivel his field of view down to a frosted tunnel. When he spoke, his voice drifted from his mouth like mist.

'As my eldest, yes sir.'

'Must have struck a chord.'

Morgan met the deputy director's gunmetal grey eyes, and had the distinct impression of falling off a cliff. The door was pulled gently closed, leaving him alone, with his mind in turmoil:

What had he started?

Sixteen

It was two hours twenty minutes from Bialystok to Warsaw, then eighteen hours on the sleeper train from Warsaw to Kiev. Trains had been chosen as Wisher's mode of transportation because of their less stringent security checks; also to give him a chance to regain his strength and bed in his new alias, business traveller Kurt Schiele.

Not that security would have been a problem, necessarily. His true identity was dead and buried, and his new papers were superbly prepared. Still, Wisher was happy to eat and sleep in some approximation of normality for a while, albeit with a knot in his stomach every time one of the sour guards muscled past.

He befriended an InterRailing student couple from England, Jenny and Dan, partly to deepen his cover, also because he was strangely craving conversation. And it didn't hurt that Jenny was quite a beauty, either. They passed a very amiable evening, drinking moderately and swapping stories. Wisher had to maintain a German accent and limit his English vocabulary in order to pass as 'Schiele'; in fact, his command of the German language was excellent, thanks to schoolboy studies in England, topped up with evening classes in the States.

There was an art to this kind of role play. Wisher tended to focus on listening and reacting rather than offering anecdotes. The challenge was to sift in snippets of truth among the general deception. Thus he mentioned that his father had been in the forces; that his sister was a journalist; that he was a keen student of martial arts. As the conversation turned to childhood, he'd even referenced the grand magnolia in his garden; he was referring to MacMillan's family past, though it had a place in his own childhood memories, too, and in his heart.

They stayed together during the next morning: Wisher had time to kill, and joined his travelling companions on a tour of the Museum of the Great Patriotic War, built to commemorate the German–Soviet conflict of 1941 to 1945. The venue was impressive, though the combination of modernist concrete and massive socialist-realist sculpture struck him as particularly gloomy.

Conflict is our business. It's what we do.

Wisher wanted to fight. More than anything, he wanted to take the fight to Blake, but that would have to wait.

Evening brought the Odessa train, and a warm farewell to Jenny and Dan. Email addresses were exchanged, Wisher's invented on the spot, of course. A handshake for Dan, a kiss on the cheek for Jenny that he tried to prevent his libido from seeping into. Judging by the curious look she shot him, he hadn't quite succeeded.

The train ground out of the station and Wisher settled back for another thirteen hours of shuddering floors and gently thrumming window glass. The sojourn in normality had been refreshing, but now his mind turned again to the task at hand.

He'd spent a day with Galloway and his associates, preparing his cover story and discussing the logistics of the mission. He was to travel alone to Ukraine and rendezvous with a contact in Odessa who would supply weapons and equipment. Together they would make their way north by car, staying close to the border and crossing on foot through a region of dense forest. A forty-mile hike would bring them within striking distance of Florescu's base on the banks of the Dneister.

The spymaster wouldn't be drawn on the specifics of his organisation. Indeed, it remained unclear to Wisher how far his influence extended beyond the cracked glass and peeling wallpaper of the mansion in Poland. But he'd certainly made an impression on Wisher with the force of his character. The older man was matter-of-fact but there was charm at play, too, and a sense of respect for Wisher's journey that was gratifying. As they talked through the past weeks Galloway had made it clear that he understood Wisher's decision regarding MacMillan, admired the pursuit of principle at the expense of orders.

And then there was their conversation on the weed-strewn patio, as the last of the day ebbed from the sky. Wisher had stepped outside to clear his head; Galloway had joined him after a few moments. Nothing was said at first; the older man seemed content to share the cool air with his newest recruit.

'Are we the good guys?'

The question was Wisher's. Galloway's response was dry: 'Depends whose side you're on.'

'It can't always though, can it? It can't always depend.'

Galloway stared out across the ratty lawn, watching absent-mindedly as night settled upon it.

'People need protecting, that's how I see it. From themselves, sometimes, from their ignorance and its consequences. And from those who have knowledge, and abuse it. That's what we do, in the end. Protection.'

Galloway turned away from the night, back to face the young man at his side.

'That's why we're the good guys.'

It seemed crazy to be even thinking about concepts

like 'integrity' in the wake of his recent experiences and yet that was the word that kept coming to mind. That was Wisher's feeling about his new employer.

He banished the thought. No one could be trusted, not really. It was all about taking action. Look at the options available to you, choose your course of action and pursue it to the limit of your ability. What else was there?

He'd been given a file on Florescu, now loaded on to a media phone that would travel with him for the duration of his mission. Fifty years old, the arms dealer boasted a track record of robbery and larceny stretching back to Soviet-era Romania. His business had expanded rapidly during the Yugoslav wars of the early 1990s, supplying decommissioned Russian army weapons into the region. This kind of contraband remained the bedrock of his trade, and he was said to have vast stockpiles of ordnance at his fortified compound in Transnistria. But he'd also diversified of late, organising protection and couriers for the Afghan heroin trade, trafficking girls out of the Baltic states, investing in technology to service the increasingly profitable Tor network, a shadow internet that guaranteed anonymity to its often criminal users.

In short, he was exactly the kind of target Wisher had imagined when he elected special agent training. He studied the photos on his phone, criminal mugshots dating back to the late 1980s that showed a lean and hungry criminal on the rise; long-range surveillance shots from more recent years showed a man of widening girth and escalating self-importance, rarely leaving his compound, favouring the peaked cap and military jacket of the petty dictator. Wisher imagined the cap falling to the ground as a bullet punched through Florescu's forehead. He recalled the first man he shot, the jet of blood as he fell back . . .

Wisher packed the memory away. He didn't need

darkness right now. He turned to his phone for distraction, intending to scan the internet news, but soon he was searching out his sister's online presence instead. She was all over the net, as it turned out, and had carved out quite a reputation as a tireless critic of western governments in general and covert interventions in particular. *Sibling rivalry*, he thought to himself, and smiled.

Not surprisingly, there had been no updates in the last few days. But there was a personal blog that Rachel checked regularly, reading and responding to the various supporters and critics who posted there. It took just a few key strokes for Wisher to create an online identity and add a comment to the list. He hoped that Rachel still believed he was alive, despite the official pronouncements, that she wasn't hurting, and that she recognised his post for what it was, a message to her. He was under the radar for now, but he *would* see her again. He was sure of it.

Wisher left his couchette around two a.m. to use the washroom. Emerging from the cramped cabin, his eyes were drawn to a skinny young woman of around twenty who was now standing just a few feet down the corridor, smoking a cigarette. She stretched out her neck towards the high window and blew out smoke into the airstream rushing past outside.

She glanced towards him, as if just noticing him.

'English?'

'Deutsche,' he replied. She was scrawny but pretty in a low-class kind of way, with dark, finely shaped eyes and a sensual mouth. She switched easily into broken German:

'You like it in Ukraine?'

Her name was Katya, she said. She was a student, travelling home to Odessa to visit her parents. She'd decided to save money by buying a standard seat instead of a bunk, but was finding it impossible to doze in the company of her fellow passengers, many of whom were drunk and intent on chatting her up.

'Maybe you can make room for me in your bunk? What do you think?'

The question actually took Wisher by surprise: he'd been too busy fancying her for it to occur to him that she was, of course, a prostitute. She'd played him well, making conversation, letting him get a good look at the body she was prepared to sell.

Wisher knew how the prostitution racket worked, what a grim and ruthless trade it was. But still he was interested, there was no denying it. It had been too long since he had been with a woman.

She crossed the corridor to stand close to him, looked up at him subserviently. He frowned:

'You got a pimp?'

She looked at him uneasily.

'Is there a man that makes you do this?'

She shook her head.

'Just me. I just need somewhere to sleep.'

'Sleep?'

She placed a slender hand on his chest. The nails were shaped and tended, which could be taken as evidence of self-respect.

'We don't have to sleep. We can do what you like.' Her voice was soft and low, full lips held a little apart. He imagined the tip of her tongue wetting them. Her eyes met his; dark pools, inviting him in.

'Fifty euros. We can do what you like.' She smiled, then added as an afterthought:

'Not up the ass. I don't like that. Okay?'

Just like that, any romantic spell that Wisher might

have been weaving around the encounter abruptly vanished. The girl pushed herself against him, hand discreetly brushing his crotch as she kissed him on the neck. Wisher eased her away. He wanted a woman, but not like this.

The girl studied him, aware that his mood had changed. 'Don't you like me any more?'

He fished in his pocket and brought out a roll of euros. He peeled off a fifty, squeezed her hand shut over the banknote.

'Buy yourself some coffee.'

She shot him a look, then shrugged.

'Sleep well, Deutsche.'

She smiled again, a person now instead of a seductress, and headed off towards the buffet car. Wisher felt a pang – she was actually better looking when she wasn't trying so hard to be sexy. He headed back to his couchette; glancing back once, he caught sight of her stifling a yawn as she opened the connecting door and disappeared into the next carriage.

Nestled in his couchette, Wisher's imagination drifted back to Jenny. Now there was an attractive woman: her elegant neck, the line of her collarbone under her vest strap, visible as she shrugged her denim jacket to the back of her shoulders . . .

He sighed, rolled over. Sleep came slowly, filled with stressful dream fragments: MacMillan's execution, Blake's betrayal, the fortress, Peshawar.

In the moments when Wisher's mind lifted out of the dream haze, he was aware of a burning need for it all to make sense. If human life was the unit of value, then those lives that he had seen end in violence, or that he had taken himself, had to count for something. It was his responsibility to make sure they did.

The train drew into the Black Sea port city of Odessa around five in the morning. Wisher had barely slept; he needed more. Taxi drivers clustered round him as he left the station, hustling for custom despite the early hour. He picked a car at random, dozed in the back as it cruised along tall boulevards, the nineteenth-century grandeur still impressive, gradually revealed by the breaking light. He checked in at his hotel, which had been booked in advance, and went directly to his room. The generous double bed was bliss after the cramped couchette. He stripped down to his underwear, pulled the curtains to block out the dawn and slid between the sheets, heading quickly into a deep, satisfying sleep.

Next thing he knew, he was looking down the suppressor barrel of a Makarov PB handgun. The trigger click had woken him; the presence of an intruder stood over him on the bed sent a mighty surge of adrenaline through his veins. Slight, black-clad, a silhouette against curtains glowing with daylight behind them . . . must have moved like a ghost to get so close to him.

And he had no weapons to hand. Stupid.

The figure crouched slowly down, until the gun barrel was just inches from Wisher's face. A ski-masked face, detail obscured by gloom that his eyes were still adjusting to. Wisher shifted backwards, calling his limbs to red alert, muscles sucking up glucose and oxygen . . .

'Guten tag, Herr— '

Wisher twisted, a spasm of movement along the length of his body, legs shifting to upset the intruder's balance, right hand slamming into the intruder's wrist as he rolled out of the line of fire. The assailant – a woman, judging by her voice – spun away from the blow, still holding the gun. Wisher surged up, using his blankets as part of his attack, aiming to entangle her head under the fabric. She slipped away from him, trained suppleness in her movements. But he got hold of her gun hand once more and dug his thumb into her tendons, this time breaking her grip. The weapon dropped but she twisted free, tumbling on to the floor, rolling and righting, adopting a fighting stance as she turned to face him.

But he had the gun, trigger cocked and solid in his hand, a KGB classic from the days of Reagan and Brezhnev. The integral silencer played hell with accuracy but not at this range, levelled at the svelte silhouette crouching by the balcony doors.

'It isn't loaded.'

The voice was accented Eastern European, the tone dry. He believed her – the weapon handled on the light side – but he pulled the trigger anyway. A dull click, as predicted.

The intruder straightened, pulled off her mask and shook out a short crop of thick, raven hair.

'I'm Maja Vacic. I work for Galloway.'

She offered a smile, so small it hardly turned her lips, and yet the expression somehow lit up her face with mischief.

'You're pretty quick for a dead man.'

Seventeen

He feels sure they will like each other, Wisher and Maja. Both have superb combat skills and a hunger for action; deeper than that runs the shared sadness in their personal histories, wounds that they are reluctant to discuss but which are the basis of their drive.

Wisher's powerful sense of justice ennobles him, but brings with it a tendency to be earnest; Maja's vitality masks a certain ruthlessness, a useful quality in an assassin, not so helpful in social situations. It's possible they could grate against each other, but Galloway would bet money on the opposite outcome.

The truck judders beneath his chair, travelling through the ancient forests of the Zhytomyr Oblast in northern Ukraine. Tevis is seated beside him, very much online; Jago drives. Screens show the various feeds from Odessa: Wisher's phone, Maja's phone, her laptop also. The device is open and its webcam relays an image from the hotel room.

Wisher has slept for a few hours. Now he is showering, preparing for the long drive that will take them to the border with Transnistria. Maja is changing clothes; half naked, she shoots a look at the door to the en suite bathroom. She lingers for a moment, waiting for an 'accidental' moment of frisson, should Wisher emerge from the bathroom and find her half-dressed. Has she forgotten Galloway is watching?

It seems she had: she flicks a quick glance towards the laptop's eye and resumes dressing. Galloway smiles; he loves this playful, flirtatious side to her. On the occasions that he surrenders to sleep, and his mind is overcome with thoughts of the illness that chisels relentlessly at his insides, he sometimes turns to her image for consolation. Not in a sexual way, but as a father might think of a child, reflecting on the being he has forged, their flaws, their charms, the ways in which they have exceeded his expectations, as indeed his biological children have done.

The smile is quick to fade. He is sending these young souls into danger, and he does not take his actions lightly.

A long game is being played out on the chessboard of the world. Wisher and Maja are among Galloway's pieces, to be advanced and withdrawn at his command. His opponent is the mysterious Consortium, which fields more than one champion of its own. Over the years, it has been necessary on occasion for Galloway to sacrifice a piece in order to out-manoeuvre his enemy. He can only hope that this will not be one of those times.

Eighteen

The call from Kincaid came in around two-thirty a.m.: get the hell to Transnistria, now. And all because of John Morgan, whose 'initiative' in the wake of the Peshawar bomb had triggered a military build-up against Florescu's fortified headquarters. Blake shook his head in amused disbelief – in admiration, almost. He had imagined that Morgan's capacity to eat shit and grin was without limit.

Officially, Blake was taking well-deserved leave following the closure of the file on Tom Wisher. Unofficially, he was the sole passenger on a nine-seat Cessna, a private charter out of Budapest, currently flying above the Romanian end of the Carpathian range. He glanced out of the window. The terrain below alternated between wooded valleys and bare peaks, snow capped in places. Blake knew he should be concentrating on getting the news of the impending attack to Florescu and helping to move his key stock of nuclear materials to safety before the Moldovans descended. He understood the priority – highly enriched uranium was a rare commodity on the black market – and yet it pissed him off that he'd had to put his own plans on the backburner, a fact that he'd made abundantly clear with some choice expletives during the small-hours call.

Blake's personal priority was Rachel Wisher. Since their encounter in England he'd found it hard to get her out of his mind. She was naturally fair, like her brother; lean, a tomboy who hardly had time to eat but still retained full lips and feminine curves. And that damn mid-Atlantic accent, so affected! She seemed to think it made her seem cosmopolitan; to him it was a sign of insecurity and it only made him desire her more.

He'd felt nothing personal towards Tom Wisher, except perhaps mild contempt for his boy scout enthusiasm, until he'd stuck a shard of wood into his face and spilt his blood, three weeks ago now. The boy should have been eliminated at the fortress in Safed Koh; instead he'd got the better of Blake, left his mark upon him. It didn't matter that Blake had successfully painted Wisher as the ultimate all-American traitor; there was still a score to be settled, a beating to be delivered in some off-the-grid location . . .

Except of course that it was not to be. Wisher had been killed, car crash, engine fire, no face left – just the sort of method Blake would have used himself if he'd wanted to stage the disappearance of a valuable asset, say. Tom Wisher had no resources, no friends, Blake had made sure of that. And yet Rachel had been there.

As he'd worked his way into her confidence, he'd grown more and more certain that she knew something significant, something she was holding back. Her only motive would be to protect her brother, but her brother was dead, laid out on a slab in front of her . . . with no face.

A beautiful woman with a secret.

Blake licked his lips absent-mindedly. He could feel his hand on the back of Rachel Wisher's neck, holding her face down on a bare wooden table. His other hand was under her belly, fingers finding the cold metal button of her tomboy jeans, jerking down the rough fabric to reveal the pale curves beneath ... It was going to happen. He could feel it in his nuts.

In truth, Blake needed a break from the game. He was exhausted after Peshawar. The dressing was off his face wound, but it was not quite healed, raw red at the seam, stitches poking out. Blake knew that Kincaid was not the end of the line when it came to the hidden structure that penetrated the Agency, but he didn't want to look further. He'd reached his level. He was a man of action, he wasn't interested in boardrooms and business suits. More than once over the last few days, he'd contemplated stepping off the treadmill, but always he ran up against the same problem: he had money, but it would take a small fortune to buy the anonymity he would need to evade not just Kincaid but the shadowy people he reported to.

Twenty minutes until touch down. Blake fished a wrap of cocaine from his pocket, sniffed up the last of its contents. He'd been clean through necessity during the Pakistan detail, gratifying to know he could cope without the drug when needed, though he'd put on a few pounds in the process. Since his return to the States he'd been making up for lost time and he had to admit the world was in sharper focus as a result, plus the weight had been falling off. All in all, it was good to have Charlie back.

There were cars waiting on the cracked concrete of the private landing strip. Taking point on the reception committee was Stefan Florescu, Arkady's twenty-year-old son, with a retinue of armed goons to back him up. Luggage in hand, Blake strode over to the young man, offered a relaxed handshake:

'How goes it, Stefan?'

Stefan declined the welcome. Instead, he nodded curtly to one of his heavies, a huge bruiser by the name of Olek, who stepped up to Blake, took his bag, and turned him to face one of the black sedans.

'You spread please.'

Blake obliged, allowing the thug to pat him down. The coke was still warm in his veins, he had no trouble in finding an easy smile as he was turned to face Florescu junior.

'You're growing up, kid.'

Blake projected respect for the aspiring young mobster. In truth, he found it all rather pathetic. Stefan was short like his father but had none of the presence. With his army jacket, bum-fluff sideburns and acne, he appeared more like the cast member of some high-school musical about dictatorship in eastern Europe. Unsurprisingly, he took Blake's compliment at face value, puffing out his chest:

'My father is waiting for you, Mister Blake.'

It was a short drive to the gates of Florescu's base, across a bleak, semi-militarised stretch of terrain. All the men Blake saw from the car window were armed; the occasional women he passed seemed weary, and always escorted.

The base itself was situated in a former factory complex that butted against the Dneister along its western edge. The vehicles passed through the check point; the route continued past a succession of warehouse buildings to the river's edge.

The group disembarked. Blake accompanied Stefan to the fore, with Olek and his crew following to the rear. They were heading toward the rear of a large wooden shed that seemed to pre-date the soviet-era concrete and corrugated iron warehouses.

There was the thud of an impact, nearby but out of sight. The wooden wall beside Blake juddered in response.

He started to tense, his senses cocaine keen: what the fuck was this about?

They rounded the corner of the building to find Arkady Florescu, his face red with exertion, pulling a throwing axe from the back wall. The wooden surface was riddled with divots: clearly this was a regular pastime for the arms dealer. A quivering young woman stood against the wall, her face streaked with tears. Florescu walked up to her, pressed the axe blade against her cheek, snarled a few phrases of Russian in low, angry tones. A maid caught stealing, perhaps. Blake's eye corner twitched – the sense of impending violence in the air was palpable.

Florescu wiped the axe handle with his shirt tail and glanced over at the new arrival, his eyes dark. Behind him, the target girl sagged, weak-kneed with relief at the stay of execution.

'What brings you to my home, Mister Blake?'

'I have news, Arkady.' Blake tried to strike an appropriately grave tone. He wasn't looking forward to breaking this particular story, particularly not to an angry man holding a not-so-blunt instrument.

'Good news, I hope.'

It was a joke, the kind you were not supposed to laugh at unless you wanted to experience immediate physical pain. Blake kept his expression neutral; Florescu snorted at his guest's lack of reaction, then continued:

'Of course it is not good news. You would not be here if it was.'

Florescu raised the axe, threw it. He was a good shot: the girl barely had time to gasp before it slammed into her chest. The arms dealer held out his hand for a towel, which was promptly handed to him by a nervous assistant. He mopped the sweat from his face and neck, threw down the towel and gestured for Blake to accompany him back into the main encampment.

Come. Tell me your news.'

'NATO liberals don't appreciate the vital role that businessmen such as yourself play in the global security market. That's why they're targeting you as the supply line.'

Blake was addressing Florescu over a dinner table stocked with rustic fare, bread, meat, cheeses, local wines. They sat outside, under an awning stretched in front of a former office block. Butane space heaters drove the chill from the air, as did the shot of ferocious plum brandy they'd just downed.

Stefan was there also, a sullen girl draped on his shoulder. Olek stood guard. Blake had been careful to make clear his allegiance to Florescu, but he didn't want to downplay the urgency of the situation, either. Soldiers were coming, and soon.

'I'm not interested in politics. I am a businessman. I buy cheap, I sell at a profit. It is simple.'

'I'm afraid the Moldovan government don't see it like that.'

Blake recalled his first contact with the Romanian, back in 1992. They'd both been rookies at the time; both had lined their pockets working as go-betweens for Operation MIAS, and taking a cut for their troubles. Blake used to joke that Florescu could be a poster boy for the American Dream; for his part, Florescu had continued to see himself as a valued ally of the West. Unfortunately that was a world view that would have to change.

The arms dealer drew on a cigar and exhaled smoke, thoughtful.

'What do you propose?'

'The army is coming. Leave them something to find. Say ten per cent of your stock, guarded by a skeleton crew— '

Florescu slammed his hands down on the table, knocking his chair back as he lurched to his feet:

'For ten per cent we will stand and fight! Let them try to take my weapons!'

Blake had expected this reaction. Arrogance and alcohol were not a great combination when it came to diplomacy. This was why he was here, to manage this pivot point, to turn it in his favour.

'You are a brave man, Arkady, but now is the time for strategy. Give NATO a victory to trumpet and a haul of weapons to add to their collection, and their attention will move elsewhere. By seeming to lose, you will end up the winner. And the special relationship between our organisations can continue, to the benefit of all.'

Blake knew his suggestion made sense, he could only hope Florescu was smart enough to see beyond his own hubris. For sure, the black marketeer's status would dip in the wake of a perceived 'clean-up' of his operation. But it would be short-lived, and with the majority of his stock removed to safe locations, he would have no problem in resuming his trade once the dust had settled.

Blake's logic seemed to have struck a chord. The Romanian was quiet for long seconds, eyes narrowed as he considered his options.

'We will leave the uranium behind.'

Shit.

The commodity that Blake had been instructed to keep in circulation was the one that Florescu had decided to dispose of. Worst of all, the reasoning made perfect sense. Trying to maintain his composure, Blake scrabbled round in his mind for a riposte.

'It's your most valuable stock . . .'

'I can make money from guns and women. Uranium has brought me only trouble.'

'But it's such a unique resource—'

'It is decided.' Florescu glowered; Blake bit his tongue. If he pushed further, he risked triggering suspicion.

The arms dealer turned to his son:

'Stefan, stop fondling your whore. I need vehicles.'

Stefan's expression was sour as he got to his feet. He didn't like the way his father talked to him. Blake picked up on the sentiment and his rising panic started to subside. In his mind, a contingency plan was forming.

Nineteen

It was definitely just sex, not lovemaking. At least it was the first time round. It was night, it was cold, and they were alone together, deep in woodland, miles from the nearest human being. They were young, fit and able – and they were attracted to each other. It was always going to happen.

They'd said it plainly to each other, looking down at the lightweight tunnel tent Wisher had just erected. The foliage was thick above them, the moon waning, and it really was pitch black outside. They'd agreed to risk an LED flashlight while they assembled the tent and shared out some rations. They'd walked twenty-five miles, they were starving and the cold was quick to find its way into their bones, despite the layers of clothing they wore.

And so Wisher had switched off the flashlight and they had slid into the tent together, and delicious relief was quick to follow. Afterwards, there wasn't much else to do in such close quarters apart from embrace. It had felt natural, playful, and if there was a small voice in the back of Wisher's mind suggesting things were a bit *too* comfortable, well, he managed to block it out.

They'd avoided sweet nothings, kept the pillow talk ironic, even digressed into strategic discussion of the mission to come. Both were tired and needed sleep, and a goodnight kiss seemed an appropriate way to draw a line under the evening. He'd leaned over, half expecting a polite peck and a shoulder turned towards him. But he'd found her lips open and inviting and soon they were at it again, this time without the excuse of urgent physical need. They were doing it because it was good, and it felt right. And because they were human beings, and they craved intimacy just as much as their bodies needed release, if not more.

Wisher couldn't remember falling asleep. The transition to dawn was seamless, perceived first as birdsong heard through the canvas that enclosed him. He opened his eyes to grey light, filtered through the tent walls, and Maja, just inches away, watching him with dark, inquisitive eyes.

'Time to get up.' She kissed him, then slipped away, shuffling backwards out into the air. Wisher dawdled for a moment, enjoying the tingle on his lips. Then he followed Maja out into the dewy morning.

She was pulling on a long-sleeved vest, the first of several layers. He glimpsed the knotted muscles of her back, lean enough for the ribs to show, the skin marked by several scars. Hard to believe how soft it had felt to his touch, how yielding, this wiry, athletic torso.

'I have to say, I just don't know what to think right now.' She spoke without turning. He walked over to join her, his footfalls shifting leaves, snapping twigs. He wanted to see her face before deciding how to respond.

'It's just fucking. It's not a big deal. It's just what people do. And I do feel lighter, you know? But we have to keep our heads clear, Wisher. We have to.'

And Wisher thought to himself, *okay, fair enough.*

'I hear you. Let's keep it simple.'

Her shoulders relaxed. She glanced round, and shot him a look of such straightforward affection that he revised his position. She deserved something closer to the truth of what he was feeling.

'Honestly, I think maybe we can have something together. Something real. But I won't go there until this is done.'

She sighed.

'I haven't been close to anyone since I started working for Galloway. I don't even know if it's possible, when we do what we do.'

She shot him a guarded look, then continued:

'But yeah. Maybe.'

'And now the subject is officially closed.'

He thought it was best to draw a line under the subject. She nodded agreement.

'No more sex until we've killed someone.'

It would have been funny if it weren't true.

'Potassium chloride. Stops the heart, hard to trace, especially if you hide the puncture wound in the ear or the mouth.'

Wisher nodded, deadpan.

'Good tip.'

Maja rolled up the syringes and phials in their fabric wrap, eased them back into a pouch on the military-style webbing harness she now wore. She was showing him the collection of concealed weapons she had brought, offering to share. She was the mission armourer, after all.

What else did he know about her? She was thirty years old, born in Croatia, a child survivor of the war that devastated her immediate family in the early 1990s. She'd worked with Galloway for three years. Her immediate family were dead. This job was her world. And she was nothing if not prepared. Webbing pouches held flares, grenades, throwing stars, even a knuckle duster.

Wisher already had a Dragunov SVD sniper rifle slung over one shoulder and the Makarov PB and silencer in a custom holster under his jacket. The decision between distance shot or close-quarters kill would depend on the state of play at the target location. He pocketed a couple of M67 fragmentation grenades, plus a simple fold-out knife, a useful all-purpose tool in forest terrain.

Maja shot him a mischievous look.

'Of course, you've already examined the most powerful of my hidden weapons.'

'You mean your feminine charms?'

'You're such a gentleman!'

Maja's words rode on a wave of delighted laughter. Wisher grinned, knowing he was being teased but happy to have amused her. Then they both heard gruff voices among the far trees, and realised they had just fucked up.

Quick looks, quicker movements. Above all, quiet. Weapons rolled into the groundsheet they had been resting on. Maja carried the canvas with her to one side, buried herself into the nook formed between two thick roots at the base of a tree. Wisher took a few swift steps towards a gulley, folded himself down and out of sight behind it. He flicked up the charcoal grey hood of his lightweight inner jacket and lifted his eye-line to the edge of the dip, pulling bracken fronds across and over his head for camouflage.

A small band of men came into view. Poachers, four of them. Backwoodsmen, with thick, rugged jackets and leather hunting caps, their eyes bloodshot from moonshine vodka, their faces all but lost to beard. Two had rifles, one a shotgun. Coils of rope and trap-wire were slung from belts. The youngest of them carried their catch, rabbits and pigeons slung over his shoulders.

Wisher had the sniper rifle to hand. He fed the slender barrel out through his nest of bracken, sighted to track the poachers as they drew nearer. In this dense forest it was impossible to get a line of fire on more than one man at a time – shoot one of them and he would instantly make himself a target. He looked across at Maja. She had her back against the tree, handgun at the ready, but she had no line of sight on the approaching group.

And they were suspicious, no doubt about it. None of them spoke; one of their number moved ahead of the others, his shotgun levelled. This was their forest, they could sense trespassers. Wisher and Maja had been scrupulous about treading lightly and keeping track of fabric snags, but still it was likely they had left traces that a skilled woodsman could spot.

The nearest of the hunters edged closer and Wisher held his breath. The man was perhaps twenty-five yards away. Too late for Wisher to withdraw his rifle barrel – the movement would be visible, and might catch the hunter's attention. Instead he sighted on the grizzled forehead and cleared his mind, entirely ready to shoot. If it kicked off, one would be dead for certain, Maja would roll from cover and take down another, with luck, then it would be two against two.

The hunter stopped, gestured for the others behind him to follow suit. He ducked under a low bough, his nostrils flared. Something had caught his attention. He knelt to examine a section of foliage. With a surprisingly delicate touch, he pinched a small leaf between thumb and forefinger. The blade hung limply, its young stalk broken.

Wisher glanced again at Maja: her jaw was clenched, tendons stringing on her neck, both hands on her gun; her chest heaved as she pumped oxygen into her system – she was getting ready to make her move. Wisher tried to signal with his eyes, *for fuck's sake, wait!*

A ragged screech broke the stillness; there was a flurry

of beating wings as a large bird burst through the green. It was a hooded crow, drawn by the carrion on the poachers belt, now protesting as its branch was disturbed. The hunters broke their silence with curses and mockery.

The crow's raw cry was hardly the same as Maja's laughter – and yet, how likely was it that a woman was at large in this wilderness? Common sense appeared to have won the moment; the suspicious poacher returned to his group, growling and swearing as his comrades teased him. Wisher kept stock still, waiting for the huntsman's inevitable last glance back before risking a move. He couldn't understand their dialect, but he imagined the conversation was turning firmly towards lunch and an afternoon of drinking after the group's early start.

He looked across at Maja. She too remained frozen, awaiting his cue that the coast was clear. He hung on till the last of the poachers was out of sight, then counted out another minute in his head. It was a long sixty seconds. He spent it gazing into the forest's depths, staring until the layers of green started merging into abstraction. His mind was on Maja. They had both let their guards down, and seriously jeopardised the mission as a result.

He couldn't be sure what the future held; but for now, the chemistry between them had to be extinguished.

Dusk brought them to a wooded ridge overlooking the Dniester, within view of Florescu's base, a conglomeration of factory buildings lying the best part of a mile downriver. They stayed behind the tree line, wary of patrols. A column of vehicles wound along the access road into the compound, headlights switching on as night drew in, a string of flickering jewels in the gloom.

They hadn't spoken about the close encounter with the poachers. They hadn't needed to. They'd also stopped cracking jokes, and kept their distance during their occasional rest stops. It wasn't awkward for Wisher: working with someone he liked and respected was as good as it got for many, and it was enough for now.

Wisher kept guard while Maja established a communications link with Galloway's mobile command unit. Using his rifle sight as a telescope, he surveyed the line of vehicles snaking towards Florescu's base: trucks and vans in the main, being directed through the gates and organised in rows on the concrete beyond. He could discern small figures running between the vehicles, steering them towards various storage depots spread throughout the complex, where other workers were ready to load them up with boxes of ordnance.

Florescu was getting ready to move out.

They'd touched base with Galloway once already, and got the heads up on the proposed military strike courtesy of a Langley mole. During the day's trek Wisher had reflected on who the source might be. He hoped it was John Morgan; he didn't like to think of the veteran agent as part of Kincaid's conspiracy, and certainly, if you weren't with Kincaid you were against him.

'The attack is scheduled for dawn tomorrow. That's around 0600 hours. We should aim to strike and be clear well before that.' Maja wore a headset, and was relaying instructions from Galloway. Wisher crouched beside her; she handed him a second headset so that he could join the conversation.

'How's it looking, Agent Wisher?'

Galloway's gravelly tone was strangely reassuring, as was his use of a formal title. They weren't working in a vacuum here; they were part of a plan, a grand design, striking blows for the global good where government and international law could not reach.

'They're on the move, sir.'

'Time's pressing. Florescu will make a show of leadership but he won't stay till the bitter end.'

'I think I should head in as soon as it's dark. We don't want him to slip the net. And all the activity on site could actually work in our favour. More distractions, more cover.'

Wisher had no visual contact with Galloway; he and Maja would be visible via the laptop webcam. Instinctively they leaned in so Galloway would be able to see them both. He imagined the spymaster's rugged face lost in thought as he weighed up the situation.

'You ready, agent?'

'I'm good to go, sir.'

Wisher meant it. He believed in Galloway and in the justice of his mission. It was time to redefine himself. Assassin.

Galloway's voice crackled in his headset.

'Then let's do this.'

Twenty

As Morgan headed into the office where Jeanette was stationed, he passed Peavey heading out – and his heart, already riding low in the water, sank still further into the gloom.

Brushing past Kincaid's oily lackey was unpleasant enough. At close quarters Morgan smelt body odour forcing its way past lacklustre cologne, observed dandruff dusting Peavey's shoulders. Some men defied grooming. The assistant offered a reptilian smile, mouthed a pleasantry that evaporated on contact with the air, and slipped away down the corridor, leaving a vaguely acrid tang behind him, like a burnt-out appliance.

The situation with Jeanette was just as Morgan might have predicted: she was in the process of shutting down her terminal and gathering her few belongings, ready to leave the office.

'I've been reassigned to advanced analysis. Thanks to your recommendation, I presume. I'm grateful.'

Her gratitude was no doubt genuine enough; still she seemed reluctant to look him in the eyes. Since he had challenged Kincaid over Tom Wisher's treachery, Morgan had been a marked man; since his decision to talk to Moldova behind the deputy director's back, he'd pretty much had the laser dot on his forehead. Typical of Kincaid to asset-strip a rival in this way, promoting Jeanette upwards and out of reach.

It wasn't that she didn't deserve it; simply that she understood it came at the cost of shunning him. He was the sinking ship; she was the last of the rats. He felt like issuing some gloomy warning to her about corruption in high places. Instead he smiled with as much warmth as he could muster.

'Good luck.'

'You too.' There was a brief meeting of eyes as she bustled out of the room – and then Morgan was alone.

He sat for a few minutes in the empty office, reflecting on his situation. He had crossed Kincaid, and he was being punished for it. That was the first layer. But what about the real-world events that triggered the clash? Why would Kincaid believe so readily in Wisher the traitor? Why wouldn't he want Florescu stopped?

Morgan switched on the computer terminal. As it booted up he mentally sifted through his years of experience working for the agency, his memories of Kincaid and Blake. The two of them were tight, but discreetly so. And protocol was always observed, at least on the surface. However they were moving as one at the moment, Kincaid the arm, Blake the fist.

The intranet went live and Morgan accessed the agent diary. Blake was out of the office, called away at short notice. A flight had been booked to Warsaw. No travel details beyond that.

Called away just a few hours after the Moldovan assault on Florescu's base was announced.

Each way Morgan turned his thoughts, they spelled out the same word. *Conspiracy.* Uranium being fed into the black market, in the hope of triggering nuclear events, justifying an escalation in defence spending and CIA influence. Now the idea had a hold of his mind, it didn't even seem unlikely. Not with Kincaid at the centre of the web. Not with Blake at large in Eastern Europe.

Morgan had sent his wife and youngest son upstate for a few days, after the veiled threat from Kincaid. A crazy precaution, surely unnecessary given his public profile and status within the agency, and yet it had felt right. He was out on a limb and he could hear Kincaid's chainsaw roaring into life.

He logged off the computer and headed out into the main office, making a point of switching off the light as he exited. Attention to detail was important right now. Out on the main floor of the Clandestine Service, he could feel the tightening of his colleagues' shoulders as he passed, the discreet aversion of gazes. He heard the prison-guard call in his head: *Dead man walking!*

Television monitors on walls and pillars around the room showed twenty-four-hour newsfeeds, ticker tapes scrolled across the bottoms of screens. A newsreader intoned:

'There were ugly scenes in the Capitol today as police clashed with several hundred demonstrators protesting against the massive increase in troop numbers proposed in response to the elevated nuclear threat level in Afghanistan.'

Jostling crowds of students and refuseniks in DC, celebrity spokespeople offering soundbites, restless cops and bearded liberals regarding each other uneasily. The video feeds were due to switch over in the early hours to track the Moldovan army via drone and satellite as they launched their six a.m. attack on Florescu. Morgan would make another statement after the foray into Transnistria, explaining how America and her friends had tirelessly pursued the terrorist supply line, another victory in the war on terror . . .

Except that the conspiracy wanted the supply line kept

open. Bill Blake had flown out to the region, undoubtedly to facilitate this very process. Why else would be Kincaid and Peavey be looking so at ease, drinking coffee and chatting in front of the monitors like suits at a soirée?

For one dreadful, rushing moment of vertigo, Morgan wondered if they were *all* in on it. Not just Kincaid, Peavey and Blake, but every other employee, all the way up to the director himself. Maybe there was no government any more, no police force, no America: just oligarchs and private armies, carving up the world. Was he the only one who didn't know?

Morgan steadied himself on the back of a chair and waited for his mind to settle. He was strung out and sleep deprived, but he was determined to see this crisis through. Kincaid and his kind might rule through fear, but they were not invulnerable. Plus he still had an ace up his sleeve – and he had King Crimson to thank for it.

Fifteen years earlier, at a Ukrainian embassy dinner organised to forge links with post-Soviet states, he'd discovered that he shared with the Moldovan ambassador a passion for progressive rock, in particular the debut album by British guitarist Robert Fripp and his band. Strange how taste in music can transcend political, social and even language barriers. The official agenda had focused on issues of economic instability and organised crime, but in his own corner of the long table, Morgan had forged a genuine friendship.

This was the reason that he had his own private channel of communication with Moldova, a cellphone SIM that was untapped and off the record, with a similarly secure receiver at his good friend Andrei's end. Any strategic advice he might offer could be implemented without the knowledge of American surveillance operations in general, and Kincaid in particular.

Morgan glanced round. If anyone had noticed his moment of light-headedness, they were keeping it to themselves. Deliberately relaxing his movements, he strolled over to join his boss at the monitor wall. Kincaid glanced round, then turned his attention back to the footage of protesters and pundits.

'What do you make of it, John?'

'I guess it's a dangerous world out there.' Morgan didn't want to chat, but it was necessary to keep up appearances.

'I guess it is.' Kincaid nodded sagely.

'Let's hope the strike on Florescu brings the threat level down.' Morgan added.

Peavey and Kincaid both turned to study him.

'It's what we all want.' Kincaid's face was neutral. Morgan smiled in return.

Like fuck you do – Sir.

The veteran agent made his excuses and headed out of the building, in search of fresh air. He had his cellphone in his pocket, the secure SIM in his wallet. It was time to play his ace in the hole.

Meanwhile, Kincaid stared nonchalantly at the news images, indifferent to the reports of civil disobedience flaring up like wild fires in city after city. The police presence appeared sufficient to keep this micro-rebellion in check; more than that, he was confident that weight of public opinion supported the war on terror. His country needed enemies, he had helped maintain the supply.

No doubt there were many faces from the CIA files among the sea of protesters, but no one in particular stood out among the crowd: Kincaid was too busy savouring the big picture.

If he had looked more closely, he might have spotted

Rachel Wisher at a London demo, her features twisted with rage and exultation as she joined the chanting of her comrades-in-arms. Rachel directed her anger towards the news camera, and it seemed like she was shouting from the screen directly at the CIA deputy director, who looked at her but did not see her. And yet if she had been in the room with him, he still would not have heard her: her ideals were as foreign to him as the wilderness her brother now ran through.

Twenty-one

'You useless piece of shit!'

Blake wasn't sure of the exact translation, but the sentiment was clear enough. A truck moving under Stefan Florescu's direction had just reversed into the steel door strut of a storage depot, then ripped its own side open as the panicked youth had tried to guide it back into line before his father stomped over to intervene. A double fail, then. Blake swallowed a grin.

Florescu senior was red-faced, barking at his son, berating him in front of his men, who made less effort than Blake to hide their disdain. Stefan's sneer was gone for now; the lad was ashen with humiliation. But the contempt would be quick to return, indeed this routine was the force that created it.

Blake could read Stefan so easily. If the lad had a stronger intellect then he would dissemble more, but sadly he was no match for his father, in that department as well as most others. Florescu was repugnant but shrewd, a quality that Blake admired. His aggression towards his son was an understandable weakness, driven by frustration at the young man's limitations. It also gave Blake a route into Stefan's psyche, a lever to work him with.

The argument between father and son ended with Stefan marching off towards the accommodation block while Florescu took over the supervisory role himself. Blake had joined the removal effort, hefting cases with the other men, literal tonnes of stock that were being relocated to a forest hideaway, to be guarded while the Moldovan army made its show of force. Straws had been drawn among Florescu's militia; the handful that would stay behind were to offer only token resistance. Money for their families – plus the fear of punishment if they broke ranks – would secure their silence once they had been arrested.

Blake gave it fifteen minutes before heading over to the accommodation block, on the pretext of a washroom visit. Stefan's door was half open; through it Blake could see the young man's girlfriend, stripped to the waist, pouring vodka on to ice. He lingered for a moment – her face was vacant but her figure was pert – then knocked. The girl looked up, stared at Blake in the doorway, her eyes blank as a rabbit's. A wooden drawer scraped, out of sight, as Blake made his way into the room.

Stefan got clumsily to his feet, his back against a chest of drawers. The lad was ill at ease, and the reason was obvious to a seasoned cocaine user like Blake. Flecks of powder on the nostrils, wiped away by a sleeve; a mirror lying flat on the top of the wooden surface behind him. Craving jabbed at Blake; the bump on the flight over had long since worn off, and the Turkish coffee jag he'd been on since dinner was fraying his nerves.

'Get the fuck out of my room.' Stefan was still the sulky teenager, despite having left that particular decade behind.

'I'm here to talk.' Blake's eyes were on the white grains dotting Stefan's cuff, the mirror's edges . . .

'What about?'

'Your father.'

Stefan sniffed, screwing up his face for a moment, then shot a look at the sullen, still topless girl perched on his bed.

'Leave us.'

'It's cold outside.' The girl pouted, wanting their rugged visitor to turn and admire her breasts.

'Just fucking go!' Stefan snapped. The girl huffed, tugged on a T-shirt and left. Blake took her place on the edge of the bed, glanced up wearily at Stefan, who shifted uncomfortably.

'You want to share that?'

Blake grinned, activating the roguish charm that had opened so many doors for him. Stefan narrowed his eyes – then smirked and turned to retrieve his stash from the top drawer.

Back outside, a short time later, the cold air was a delicious pleasure on Blake's tingling nasal septum. The drugs had sharpened his game: he'd bonded well with Stefan and now they were headed out across the base to the warehouse where Florescu's most precious asset was stored. Blake directed Stefan to the driver's side of a small truck; Stefan played along well, head ducked and subservient to Blake's broad gestures. They hardly stood out amid the furious activity throughout the compound; certainly they looked like they knew what they were doing.

The plan was simple enough: they were going to steal as much of the uranium stock as they could manage between them.

Blake had correctly judged that a resentful son might be willing to scheme against an overbearing father, but he had actually underestimated the vigour of Stefan's paternal dislike.

The lad was smarter than he appeared, too – not much of an achievement, admittedly, but a relief nonetheless. Blake had visualised having to spell out the nuts and bolts of his proposal, but Stefan had no trouble at all in grasping the basic economics. There were plenty of guns in circulation, very little weapons-grade uranium, plus an active demand, stimulated by Blake's intrigues among some of South Asia's more fanatical residents.

In short, there was a small fortune to be made, irrespective of the various geopolitical implications that Blake cared less and less about. Enough money, perhaps, to finally satisfy his avarice. Enough to fund his exit from the grid, goodbye and fuck you very much to Kincaid, Morgan and the rest of them, all busy defending their little fortresses of self-righteousness and self-interest, all utterly the same to his cynical gaze. Time to move on.

Young Stefan Florescu was an unlikely new player at the poker table. Maybe it was the Charlie talking, but Blake couldn't help feeling he could make something of this young man. Stefan had revealed ambition, claiming a small network of loyal men among his father's private army. He also had contacts in Odessa who he thought might be able to ship the contraband once it had been spirited away. It was an impressive contribution.

Blake climbed down from the truck and stood watch as Stefan reversed through the warehouse doors. This time there was no clumsy collision. The store was away from the main thoroughfare, a stroke of good fortune. Still, there was no time to waste. Once inside, they pulled the doors shut and worked by flashlight, transferring crates into the rear of the vehicle.

The metal blocks were packaged individually, nested in foam beds with a lead surround, inside crates labelled on all sides by the familiar trefoil warning symbol. The blocks were not dangerously radioactive on their own, but needed the protective lining to prevent accidental fission – a remote possibility, but an alarming one – while they were in proximity to each other. Each crate weighed around one hundred pounds; there were twenty-nine in total. After they had shifted twenty crates between them, they were both sweating and the rear of the truck was low on its suspension. The vehicle had rough terrain to face and they couldn't risk a broken axle; yet Blake was reluctant to leave any stock behind. Another four crates filled the passenger seats and footwells. In the warehouse they'd been stored at a distance from each other, spaced apart on the floor. Now they were packed together, their protective housings in actual contact with each other.

Blake shot Stefan a look, trying to gauge if the young man had any idea of the utter recklessness of their plan. The lad grinned back; he hadn't felt this important in years.

That was when Damir entered. The young Croatian was barely seventeen but had been in Florescu's entourage for three years already, first as a drug mule, now as a sentry and loyal dogsbody. He'd caught sight of flashlight flicker at the warehouse windows and decided to take a closer look. Now he found himself pointing his gun at Stefan Florescu, caught in the act of theft.

Despite his surprise, his rifle barrel did not waver. Whatever was unfolding, Damir felt sure he could turn it to his advantage. He'd never liked Stefan, never trusted him. He was about to say something to that effect when Blake's thick fingers clamped over his mouth and his hand was twisted painfully from the rifle trigger. The agent had been around the back of the van and had moved into shadow at the creak of the warehouse door. Now Damir was writhing and powerless in his bearlike grasp.

A look shot between Stefan, still startled by the intrusion, and Blake, grim and certain. The mood transmitted swiftly from older to younger man; Stefan snapped open a pocket knife, took hold of a tarpaulin and stepped up to the squirming sentry. He finished him swiftly and silently, catching the blood spill in the tarp. Blake lowered the shuddering body into its shroud, together he and Stefan rolled the corpse up tightly, then carried the bundle to the back of the storeroom and stashed it there. Again Blake was impressed: he'd seen the father in the son, ruthless and pragmatic when the need arose. His confidence went up a notch.

Time to move out. The last five crates were heaved into the cargo trailer, stacked double. Blake and Stefan hurriedly piled blankets and empty boxes over the labelled crates, then closed and padlocked the truck's rear pull-down door as an extra precaution against discovery. They shook hands, and Stefan climbed back into the driver's seat. Both had GPS on their phones, and had agreed a rendezvous point for the following evening, a village fifty miles down river, again organised via Stefan's contacts.

Blake walked alongside the truck part of the way towards the main gates, where another van was waiting to exit the compound. The lights were bright, but he made no attempt at concealment. Instead he slapped the rump of the truck as it pulled away from him, waved to the guards as the vehicle pulled up at the barrier, then turned and strode back along the main thoroughfare of the base. He moved quickly, projecting brisk efficiency; when he shot a casual look back towards the gate, he saw that the truck had made it through unchecked. So far, so good.

He returned to Stefan's room to find his girl drunk and dozing. He didn't ask permission, he just took hold of her. With her face pushed down into the pillow, it was easy enough to imagine that it was Rachel Wisher's muffled grunts of pain that he heard, Rachel's hair that he twisted tight between his fingers. He finished quickly and left the sobbing girl in search of somewhere to clean up, concerned that his absence would be noticed by Florescu. He was far from being out of the danger zone, but still, he had a positive spring in his step as he pushed through the swing doors into the washroom. Who didn't love it when a plan came together?

Certainly he wasn't prepared for the ski-masked, black-clad figure that he found edging slowly towards Florescu, silenced handgun aimed and ready, poised to execute the arms dealer at point blank range.

Twenty-two

It was called a 'haptic belt' – an array of vibrating units, much like those found in a cell phone, but here mounted on the inside of an elastic strap that sat around Wisher's midriff, against his skin. He'd hardly had time to test out the prototype device before setting off on his run into Florescu's camp, but Maja had assured him its use was intuitive, and she was right.

The belt allowed Maja to steer Wisher by triggering individual vibrating units that were oriented in the direction he needed to take. As he progressed, Maja directed him by GPS, cross-referencing his position with a static map and a live satellite feed to her tablet computer. It was a brilliantly simple and efficient technique that depended on a strong rapport between the belt-wearer and the map-reader – and Wisher and Maja certainly had that.

The belt also worked in reverse: in 'homing' mode it would automatically steer the wearer towards its base unit or another specified location or transmitter. Right now it meant that Wisher could focus his attention on the rough terrain under his feet and the branches coming towards him out of the darkness, confident that Maja would signal changes to his route as required.

Wisher ran low and fast, keeping inside the forest. He wore all-black stealth clothing: lightweight hooded top over a Kevlar vest, ski mask, leather gloves. A headband-mounted video camera relayed a live image to Maja's computer; it was also being watched by Galloway in the mobile command unit. Wisher had grenades and flares in his webbing harness, and more explosive charges in a small knapsack, should he need to create a diversion. The Makarov was in a customised holster, its silencer already screwed into place, and he had the Dragunov sniper rifle with night sight slung over his shoulder.

The forest reached to within fifty feet of the perimeter fence at its closest point. Wisher crouched low, right at the edge of the foliage cover. Through binoculars he could follow the activity inside the base. Even at first glance there were twenty to thirty men engaged in loading and despatching Florescu's armaments; he guessed there would be at least double that number at large within the compound, with more coming and going as vehicles arrived and were dispatched. He could hear their voices in the distance, above the background of engine noise and loading clanks.

There was a sentry tower above the main gate, one man on duty. This lookout held binoculars too, Wisher observed, but his attention was directed away from the base, down along the road that snaked away beside the river's edge, turning up through the trees after about a mile. There was no sight of his target yet, though in truth it would be hard to identify Florescu at this range, particularly as the men were largely dressed against the cold night with hats and turned-up collars. So much for the sniper shot: the kill would have to be at close range. He took off the Dragunov, tucked it into a tree hollow. Four feet in length, it was just too cumbersome to stay on his back during an infiltration run.

Through the wire, Wisher watched a small truck progress along the central concourse, over-laden and perilously low on its suspension. A foreman slapped it on its side and it set off towards the main gates. The two guards on duty seemed to know the driver and stopped to make conversation. While their attention was occupied, Wisher broke from cover and bolted for the fence.

Work lights cast a thick block of shadow from a warehouse close to the perimeter. Wisher quickly merged with the darkness, his back now up against the fence. Only the front-gate guards had a direct view down this back alley. There was CCTV coverage also, but Wisher was gambling that the security monitors were unmanned; with just hours until the base was evacuated, it would surely be all hands on deck.

Wisher cut through the fence – quicker than trying to negotiate the razor wire on top, and it provided a concealed exit point, too. He stepped through, roughly sealed the mesh behind him. A few steps took him to the warehouse wall; he pressed himself against the concrete blocks and started edging left.

'Man approaching. Twenty yards and closing.'

Maja's voice crackled in his earpiece, the first time she had spoken since he left the ridge. Shortwave was the most reliable audio link in this neck of the woods, but it was easily intercepted. The haptic belt buzzed, giving him the direction of the approaching hostile as viewed by Maja on her satellite feed. Wisher slipped a dentist's mirror from his pocket, crouched down and used it to peer round the corner of the building.

The sentry was just twenty feet away, relieving himself. He wore a scarf up to his nose, cap pulled down, donkey jacket. Mist rose from the now damp concrete as he turned away, zipping himself up. Wisher crept up behind him and took him down, clubbing him with his pistol butt then dragging him back into the shadows. Donning the guard's outfit would mean sacrificing the hcadcam, but it made crossing fifty yards of open ground considerably less daunting.

'You've got two men out on the asphalt. One heading west, one entering from the north . . .'

Maja was advising caution, but there was no time to waste. Either his disguise was going to work, or it was not.

Wisher pulled down the guard's hat, turned up his jacket collar, hefted his rifle and strode out into the open. His destination was the three-storey office block that had been roughly converted for residential use. Across the asphalt, an armed man waved to him, beckoning him over. Wisher waved back, but kept his course towards the trestle tables that marked a path to the main door.

'Hey!'

A gruff voice cut through the chill air, clearly directed at him. He kept walking.

'Hey, *voye!*'

The voice was getting closer; Wisher turned to face the speaker.

It was Florescu himself, twenty-five yards away and scowling in Wisher's general direction. Too far away to be sure of a kill with either the silenced pistol or the ex-service rifle he was holding. And there was a truck pulling on to the concourse where they stood, backing up towards the accommodation block: more witnesses.

Florescu shouted at him in Russian, something about helping with the loading, and pointed back towards the warehouses. Wisher nodded, trotted off in the direction indicated. At least he had escaped detection. And behind him Florescu was heading into the accommodation block, the perfect opportunity for a covert hit. As soon as he was round the corner Wisher doubled back on himself, jogging alongside a moving lorry for a few yards, using the cover to make a run for the back of the former office building.

He found a fire escape and quickly scaled it. On the top floor he elbowed through the door glass and let himself in. The corridor was dark, which suited him just fine. He shed the borrowed jacket and hat, pulled his ski-mask back over his face, adjusted the video camera on its headband. It occurred to him that he had not felt the nudge of the haptic belt for some minutes – but then he was indoors now, satellite eyes could not guide him. At least Maja would be able to follow his actions via the video feed, as would Galloway. There was a microphone bead on the earpiece wire, tucked inside the collar of his undershirt. He fished it out, pushed to activate.

'I'm going in.'

He unholstered the Makarov PB, felt the weight of it. The silencer barrel gave the weapon a tendency to tip forward; he adjusted his grip to compensate. In the gloom of the corridor's end, the only illumination came through part-opened doors, letting in grey fractions of the flood-light glare outside. Wisher was a wraith, a black form moving in shadow.

Slowly, he stretched out his arm. He ran his gaze along the dark fabric of his sleeve, imagining the sinews under-neath. The black leather of his glove merged seamlessly with the dark handle of the pistol, the long barrel seemed to his imagination more like a blade than a handgun.

Assassin.

A role that stretched back through history, to the first kingdoms, the first courts. A tradition of deadly force, deployed by nobles and traitors alike to shape the affairs of men. He was no longer the player, he was the chess piece. Not the pawn, but the knight for hire, the 'free lance'. He was the weapon of choice.

Rooms were laid out along either side of a single corridor that ran the length of the building. Wisher moved with fluid efficiency from door to door. It felt like dancing, this wraith-mode, smooth lines, no sharp edges, flowing like smoke. But the rooms on this floor were empty, it appeared; even the suite at the far end that surely was Florescu's personal lair, judging by the rugs and bedding that had accumulated there.

There were washrooms either side of the central stairwell, male and female. Wisher checked both; the stench from the male latrine was foul, the sprung hinge whined as the door pulled shut. Wisher softened the motion with his hand; the sound would be lost amid the vehicle noise outside, he felt sure.

The stairwell was brightly lit, reminiscent of a school with its polished cement steps and enamel-painted metal handrail. Wisher pushed through glass safety doors and crept downwards, aware that he was in plain sight now, black-clad against the white walls. The stairs turned and he saw a figure on the floor below, walking past behind the glass doors that marked the entry on to that level.

It was Florescu, heading for the washroom. Target acquired.

Wisher edged forward, leading with his gun hand. He'd packed his scruples away. Florescu was a deserving target. The scale of his base bore testament to that. The armaments that the Romanian supplied would take hundreds of lives in the world's war zones. The weapons-grade uranium he was trading could kill many thousands more. He needed to be stopped.

Wisher was half-way towards the stairwell door when another figure appeared, a maid carrying a box she could barely see past, pushing through the doors and out on to the stairs. Wisher ducked back against the wall, on instinct

– but there was no way to conceal himself. If she looked up . . .

The silencer barrel of the Makarov jutted forward. The maid wore a headscarf: the black cotton would soak up the blood jet, if he fired the gun. But he knew in his gut that he couldn't shoot. Not this innocent woman.

She hesitated at the top of the stairs. She had to peer round the box she held in order to see the first step – and in the process she obscured her view of the spy clad in black, standing just feet away from her. Silently, he lowered his gun as the woman proceeded out of sight, fully occupied with negotiating her descent. Wisher drew breath: as soon as the maid was gone, he made his move.

Light, quiet steps to the glass doors. Through and turn right. Gloved hand on the washroom door, easy on the hinge as he slid through. He held the door, let it fall back. Pressed himself against the wall of the short corridor leading into the room, gun in hand, pointed like a blade. He edged forwards.

Florescu was at the sink, silhouetted against large windows of frosted glass, through which the exterior lights glowed. There was a mirror: Wisher could see his own reflection, but the water's rush would cover any sound. Florescu bent to the cold flow, splashed his face. Wisher stepped away from the wall. His mind formed a line in the air, eye to iron sight to target skull. He held his breath.

The sprung hinge gave him a split-second of warning. The door behind him was swinging open. He turned—

And saw Bill Blake.

Memory and emotion rushed, threatened to overwhelm him. The split-second divided further, broke into fragments of time. He had to act *now*.

But it was already the next moment, and Blake had seen Wisher: a masked assassin, targeting Florescu.

Wisher pulled the trigger without looking. The silenced gun hissed and a bullet flew towards the arms dealer. In the same shattered instant, Blake was lunging at him. Wisher swung his gun hand round, knowing he would not be quick enough, but knowing also that the weapon would draw the attack. Blake did indeed snatch for the Makarov: Wisher slammed an elbow into the older man's face, felt it sink in and do its damage. The scar on Blake's face that was barely healed broke open, dribbling fresh blood.

Blake kept hold of Wisher's gun hand, managed to block a second blow to the face. The two men were just inches apart. Their eyes met – was there recognition from Blake? Did Wisher's furious blue eyes boring into his connect him back to Peshawar, to the hotel room where he had fought this young man once before?

Wisher pushed forward, got his forearm against Blake's throat, slamming his head back against the wall. Blake's free hand was jabbing and clawing at Wisher's side, but Wisher's surges of force were having more impact, squeezing breath and life out of his enemy. He braced back against the other side of the entrance corridor, triangulating his efforts, directing his strength and will towards the apex, the pressure point at Blake's windpipe.

He wanted this, wanted it too much. The desire for revenge flooded him, overwhelming whatever noble purpose he might have constructed for himself. Wisher had entered this room intent on making the world a better place; now it was his anger only that was being served, rage that called out to be quenched . . .

A sharp new pain tipped the balance – the fingers of his gun hand, being twisted off the pistol grip – Florescu!

The bullet had ripped through the meat of the racketeer's trapezius but he was still very much alive. One arm
was compromised by the wound; the other was joining
forces with the half-asphyxiated Blake to liberate the gun
from Wisher's failing grip.

Wisher squeezed the trigger; the gun sneezed twice
but the rounds missed flesh and bone, instead drilling
harmlessly into the ceiling. His fingers were giving way;
aiming to buy time, he threw the gun down deliberately.
Florescu turned to chase it as it skidded across the washroom tiles; Wisher released his grip on Blake and swung
instead at the side of Florescu's head, landing a clean
blow even as Blake sagged to the floor, gasping. Florescu
stumbled forward, Wisher drove into the back of him,
both hands gripping the racketeer's head like a rugby
ball, pushing forward and down, slamming his temple
into the edge of the sink. Florescu's head jerked back as
his body slumped beneath him.

Wisher spun on his heels: Blake had crawled across the
floor, was stretching for the handgun . . .

Wisher leapt across the washroom. He pounced on to
Blake's back, knocking out whatever breath the burly
agent might have mustered. The gun was pushed away,
skittering under the sink. Blake writhed and heaved
under Wisher, jolting him upwards. His head slammed
into the towel dispenser; the curved door of the device
was knocked open and a roll of tough linen coiled out,
spilling on to Wisher as he forced his weight back down
on Blake beneath him.

Wisher grabbed hold of the fabric, looped it round
Blake's neck as the older man tried to lift himself up once
more. He twisted the material on itself to form a thick
rope, twisted it again to increase its constriction around
Blake's windpipe. His former colleague gasped and

arched, but Wisher kept him pinned down. From this position he could kill him. No doubt about it.

But now Florescu was stirring. He must have a skull made of cast iron! Wisher pulled harder: he needed Blake to die right now. The man's face was bright red, he hadn't drawn breath in twenty seconds, but his neck was like a tree trunk.

Across the floor from Wisher, Florescu groaned, unstuck his eyes – and saw the assassin on top of Blake, strangling him. Wisher's eyes flicked to the gun lying in the shadows.

Stupid, stupid!

Florescu picked up on the eye movement, spotted the weapon for himself and started scrambling for it. Wisher cursed – Blake still moved beneath him, not finished yet. He released the fabric knot, leapt clear of Blake and grabbed alongside Florescu for the gun.

Faces close, Florescu flashed a grin, secret knowledge: he held a concealed knife! The Romanian jabbed at Wisher, who recoiled, too late. His Kevlar jacket blocked the blade from sinking in between his ribs, but now Florescu had the Makarov. He staggered to his feet, aiming down. Wisher sprang upwards, right into his opponent's centre of mass. He heaved him up, all two hundred pounds of him. The gun caught on the edge of the sink and another round hissed from the silencer barrel, narrowly missing Wisher's foot. He lifted the arms dealer up and over the row of sinks, his whole frame straining with exertion as he hefted the big man towards the frosted windows. The glass gave way spectacularly and Florescu fell out of sight. It must have been at least twenty feet to the ground below, far enough to break a neck, if he was lucky . . .

Wisher snatched up the handgun, trembling, pointed it out of the window as he leant forward.

Florescu was *right there*, just a few feet away, sprawled on top of one of the trucks reversed up at the entrance to the block! If anything, the short fall seemed to have knocked some sense back into him. He was already barking orders:

'Up there! Shoot him!'

His confused men turned their attention, and their guns, upward to where Wisher stood, a black wraith framed by the broken washroom window.

The first of the gunshots came as Wisher was ducking down. A hail of bullets quickly followed, escalating as more and more of Florescu's workforce directed their weapons at the first floor window. Glass blew like snow, every last fragment knocked from the frame, whipped up and further shattered by streaking lead. The metal window-frame itself buckled, then fell loose. Even the concrete that held it was starting to crumble. And across the floor, now frosted with broken glass, Blake was groaning.

Sweat streamed down Wisher's face, inside the ski mask. Blinking salt water from his eyes, he shrugged off his knapsack, pulled open the Velcro straps. Inside was a night-vision headset, duct tape, detonator wire and twenty pounds of C4 explosives. Not the sort of package you wanted to wave around in a firestorm, but right now it was the only exit strategy he could think of.

He slipped a seven-second grenade from a webbing pouch, pulled the pin, started the count in his mind. No going back now. He dropped the grenade into the knapsack . . . *one* . . . straps back down tight . . . *two, three* . . . throw the damn thing up and over his head, out through the broken window . . . *four* . . .

Wisher was slithering away, across the sea of broken glass, picking up cuts and scrapes as he reached the small entrance corridor, the door on its sprung hinge . . . *five, six* . . . bullets still reached the walls around him, chipping off paint and plaster. He stretched to grab the door handle, pulled himself through.

The blast was deafening, the force of it slammed the washroom door shut, bowling Wisher out into the corridor. He rolled to his feet and sprinted for the fire escape. It wouldn't take Florescu's men long to think of spreading round the back of the building, if they hadn't done so already.

Wisher barged through the fire escape, clattered down the rear metal stairs, dropped the last few feet to the ground and started running. The briefest of glimpses across the asphalt as he broke cover showed that the truck had been totalled. Guards were shouting for help, fighting the flames, running into the building with rifles raised. There was more than one man down; Wisher saw splashes of blood red, bright in the work lights, dark bodies on the ground, twisted and ripped open. No way to be sure if Florescu was among them. Keep running.

He made it behind the nearest warehouse without being seen. A voice rose above the chaos behind him, shouting orders – Florescu, still alive and incandescent with rage, from the sound of it. A few more seconds took Wisher back to the hole he had cut in the fence. He pulled it open and wriggled through. In moments he was back under cover of the forest, running in the direction he had come, up the slope and away from the compound – but without the benefit of the haptic belt's nudges to guide him through the pitch dark. He could only assume it was malfunctioning. He squeezed the microphone bead, whispered breathlessly as he sprinted:

'Maja, Blake's here! Fucking Blake!'

Twenty-three

'You've got two men out on the asphalt. One heading west, one entering from the north.'

Careful, Wisher, Maja thought to herself as she passed surveillance intel down the wire to him. His video feed had been relegated to a side pocket just moments earlier, after he had overpowered a sentry and stolen his coat and jacket. The plan had been to maintain a video link at all times, yet she understood his strategy and his need for urgency. She was like him in that regard.

She cared about Wisher's fate in a professional sense – they were team-mates after all – but also she couldn't deny that the thought of sex with him again had slunk across her mind more than once, if only to be picked up and bodily removed, like a cat being put outside for the night. A warm, heavy, purring cat.

Maja was heterosexual but she didn't particularly like men, which was a problem when it came to relationships. Tom Wisher, however, was a refreshing change. Maybe it was just the context of their shared mission, but he seemed free of the bullshit that guys were so fond of. He wasn't trying to lure, or seduce, or coerce her. He just seemed to like her.

It didn't hurt that he was good-looking and fighting fit. But it counted more that he was lean on the inside, like her, stripped back of the romantic crap that men and women were compelled to throw at each other. Last night they'd been two animals, doing what animals did. Did it have to be more complicated than that?

Maja had rehearsed this line of thought enough times to know there were flaws in it, and that biology was not the sum of human experience. If she ever got round to therapy, she expected she'd be told it was a defence mechanism, along with the coldness she could slip into like a favourite sweater, when she was ready to end a liaison, or a conversation – or a life.

When Wisher had suggested there could be more than just sex between them, he should have blown it according to her rules. Yet in truth she'd also glimpsed something like the shared future he was hinting at, and dishonesty seemed wasteful. She would see how things lay once the mission was finished. At least there would be no bullshit.

One thing did still bug her, though: the method of Wisher's recruitment. From what she knew, the other operatives she'd met – Jago, Tevis, Ramona – had been approached by Galloway in the same way she had: cautiously. Yet everything about Wisher's extraction from England smacked of recklessness, desperation, even. What made him so special?

'Hey, *voye!*'

She heard the shout in her earpiece, relayed from Wisher's kit, indistinct but still audible. It meant he had been spotted. The satellite image on her tablet screen was indistinct, and lagged by at least a second. She could see Wisher emerging from behind the warehouse and being approached by the figure stood in the centre of the asphalt concourse, presumably the one who shouted. A truck was backing into the space also.

The cluster of pixels that was Wisher paused, then changed direction. No panic in the movement: the disguise had been a good idea. She checked the clock:

just heading past eleven p.m., plenty of time to make the kill, get back to camp and pack up before the military strike kicked off. Maja took a breath and shifted position. The haptic belt joystick control was still in her lap; she set it to one side, for later.

That was when Galloway cut in to her audio channel: 'Maja, respond.'

'I'm here.' Something about his tone made the hairs of the nape of her neck tingle. There was a problem.

'The Moldovan attack is at midnight. Not 0600. Midnight. Is that clear?'

Maja held her breath as the information sunk in. Midnight. Less than an hour until the area was swarming with soldiers under instruction to arrest Florescu and shut down his operation. The assassins had moved promptly for fear that Florescu would slip the net. But the net was sweeping faster than any of them had realised – a failure of intelligence on the part of Galloway and Tevis that had put Wisher and Maja directly in the path of an advancing army.

'Advise, sir.'

'Notify the asset. Prepare to withdraw. It's going to be chaos down there.'

'Sir.'

Maja understood why Florescu had been targeted for assassination, and she knew that his arrest would be considered a failure by her superior. Galloway did what he did because the system was riddled by corruption. Florescu must have been shielded by some part of that system, or their mission would not have been deemed necessary. Possibly the Moldovan assault represented a legitimate effort to bring the law to bear on a known criminal. But corruption had a way of protecting its own.

And Wisher was close to his target, tantalisingly close.

Maja had undertaken twenty-two missions for Galloway in the three years she had worked for him. Seven had been aborted, like this one, due to security concerns. Her boss valued his team. She was disappointed: excess adrenaline swirled inside her head like water searching for a drain. But she trusted Galloway's judgement. Calling Wisher back might not be so easy, however.

She'd been following the satellite feed, seen Wisher head off in one direction then double back towards the accommodation block. He'd got the scent; he wasn't going to like this. She readied a phrase in her mind, reached for the bead mike on her earphone wire.

And heard a footfall.

Quiet, but close. Unmistakeable.

Awareness raced out from her like a pressure wave, into the inky darkness that spilled between the trees. It *could* be an animal, a deer, for instance. But that wasn't the image that had formed in her mind to fit the sound, the twig snap and the shift of leaves around it. Not a slender hoof; she had heard a boot. It didn't occur to her that she had been less than vigilant. She was good at what she did; if someone had gotten this close, they must be good too.

She already had a gun in hand. She was close to a tree trunk, now she backed against it, silently pulling herself free from the wires that linked her to her tablet computer. She had a night-vision headset in her kit bag, but it was cumbersome to fit and set up. There was a night-scope set up on her rifle, too, and within easy reach. She picked up the weapon, but held off activating its image enhancer. Her eyes and other senses were attuned to the dark; once she started using technology to assist her, this sensitivity would be dulled.

She peeled away from the tree trunk, stepped lightly

into the gloom. Her tablet screen glowed behind her, a lure for any stalker. She moved swiftly from tree to tree, keeping the light source in the corner of her eye as a reference point. Looking back from fifty feet out, the nest of her equipment was flickering like a camp fire, casting shadows into the surrounding thicket.

She heard the noise again, a few yards further into the forest. This was not paranoia; she trusted her senses.

She leaned around the trunk she was backed up against. Some moonlight trickled down through the leaves above, enough to make visible a clearing among the trees, in the direction of the sound. She dodged a few steps towards the grey pool of light. Tree trunks loomed at its edge, dark sentinels fixed amid the vague shimmer of leaves. Then a slice cleaved away from one trunk, black against darker black, movement without form – it was her quarry, slipping into the shadows.

Maja darted out across the clearing. Whoever was spying on her, they were about to get a *much* closer look.

Then gravity failed, and the world was turning upside down. A jolt shot painfully through her frame as she flew into the air.

A hunter's noose, tight round her ankle, hauling her up, leaving her spinning. *Fuck.*

She closed her eyes, the better to feel her way. She had to be quick. At least both hands were free. She grabbed for her webbing belt, pulled open a pouch, one hand ready to catch the pocket knife as it fell out. The blade had a button release; as it flicked open she was already folding upwards, one leg hooked behind the other to steady herself, her free hand reaching out . . .

Foliage rustled to one side, her captor emerging.

She took hold under her bent knee. She was folded up tight on herself, hanging like a huge pupa as she sawed at the rope holding her. The blade was razor sharp and made quick work of the line. The last strands snapped under her weight and she fell eight feet or so to the floor. She hit the ground awkwardly, nothing she could do but stay loose and soak up the force of the impact.

The breath was knocked from her; she drew hard on the chill air to replace it as she rolled out of her landing sprawl. A figure blocked the movement, the twin black holes of a shotgun barrel pointed down at her. She kicked up from the ground, knocking the shotgun to one side. Her attacker let off a round on reflex. The muzzle flare lit up the clearing, and she saw him. It was one of the poachers they had seen yesterday. The leader, the one who had heard her laughter, who had followed a hunch there was game besides rabbit and pheasant to be had in this particular stretch of forest.

Maja kicked again, low this time, buckling the poacher's knee. Quick to her feet, she felt a second presence behind her and swept backwards with her knife hand. The blade found shoulder flesh, the second attacker grunted in surprise and pain. But a third man was springing from the dark, unnoticed until he pounced: they were seasoned hunters all, used to stalking the most skittish of prey, and their skills in this terrain were equal to hers.

She jabbed again with the knife, only to feel her wrist caught tight as a wire noose was slipped around it. The restraint bit into her skin, drawing blood. The stabbed man turned her, slapped her across the face. She struck his throat in return, her hand flat like a shovel blade. He gasped and fell back, but now she had the first poacher right behind her, gun pushed into the curve of her neck. He was a big man, and his weight bore down the length of the shotgun barrel, forcing her to the ground, to her knees.

The three of them had Maja ensnared. The fourth, the youngest, had not returned with them. One twisted the snare wire round her wrist. One kept her pinned by the gun. The third, the man she stabbed, kicked her in the stomach, hard. She folded her free arm tight into her body, as if to defend herself. In reality she was fumbling in pockets, searching for a weapon.

A flashlight was switched on. The shotgun man grabbed her by the hair and twisted her face to the light. She felt her pupils shrink in the glare, the vague forms of the darkness instantly erased. She kept her eyes down, vision swimming.

Think, Maja. Buy time.

'I work for the government.' Her Russian was text-book, she'd sound like a cop to them. And she was spying on Florescu; they surely have her placed as some kind of special agent.

'I can get you a reward.'

The man with the shotgun pushed down again. He was the leader among them. His voice was thick with dialect:

'How much?'

'American dollars. Euros. Ten thousand. Maybe more.'

It wasn't a bad prize for a night's hunting. But Maja knew the negotiation would not be that simple, given the opportunities presented by a captive female.

They didn't seem to need to speak to each other, these forest men. The light still blinded her, but she imagined the looks that shot between them, the weighing of options. The wounded man stepped closer, shining his flashlight straight down. She could see her silhouette on the ground in front of herself, the dark mass of her head encircled by light, like an angel.

'Suck my cock if you want to live.'

Grunts of approval from the other poachers. After all, they could still claim their reward if they didn't damage her too much.

Maja was no longer in the woods of Transnistria. She was back in Vukovar, in the hospital where her mother had worked. She was with the hundreds of medics and patients rounded up by Serbian forces and transported to the woods outside the city. She was one of the few who had scrambled to safety in the confusion, who had hid among the trees as soul after soul had been set free from its flesh, body after body had been cast into the open ground. This was her darkest place, the source of her fear, her coldness, her strength. This was the making of her.

Aged nine, she'd seen what inhumanity was possible in the name of country, of ethnicity. Some part of her had died on that day, some soft part of her inner self had petrified. These men would never dominate her, not if death was all they had to threaten her with. She'd rather let the shotgun liberate her brain from its cave of bone than bow to their vile wishes. But right now she didn't need that last resort.

The injured man set down the flashlight, fumbled his fly open with the one arm that worked. Maja looked up. She could see him now, lit from underneath like a movie villain. She grinned fiercely, flicked out her free hand. A throwing star – the four-pointed steel shuriken, a favoured weapon of the ninja – flew from her fingers, glinting as it crossed the few feet between them. She kept all her blades sharp; this one popped the man's eyeball and embedded itself in the orbit, blood and jelly oozing round it.

Surprise bought her the moment she needed to pivot on one knee and knock aside the shotgun behind her. The second round discharged; the hunter straight away cracked open the barrel, shook out the spent cartridges. The wire snare jerked at her wrist, drawing more blood; she spun on the ground and took out the legs of the poacher who held her leash. She kicked at his face, viciously, determined to empty his mouth of teeth. Tethered to him, she rolled closer, opened his neck with the tip of a second throwing star. Blood pumped all over, the dying body spasmed. She turned, threw the star at the shotgun man. It stuck in his forehead, the thickest part of the skull; grotesque, but it didn't penetrate the bone, didn't stop him snapping shut his reloaded weapon and aiming it.

Maja rolled again: this time the snare wire came with her, the dead man's grip on it released. Her own rifle lay where she had dropped it, she snatched it up, turned—

The hunter's forehead blew out in a spume of blood and brain matter. The throwing star fell close to her, returned to sender, its tip embedded in a rough triangle of bone. The hunter dropped to his knees, fell flat on to what was left of his face.

Wisher stepped from the forest, lowering his night-scope. He was red-cheeked and breathless from running; his eyes held darker feelings. Maja got to her feet, pulling the snare wire from her wrist, flinching at the pain. She could hardly look at him.

'I didn't need you.'

Sensibly, Wisher said nothing.

A groan rose from the ground; the last poacher was still alive, though blind in one eye from the shuriken. Maja walked over to him, crouched down into the glow from the flashlight beside him. She glanced up at Wisher; he watched her silently.

She had a syringe in her hand, drew potassium chloride from a phial. She straddled the fallen hunter, held the syringe to catch the light as a droplet trickled from its needle tip. The hunter's one eye darted in fear, his voice croaked:

'Nyet . . .'

Maja sunk the needle into the man's neck vein, pushed the plunger.

'I wish it hurt more.'

She placed her hands on her victim's chest, feeling the desperate thump of his heart. Two or three strong beats, and then it would skitter and stumble; seconds later it would stop altogether.

Maja looked deep into her victim's eyes. There was an element of childlike fascination as she watched his life slip away, felt the animating force leave his frame. She was judge, jury and executioner, a role she had taken upon herself more than twenty years earlier. Justice had been done, grim satisfaction was the reward.

'Maja.'

It was the first word Wisher had spoken since his return. Maja turned her back on childhood and the pit in the woods, returned her attention to the present. Her eyes found Wisher crouched in the darkness at the edge of the clearing, sipping from his water bottle. Was he judging her now? She really didn't care. She got to her feet, a shadow reaching out of the silver LED light.

'I heard from Galloway. The attack has been brought forward. The soldiers are nearly here.'

And because he didn't seem to react, she clarified:

'We need to go.'

Wisher stayed low. He screwed the cap back on the canteen, his face as dark and brooding as her spirit.

'You can leave if you want. I'm not going anywhere.'

Twenty-four

'Did you know?'

That is Tom Wisher's question, directed up through the atmosphere and into space, reflected back down to the antennae of the command truck in which the man called Galloway is seated. The vehicle drives south through Ukraine, less than one hundred miles away now from Wisher's forest location. The young agent is referring to Blake's presence in Transnistria, at Arkady Florescu's base.

Galloway does not reply straight away. He has already called off the mission and ordered his agents to retreat. He doesn't want to risk two high-value assets in what may soon become a war zone. But Wisher is refusing to comply. He needs an answer.

Honesty is rarely the best policy in Galloway's line of business, but sometimes it can work. And time is desperately short. Already Tevis's screens are showing the heat signatures of Moldovan military vehicles and troops discreetly massing in the vicinity of Florescu's compound, six hours ahead of schedule. Galloway has eyes and ears at the heart of Langley, and yet somehow the change of plan occurred without his knowledge. This fact excites him as much as it infuriates: could it be that he is not alone in waging a private war against the Consortium?

Withholding the information about Blake was a judgement call, but Galloway can see how it will seem like manipulation. Now the young assassin feels betrayed by his new employer – and distracted by his hunger for revenge.

And so Galloway tells the truth: he knew Blake had been dispatched to Transnistria. He knew there was a chance that Wisher would encounter him, but he chose not to inform him of this fact, in order to keep him focused on his designated target.

The call ends as he feared, abruptly terminated at Wisher's end. The order to leave the fire zone has been ignored. His newest assassin has gone off mission. Galloway slips off his headset and takes a deep breath. Seated at the console beside him, Tevis shoots him a look.

The outcome is problematic, but does not surprise him. The spymaster knows Wisher better than he might realise. Since childhood he has been ready to fight for what he believes in; the loss of his father only served to intensify this drive. Florescu is the job, but Blake is Wisher's cause, revenge his personal mission. Having him so close will be overwhelming.

Galloway sits back, watches the data streams, and reflects. Tom Wisher is not a soldier, and the rogue unit he has signed up to is not an army. But he is a warrior, highly trained, as is Maja. If a battle breaks out, they are better equipped than most to survive it.

The Moldovans will try to take Florescu prisoner if at all possible, rather than kill him. Their government will want a trophy to parade as proof of their commitment to international law, never mind that this will fail to properly end the threat the arms dealer poses. If Wisher remains out in the field, in pursuit of Blake, there is a chance he will try to eliminate Florescu also, and complete his original mission. If Maja remains with him, the odds will only increase.

It's not much of an upside, but right now it's all Galloway has.

Twenty-five

The first thing Blake knew, he was being dragged downstairs by two of Florescu's lieutenants. The fight with the assassin had left him barely conscious of the explosion that had followed, but still the blast had impacted on his senses. Images came to him blurred and out of focus; sounds were distant and tinny. More vivid were the various aspects of pain: the bruises and raw skin around his throat, the glass cuts, the throb of his facial wound reopened; the impacts of his shins against the cement steps.

The cold air helped bring clarity. Blake managed to lift his head, and saw the destruction Wisher's improvised explosive device had wrought. Florescu, miraculously, had survived the blast. The truck outside the window had contained mattresses and bedding; when Florescu had leapt for safety, he'd ended up shielded by the vehicle. It was the men within a radius of thirty feet who had suffered the most. Two had been killed outright; the arm of a third lay on the asphalt, meat trailing from its shoulder joint. The injured man had been given morphine, and would join the dead soon.

The living encircled Blake now, pointing guns and grimacing. Florescu's left arm was held in a sling made from a woman's headscarf; his right hand gripped his throwing axe, retrieved for him by one of his men. His heavies pushed Blake to the ground. Florescu paced, enraged.

'Who was it? One of your spooks? Is this a double cross?'

Blake shook his head, tried to speak. A dry croak was all that came out. Florescu shoved him with a boot sole so that he slumped over, still half dazed. The Romanian leaned in close, all sweat and cigar breath as he held the axe blade to Blake's throat:

'Don't you lie to me. If you lie, I'll know.'

Blake glared back, his own anger rising. He would give no ground to this thug. He swallowed, lubricating his throat. Still his voice rasped like rusting metal:

'I just saved your goddamn life.'

The group was quiet; enough of them would have heard his words and felt the truth of them. Florescu was lucky Blake knew how to fight, luckier still that he had entered the washroom at that precise moment in time.

Maybe he should thank the whore, Blake thought to himself.

Florescu passed his axe to one of his men, then offered a hand to Blake to help him stand, a show of conciliation. As the agent got to his feet, Florescu leant close, whispered:

'This isn't over between us.'

The comment was meant for Blake's ears alone. The arms dealer suspected the assassination attempt was linked to Blake and he could well be right. But now was not the time to resolve the issue. Blake dusted himself down; he was in a sorry state, beaten and bleeding, his suit soiled and torn. Florescu shouted out to the men who had gathered, awaiting orders.

'We're moving out! Where is my fucking useless son?'

A text alert sounded on Blake's phone: Stefan had left the main road unnoticed and was now en route to their own private rendezvous point. The news provided a moment's distraction for Blake, as the van he rode in clattered down the road that led from Florescu's compound into the forest. His vehicle was one of twenty travelling in fairly close formation. Headlights were switched off and as the procession entered the cover of the trees, its speed was reduced to little more than twenty miles an hour. In the near pitch black, they couldn't afford a collision that might slow the whole convoy even further. Various drivers had either night-vision goggles or scopes, one was using the 'image enhance' mode on a cheap camcorder. One way or another, they were finding their way in the dark.

Two hours' drive and they would be the best part of fifty miles from the location, regrouping at a small logging town downriver, where storage barns could conceal them from surveillance. Blake would slip away from Florescu senior at this juncture and proceed another fifty miles or so in the direction of Odessa, where Stefan would be waiting.

Two hours for Blake to chew on the question that currently inflamed him, forcing his exhausted brain into endless circling lines of thought: who the fuck had just tried to kill him?

The target was Florescu of course, but the determination had been directed towards him also. He'd almost felt like the focus had shifted to him once he'd shown his face, like his demise had become the priority. What's more, he'd lost the fight: by rights, he should be dead. Straddled, choked, gasping for air, he'd felt unconsciousness rise up and known for sure that the dark wave would take him under for good. His life had started to unravel before his eyes, in all its bile and beauty.

A shudder passed through him. Emotions were

stirring beneath the surface of thought, feelings he wasn't used to and wasn't at all comfortable processing. He resisted the surge, set up shop instead in the front part of his mind, taking a firm grip on the sharp tools of reason that lay about him.

Blue eyes. That ruled out Arabs, Asians and pretty much all Africans, but could include American, European or Baltic peoples. The presence of video support implied a sophisticated paymaster. The assassin was well equipped: silencer pistol, explosives. All of this suggested mainstream spook, not some kind of rogue asset. So who, then? CIA? It seemed highly unlikely to Blake that there was a deeper game afoot in the Agency than his own. British? Maybe – but why? Kincaid's links with MI6 were rock solid, the agenda very much a shared one, above and below ground. Russian, perhaps?

It just didn't add up. The impending military strike had the full endorsement of the intelligence community, not to mention the support of governments in the adjacent nation states. Why would any of these parties feel it necessary to mount a separate assassination run on Florescu?

Blake knew that Kincaid played a deep game, he would have expected nothing less from one of the few people he regarded as more ruthless than himself. He presumed the deputy director reported in private to people outside of the CIA, and he had made a conscious decision not to find out who. He was getting what he wanted out of the alliance, plus he had room to run his own deals on the side. He really didn't need to know more.

It was often the case, during their conversations, that Kincaid would skirt round certain topics. Blake had always presumed that this was for his benefit. But during their recent exchanges, he started to wonder whether this habitual evasiveness was an indicator of something more sinister. Could the general be scheming against his loyal foot soldier?

Blake had been hitting the coke hard prior to his sojourn in Peshawar, and he'd dismissed his suspicions as drug-induced paranoia. But now the feeling returned with a vengeance, speeding his pulse, pushing sweat out of his skin. Was he being set up? He hadn't had an opportunity to touch base with Kincaid since the assassin had attacked Florescu. Now he found himself wondering if it would be the smartest move. Could Kincaid be behind this? Was *he* the real target, not Florescu?

Through the windscreen Blake could see the Romanian standing in the open-top jeep ahead of him, braced against the roll bars, his cigar smouldering, every inch the tin-pot general. The fact that he now wore a combat helmet and not one but two flak jackets only added to the impression; he even had motorcycle outriders. Another time, Blake would have found the sight darkly amusing; right now, he was struggling to control a trembling that was building somewhere in his midriff and spreading out through his body.

The driver beside him shot him a nervous glance. Blake clutched the dashboard and gritted his teeth. He didn't know if it was exhaustion, shock or a reaction to the drugs, but something was happening inside him. His hands and face were itching, a tic flickered in his cheek. The world around him receded.

Blake squeezed his eyes shut. He would not give in to fear. Heat was growing inside him, in his solar plexus, spreading up his spine. Accelerating now, reaching the back of his neck, glowing tendrils surrounding his head, pushing upwards and out.

Blake had spent a few hours studying meditation back

in the day, while recuperating from his teenage leg injury. He'd listened half-heartedly to his tutors' New Age waffle about 'prana' and 'chakras', then dismissed the whole subject as hippy nonsense. Now, caught in the grip of a wild rush of body chemistry, he recalled a fragment of that teaching, something about a serpent coiled at the base of the spine, pure life-force waiting to be harnessed.

Kundalini was its name. The dragon within. Mystical gobbledygook, of course – and yet here it was, strength rising inside him, unbidden, at his lowest point, when there was nowhere to turn, nothing to hold on to. Just chemicals, maybe, but he hadn't realised how much he needed something to believe in, and now he had it.

Panic transformed into something approaching ecstasy. Blake had felt his own life-force, surging within him, a physical sensation that transcended cynicism. In an instant, his pains were cast aside, the scars and aches. He was the dragon reborn. He could survive this. He could win.

Blake opened his eyes, utterly aware. Ahead was darkness, the glowing tip of Florescu's cigar, the sides of vehicles showing as grey shapes in the spill of moonlight. Yet in the inky black that surrounded the road, something was glinting . . .

It was the briefest of impressions, but in his heightened state, Blake was in no mind to let it slip by unchallenged. He climbed out of his seat and into the back of the van, started shifting through the boxes stacked there. He'd helped pack its contents: among the ordnance, there was a crate of distress flares. He pulled off the lid and as he'd hoped, there was also a flare gun inside.

The van had a side door; Blake slid it open, balanced against the stacked crates, and aimed into the trees. The driver shouted out in dismay, fearing his cargo would tumble out. Blake ignored the cry, fired off the flare.

A smoke trail laced between the trunks. The pyrotechnic exploded with magnesium brightness, illuminating the forest. The whole convoy could see what the stark light revealed: soldiers, creeping through the wooded slope that led down to the road. The Moldovan force, six hours ahead of schedule!

The flare provided only the briefest of warnings to Florescu's men. A Moldovan ambush was in place and ready to unfold. An explosion shook through the branches; up ahead a large tree tipped and fell across the road, blocking the route forward. Guns burst into life; tracer rounds seared through the night air above the convoy, helping the shooters adjust their aim in the dark. A megaphone voice crackled orders in Russian:

'Put down your weapons. You are surrounded! Surrender immediately and you will not be harmed!'

Florescu's car screeched to a halt; one of his outriders lost control of his motorbike and tumbled off it into a ditch. The driver in the van with Blake slammed his own brake pedal down and the vehicle skidded to a stop, sideways across the road.

The army gunfire was not aimed at the convoy, but above it. A second megaphone voice joined the cacophony, ordering a surrender, but it was Florescu's voice that cut through clearest:

'We have been betrayed! Fire at will!'

The driver was beside Blake, in amongst the boxes, loading a rocket-propelled grenade into a launcher. Blake looked down the line of trucks and cars behind him: there must have been thirty men, Florescu's bandits, grabbing weapons, diving for cover behind their vehicles. In the next instant, this ambush would become a bloodbath.

Blake leapt down from the van, and simultaneously the years fell away from him. He was a young man again, hunting in the White Mountains of New Hampshire. The weight he carried was the pack on his shoulders, to be borne lightly, not the meat and fat of middle age. If his heart gave way, if its muscles were to tear, its chambers rupture, then so be it. He would not let it slow him now.

The gun-fire lulled. Florescu's men had taken cover, the surrounding army was pausing to see if the order to surrender would have an effect. The crashed motorbike lay on the ground thirty feet along the road from Blake: his way out of this. He edged round the back of the van and saw Florescu crouched behind the jeep up ahead, trademark axe in hand.

Florescu saw Blake – and his face twisted with rage. No doubt in his mind that somehow Blake had double crossed him. He stood up, raised his throwing arm – and a bullet drilled silently through his neck. A sniper shot from high ground, precisely targeting his weak spot; Blake ducked back behind the side of the van, his insides tensing – the assassin was still at large!

Florescu was not dead, though his injury was surely mortal. He clawed his way across the mud towards Blake, face racked with pain and anger, curses spitting out with blood from his mouth. His combat helmet was working itself loose as he crawled; another noiseless impact, this time a bullet to the back of his head, and he was still.

The van wall at Blake's back shuddered as the driver hunched inside the vehicle staggered from the recoil of the grenade launcher. This was the moment to run. Blake burst from cover as the projectile arched into the forest; as it exploded, he was lifting the motorcycle from the road and kick-starting it. As the light and noise from the blast spread through the woods, and retaliatory gunfire started to rain down upon the convoy, Blake was speeding off-road in the opposite direction, down the slope, away from the oncoming army and in among the trees. Bullets flew around him, tracer rounds scratched glowing lines on either side. Within seconds he was out of range, tyres thudding on roots and potholes, headlight guiding him over the rough terrain.

Then the land shook, a massive explosion. Blake stopped the bike and looked back toward the road. One of the ordnance-packed trucks had been totalled and a massive fire was raging. Figures were running in panic away from the convoy, anticipating further detonations as the flames spread.

As Blake watched, fascinated, a slim black figure ran across his field of view, silhouetted against the flames. Moving like an athlete, focused, not afraid: the assassin, heading in his direction. He must have spotted the headlight.

Blake slammed the motorbike into gear and roared away, lights now switched off. Whoever had shot Florescu was hunting him, armed at the very least with a rifle and night-sights. The motorbike was his only advantage, but without the headlight beam the ground was treacherous. He traversed two hundred yards but he was barely above running pace, constantly stopping and starting, steering wildly to avoid obstacles that loomed out of the dark.

Moonlight spilled through a break in the leafy canopy; determined to make some distance on his pursuer, Blake twisted the accelerator and surged forward. A thick tree root sent a shudder through the motorbike's suspension; Blake twisted the handlebars to compensate and the rear wheel spun outwards, dragging the machine from under him.

He hit the ground, rolled away from the bike.

Darkness was thick around him. Shouts and occasional gunshots could be heard in the distance, against the roar of burning vehicles. Flaming orange pulsed among the tree trunks, back along the route he had taken. Blake burrowed backwards, jacket shucked over his head. There was plenty of loose cover to conceal him, he just hoped he was quick enough. Shuffled back into a depression in the ground, he held his breath and waited.

Cautious footsteps approached. Blake turned inward, in search of the inner strength he'd experienced so acutely just a few minutes earlier. He couldn't risk breathing. He didn't even listen or try to visualise the assassin now circling the crashed motorcycle. He focused on the dragon coiled within him.

He took hold of the single flare he had concealed in his jacket pocket. His fingers felt for the end, the correct orientation. Body tensed, he grasped the pull-string.

He recalled the dark figure who had so nearly snatched his life away on that washroom floor, little more than an hour earlier. He remembered the painful blows and the towel wrapped tight around his neck, chafing away at his skin. His mouth twisted: this could be sweet.

Heat was building inside him. He drew in air and launched himself up from under his camouflage, ripping the pull-string as he did so, jabbing forward with the flare, averting his eyes as it exploded with light . . .

The assassin was *right there*. He had turned at the movement, eye pressed to his night-sight – now he was staggering back, blinded by the force of light. Blake went for his assault rifle, wrenched it free from his grip, jabbed the stock back into the ski-masked face, twice, hard. The assassin was down and Blake had a foot on his throat, bayonet pressing into the masked face, cutting the fabric – that blade was *sharp*. The flare still burned on the forest floor, enough light to get a look at his assailant.

And that was when Blake realised that this was not the

man who had attacked him in the washroom earlier that evening. This assassin was a *woman*.

Her shape was evident, even disguised by the androgynous uniform of black-on-black clothes and body armour. And the eyes, visible through the ski mask, were almond shaped, dark at the centre instead of pale blue.

Blake didn't believe in coincidence. There was no doubt in his mind that this woman was a comrade of the man who had tried to kill him. He pushed down on the rifle, knowing the bayonet tip would be breaking the skin of his captive's cheek. With his free hand he jerked at the audio wire heading under her ski mask, ripped out her earpiece and mike bead.

'Who sent you? Who do you work for?'

Blake knew that the bayonet blade must be more than a centimetre deep into the assassin's face, and yet her eyes showed only defiance. When she spoke, she spat out blood:

'You'll – never know . . .'

Blake didn't have time to waste. He sensed this woman's resolve, her professionalism. She was as tough as him. But maybe her comrade was cut from a different cloth.

'Ever heard of the femoral artery?'

She said nothing; he continued:

'It's in the upper thigh. You don't want to take a bullet there. If you don't stitch up the hole you'll bleed out in minutes.'

Her eyes, glaring at him in flickering flare light, showed the slightest trace of fear. Pity the clock was ticking: the sadist in him would have enjoyed drawing out this moment.

He sank his weight into the boot that pinned the woman's neck. She clutched at him, tugging at his trouser leg, trying to find leverage, without success. She was pinned like a butterfly. He lifted the assault rifle, jammed the bayonet between her legs, into the meat of her thigh, and twisted. She let out a grunt of pain; blood started to pump, red against the blade, visible in the last sputtering of the flare's light.

'Now your little friend has a choice. He can chase me or he can try to save you.'

Blake slipped away into the gloom, leaving the assassin clutching at her leg. Once cloaked by darkness, he calibrated his pace for distance rather than speed. He was running on empty and what mattered most right now was to keep going.

He had bought himself some time. He'd soon find out if it was enough.

Twenty-six

'You take Blake. I'll take Florescu, if he's still alive.'

That was Maja's proposal. She had sided with him in the wake of his exchange with Galloway; she said she understood his need for revenge, which somehow made him want to argue the other side of the case.

It wasn't about revenge, that was what he told himself. It was pragmatism. They had an opportunity not only to eliminate the arms dealer supplying weapons-grade uranium to terrorists, but also to sever a tentacle that snaked back into the heart of the CIA, namely Bill Blake. Galloway's caution was based on protecting his assets; but he hadn't fought hard for his corner when Wisher had gone against his orders. It was almost as if he accepted that this was all he could expect from an assassin who had no contract, no official salary, who was driven by an idealistic need to make the world a safer place.

At least, that was Wisher's motivation. As to what drove Maja . . .

Wisher looked at the woman sat cross-legged across from him on the ground. She had both their cell phones and was setting them up so each could track the other's GPS. There were thirty-seven minutes till midnight, the designated time of the Moldovan strike; in seven minutes they planned to separate and take up positions on either side of the forest route being driven by Florescu's convoy.

Wisher knew that he utterly desired Maja physically.

Before her, he wouldn't have said he had a 'type'; from now on, he would measure every other woman against her and find them wanting, he suspected. Psychologically, however, she was darker, more damaged, than anyone he had ever been close to. Her approach to the act of murder disturbed him profoundly, more than he could process while he wrapped up the mission at hand. He was afraid there was no way back for her; afraid, too, of finding that he was somehow the same as her. Hadn't he wanted to rip Blake's throat out, just a short while earlier?

It wasn't the same, he was sure of it. Righteous anger had filled him, but remorse would have followed quickly behind it, had he managed to finish off his nemesis. Maja, however, showed no such compunction in killing the poacher who had attacked her. If anything she seemed calmer after the event, some highly strung aspect of her personality soothed by the execution of her craft. It didn't fit with what Wisher understood about right and wrong, what he felt about the human soul. Yet still he wanted to know her, to understand her, to help her if he could.

He sighed, admitting the truth to himself: he wanted to save her, stupid bloody white knight that he was.

She handed back his phone, got to her feet. They were all set.

'Hey.'

He took hold of her gently, his hand round the back of her head as he pulled her to him. Their lips touched lightly. She didn't fall into the kiss, didn't pull away from it either. But the warmth wasn't there on her side. Of course not. It wasn't the time.

Maja regarded him soberly. He peeled down his ski-mask, turned from her and slipped away into the forest, heading downhill. She was going to return to the ridge viewpoint, to observe the exodus of vehicles from

Florescu's base and signal him when the last of the convoy had departed.

A few minutes' run brought Wisher to the road. He hid behind a gnarled trunk while a dark truck drove past, its weary engine rattling so conspicuously, it made the lack of headlights pointless. When it was gone, Wisher darted across the way and looked for a hiding place with a clear line of sight back to the road.

Maja's voice piped up in his earpiece:

'That's the last of the trucks. Twenty-one at my count. Florescu's three from the front, looking like an ass. I haven't spotted Blake yet.'

Wisher nestled in a shallow gully shielded by a clump of fern, and lined his sights on the road. The Moldovans weren't looking for a gun battle; their aim was for arrests and captives to parade. The challenge for Wisher and Maja would be to take out their targets without triggering an escalation of the impending confrontation.

The minutes ticked past. Wisher cleared his mind, tried to focus on the task. Blake with cross hairs on his forehead. Blake who deserved to die . . . for what? For betraying Wisher? For causing MacMillan's death? For aiding Ahmed's nuclear plot? Which was the particular reason that made him expendable?

Again, Maja spoke:

'Soldiers are here.'

Wisher scowled, pushed his eye up to the night-sight, sent his focus out into the eerie green world revealed through it. Across the road, he saw Moldovan troops moving quietly into position. Explosives were strapped to the trunk of a large tree that overhung the main route through the wood. A shudder of anticipation passed through Wisher; he was in the perfect spot. No doubt there would be a similar charge being rigged further back along the road to block the exit. Fish in a barrel.

He heard the convoy before he saw it, roughshod engines growling and grinding, the whole procession managing little more than a crawl through the darkness. His scope was quick to pick out Florescu, stood in the back of a jeep, swaddled in protective gear.

In the van behind Florescu, seen through the side window, the passenger was out of his seat – Bill Blake, clambering from view into the back of the vehicle.

Wisher lined up his sights. He contemplated letting loose a volley on the side of the van but thought better of it – who knew what ordnance might be stored in there? The point here was surgical precision, not mindless destruction.

Then the flare went off.

Soldiers were revealed. The charge detonated and the tree fell. The convoy ground to a halt. Tracer rounds streaked overhead, barked orders echoed among the trees. Blake was out of the van; Florescu was charging towards him, swinging his axe.

Then Florescu was down, blood spouting from his neck: Maja's handiwork, shooting from up the slope. Blake dodged between the stalled vehicles, out of Wisher's line of fire. The young agent cursed and broke cover, darting along the line of the convoy, rifle levelled, navigating by night-sight. At the same moment, Blake came back into view – on a motorbike, speeding away from the chaos on the road. Wisher fired a round, struck a tree trunk.

Maja's voice crackled:

'I see him. I can circle round—'

A rocket-propelled grenade burst lit up the forest behind Wisher, gunfire popped and cracked in response. On instinct, he dived for cover. That instinct saved his life.

Stray rounds ignited an incendiary and a truck went up. Flames shot out and above Wisher in his hollow of earth, deadly shrapnel riding the blast wave, chipping away leaves and branches as it embedded in the trees around him. Suddenly the air was thick with bullets, gunshots reduced in volume to finger-clicks in the booming silence of the aftershock. A tiny voice spoke, an insect in his ear:

'Wisher? Are you okay? Wisher?'

Wisher stayed flat against the ground, sound and the solid world reconvening around him, all too dangerous with bullets and debris pinging all over, claiming limbs and lives, another truck bound to blow at any second. He couldn't stay where he was.

'I'm okay. Where's Blake?'

'Still on two wheels. I'm on it. Heading south. Track me on haptic. Out.'

Maja's mouse voice was gone.

Wisher slithered across the ground, raking up dirt with his boot edges as he propelled himself forward. Fifty feet and there was cover, the thick trunk of a larch that he could tuck himself behind. Back on the road, the firefight was losing ferocity as news of Florescu's death spread along the convoy. Demands for surrender echoed again among the trees and wrecked vehicles, and this time they were heeded. Florescu's men were employees, not zealots, no glory for them in a bullet-borne death. The gun barrels that poked out from the convoy now had T-shirts and handkerchiefs tied to them; emboldened troops stepped out of cover, started to coordinate.

The haptic belt buzzed a change of direction for Maja. Wisher stepped away from the tree trunk. Immediately, a gun-shot kicked scales from the pine cones hanging just above his head. He ducked back, a voice shouted out in Russian:

'You are under arrest! Surrender your weapon and step out with your hands up!'

A targeting laser beam showed faintly against the misty air, level with Wisher's eye-line. He slipped the dental mirror from his pocket, held it up to the lens of his night-vision scope. He tilted his rifle to get a reflected view of the sniper pinning him down. It meant the barrel protruded round the edge of the tree protecting him, drawing another shot, worryingly close. But he saw his quarry in the green glow. A young man, younger than himself, maybe twenty years old, tall and skinny. He wore body armour; his combat helmet made his head seem huge in outline.

'This is the Moldovan army! Surrender your weapon!'

The soldier was a good aim but he had left himself exposed, too confident that he was controlling the situation. Wisher could throw a timed grenade and be back on Blake's tail in seven seconds.

But this was a young soldier engaged in international police work. This was one of the good guys.

'I'm American! You speak English?'

'Throw out your gun!' The response was shouted with a heavy accent, but clear enough. In Wisher's earpiece, Maja whispered:

'I found the motorbike. He must be close . . .'

Wisher's insides lurched: he didn't want Maja facing Blake alone. Yet he could hear the soldier calling in the hostile contact, requesting backup. He shouted out to him, desperate:

'I'm on your side!'

'Throw out your gun and we can talk!'

No time, no time. Maja was just yards from Blake, backup just seconds away from the Moldovan.

Wisher took a snub-nosed Colt from his webbing belt;

pretty much the only American gun in Maja's armoury. He palmed the small revolver, threw his assault rifle out into plain view.

'Come out with your hands up!'

Wisher crouched down, then reached up with his dental mirror to the faint line of the targeting laser. He held the instrument by the tip of its handle, lifted it delicately towards the beam, angling it perpendicular to the line. He really didn't want to lose a finger, but he didn't want to kill this lad, either.

The mirror caught the red dot and reflected it back over to the soldier, who fired at it on reflex. Wisher leant out from the base of the tree trunk, aimed the Colt low and shot off two rounds. The soldier cried out as a bullet struck his shin, dropped to his knees in agony. Wisher burst from cover and darted over to the youth, black against black. He took hold of his rifle, kicked at the fallen man's face until he let the weapon go.

Wisher aimed the weapon downward. The laser dot danced on the soldier's forehead, mortal fear shone in his eyes. Wisher lowered the rifle. He knew the young man wouldn't be able to see him in the darkness, but he could still hear him.

'I'm sorry.'

Wisher ran away into the forest, leaving the Moldovan bewildered – and incredibly relieved.

For his part, Wisher felt some sense of relief also, that he had spared a life and managed to avoid another self-inflicted wound upon his already troubled conscience.

Unfortunately, he now had another problem.

'Maja?'

Twenty-seven

She wasn't answering, which meant trouble. It was hard for Wisher to pick up speed when he was obliged to keep his rifle's night-sight to his eye. The forest seemed vast now that the road was some distance behind, and very similar whichever way he looked: the glowing struts of trees, tunnelling to eerie darkness in between. Maja had found the motorbike, which meant she must be nearby, within half a mile, surely. But that was still a hell of a sector to search on foot, and time was crucial, especially if she'd gotten into a situation.

Wisher stumbled to a halt, breathless and mentally cursing his stupidity. He still had the haptic belt, and he had Maja's GPS in his cellphone.

He switched on his flashlight; it seemed possible the soldiers would not sweep this far south of the road before daylight, and now was not the time to fumble by hand for the right connectors. He had a number of electrical leads in a waterproof pouch. Holding the torch in his mouth, he quickly located a mini-USB and hooked up his phone to the belt's control board. The map function found Maja's GPS: the range was three hundred yards, due southeast, thankfully close by.

Wisher switched off the flashlight and started his run, scope to eye, haptics guiding the way.

He couldn't see her at first, and feared she had been separated from her phone. So he called her name, softly, and after a few moments, her hand emerged from what had looked like solid ground, but was revealed to be a rough ditch in the forest floor, the nearest cover she could find.

He rushed to her side, helped brush the dirt from her as she slowly sat up. He knew she was injured, could tell straight away from her laboured movements. Her face was ghost pale, the eyes obsidian in the night-vision view. When he flicked on the flashlight, he saw that she really was white as bone, her expression taut with suffering.

'Turn it off,' she snarled, her few manners stripped away by the pain. He ignored her, exploring her with the beam, pulling off his own mask to see better.

'Where are you hurt?'

Fear flooded her face and she glanced down. He followed her eyes, saw her hands clutched around her thigh, fresh blood pumping out between her fingers.

'I can't stop the bleeding.'

He saw and understood. He'd learnt anatomy and wound care as part of his training. He knew about injuries to the femoral artery. He felt the intention behind this cruel act of violence.

'Blake?'

She nodded.

'To slow me down.'

Maja's response was cold and focused, her fear controlled.

'I got a bug on him. RF pinhead. Range is shit, just a few hundred metres. But you can catch him. He's got a head start but he's fat and he's slow. You can do it.'

Wisher was hardly listening. He searched his pockets, fished out a Zippo lighter and a small packet of flares.

'Do you have pain relief?'

She nodded.

'Dilaudid.'

'Take some.'

'You have to *go*.'

Despite her situation – or was it because of it? – Maja was actually pleading with him. The tone of her voice, the weakness revealed in it, chilled Wisher more than he expected. He snapped open his pocket knife.

'This is going to hurt. A lot.'

She didn't argue. She lay back, positioned her leg as best as she could to give him access to her injury.

Flashlight in mouth, Wisher cut away the dark fabric. The knife wound on her thigh showed clearly each time blood pumped out of it. Maja had her thumb dug in above the cut, trying to pinch the vessel closed. It wasn't working. Her free hand was fumbling a blister pack of pain meds toward her mouth.

Wisher took out a flare and jabbed his knife blade into the end of it, cutting away the projectile fuel, leaving the pyrotechnic part of the device intact, still fixed on the end of the blade. It was a distress signal, designed to be fired from a pen launcher. Its incandescent payload would burn for just a few seconds – but at an intense heat.

'It'll be quick.'

Maja nodded. Wisher's hand was shaking as he sparked the Zippo. The flame caught and he held it to the pyro. For a breathless moment it seemed that the flare would not ignite. Then it hissed and burst into blinding light, coloured vivid red, spewing bitter, bonfire-night fumes. Squinting, his eyes watering, he pushed the flare into the wound.

Maja let out an animal howl of pain as the flare seared the meat of her leg. A count of one and Wisher lifted the incandescent ember away from her, moving it carefully until it was clear, then throwing it to one side, where it swiftly fizzled on the forest floor.

A thread of smoke coiled from the burn, twisting in the flashlight beam. Wisher was almost afraid to look but Maja was alert, energised by agony. Wiping tears from her eyes, she leant forward to inspect herself.

'Shine the light there.'

Wisher complied. The wound seemed bigger than before, deeper. The flesh was red and blistering. But the blood flow had been reduced to less than a trickle. A battle had been won, not the war; Maja was still critically injured, and they both knew it.

'I can clean it. Go.'

Her face was a skull, sapped of its beauty, its functions laid bare. But her eyes were fierce. He put his hand to her shoulder, gentle, bearing her pain in mind.

'Wait for me here. I'll be back.'

She grabbed hold of his jaw and pulled him close. Her hand felt waxy against stubble and sweat and grime.

'Find him. Kill him. Do it.'

And so Wisher ran. The trees were less densely packed in this part of the forest and moonlight was filtering through, enough to give some form to the ground and allow him to progress without night-sight. The RF receiver was linked to the haptic belt, awaiting the first hint of a signal. He imagined himself as a marker on a map, sweeping out a wide circle of detection. Three hundred yards of range would make a diameter of six hundred yards around him. The forest was big, statistically the odds were against him. And yet his gut told him Blake would head in this direction, Blake would have the map in his mind's eye too, he'd want to get to the river and find a way across, the surest way to ditch a tail.

Blake filled Wisher's thoughts like a bloated sac with a human face, bulging outwards to fill every inch of his mental space, pushing other thoughts from his mind. Blotting out the image of Maja in a shallow grave, half-bled to death. Obscuring the persistent line of reasoning that said he, Wisher, was to blame.

He could have killed the Moldovan soldier. The young man was shooting at him: it would have been self-defence – not perhaps of the urgent, knife-to-the-throat kind, but surely a legitimate 'me or him' situation.

Except of course that there *had* been a way past without killing, but it had taken thought, and precious minutes of time. If Wisher had known the true cost of indulging his conscience, would he have done so?

He brought his focus back to Blake as his feet thudded on the dirt and he ran through the forest. He hated Blake. Bloated, ugly, putrid Blake, floating in his mind's eye, no, in a pool of his own blood. Dead Blake, thrown to the dogs, left for the wolves, meat gnawed away to the bone, a red, ragged skeleton in the wilderness.

Wisher felt a tickling sensation under his ribs and slammed to a stop against a trunk, gasping for breath while trying to hold still, even as hope surged.

There it was again, the buzz of the haptic belt. A signal that Blake was in range, southwest of Wisher's current position.

The young agent rolled up his ski-mask, fished a choc-olate ration from his pocket, and tried to eat it without rushing. He had a trajectory; now he needed fuel. Blake was around three hundred yards away. Probably he was down to fast walking by now, five, maybe six miles an hour. Wisher was tired, but he probably could do a six-minute mile, even on this terrain, in the dark. One seven six oh yards in a mile . . .

Wisher couldn't do the maths. He unshouldered his assault rifle and resumed running.

Within two minutes he had reached the edge of the forest. The signal from the belt had been increasing in strength and frequency. He was very close now.

Clear night sky above, gibbous moon. After the gloom of the wood it was almost like daylight, distance and perspective restored in the silver radiance. The ground was becoming marshy underfoot. The river was near, he could hear its distant flow, separating out from the rustling of leaves and night creatures.

Suddenly, he glimpsed him, a dark spot moving through tall reeds. Wisher got the scope to his eye but Blake was out of sight again, lost among cover at the river's edge.

Wisher pushed forward. The terrain was harder to traverse with each step, clogged with rank marsh-plants, turning to mud that sucked at his feet and held them under. It was hard to keep quiet, too; the struggle to maintain a silent approach had reduced his speed right down. It would be the same for Blake, but these last few yards were proving tough to close.

Wisher crept on, up to his waist now in the murk, rifle lined up and ready. Then an outboard motor revved, and suddenly the stakes changed. Blake had found a boat!

Wisher burst into action, splashing wildly through the reeds, gun held above his head. He pushed past a body floating face down – some unfortunate night fisherman with a bayonet hole in his back – and broke through the reeds into a stretch of open water.

A petrol engine growled, and a boat prow drove towards him. Blake was at the tiller, river-soaked and wild-eyed, steering deliberately to bear down on his pursuer. The vessel was small, just a flat-bottomed rowboat with an outboard motor. But Wisher was submerged up to his chest, hardly able to manoeuvre.

The boat struck him a glancing blow. He reached up and snatched a hold of the side with one hand, the other still holding his rifle. Instantly he was pulled off his feet and dragged through the water, shoulder straining at its socket, legs trailing dangerously close to the propeller's churning blades. His face was half submerged, his vision blurred, the moon a wavering coin, now blotted out by a black shape rising . . .

Wisher released his grip, just in time. Blake's bayonet sank into wood instead. He was off the tiller, the boat was turning of its own accord, wobbling. Wisher broke the surface to find Blake staggering, falling on his ass as the small hull bucked under him. Letting go of his rifle, Wisher grabbed the side with both hands and hauled himself up.

The boat tipped again. Blake staggered, losing grip of his own gun, the one he took from Maja. Wisher rolled into him, grappled the rifle away, and forced him down into the bottom of the boat. Face down, Blake braced a foot against the seat board, but the advantage was Wisher's. He already had the Colt in hand; he pressed it up into the soft tissue under Blake's jawbone, and the big man was suddenly very still.

'Turn over.'

Blake righted himself slowly; Wisher kept the gun barrel pressed into its fleshy nook all the while. The outboard motor buzzed like some huge, angry insect. Wisher stared down at Blake with watering eyes, not from pain, but from a building nausea, exhaustion mixed with anger and noise and adrenaline, threatening to shut down his thinking brain.

Blake spoke quickly, desperately:

'I don't know who you are or what you want, but I have some very powerful friends. Whatever you need, I can get it for you.'

Wisher reached for his ski mask. He couldn't help himself. He needed Blake to shut up. He needed him to *know*.

'Holy shit!'

The mask was off, and Wisher was revealed. At first Blake was stunned – and then a grin spread.

'And you went to all this trouble for me? I'm flattered.'

'Florescu was the target. You're just the icing on the cake.'

Stupid tough-guy posturing. Why was he even talking to this bastard? Just kill him and be done with it! And yet he hesitated. Blake could feel the reticence, the damned conscience rising up. Contempt was his response, it burned in his eyes:

'You think you're so much better than me. You're still a spook, a little boy with a gun, hiding in the shadows.'

'I'll never be as low as you. I'll never be as cruel.'

Blake's expression was sly. Despite the gun pressed into his flesh, he was calm. He knew how things stood.

'I'm an unarmed man, Tom. If you shoot me now, that's as low as it gets.'

And there it was, the nub of Wisher's hesitation. He wore the garb of the assassin, but inside he was the white knight. He knew it; Blake knew it. He gritted his teeth.

'This is justice. For MacMillan.'

'Yeah, right. It's got nothing to do with revenge at all.'

'Screw you, Blake.'

Blake actually laughed, then spluttered as Wisher pushed the gun barrel hard into his soft tissue. Half choked, he rasped:

'This is good, Tom. Seriously. I've never felt so close to you, buddy.'

The scorn burned like battery acid. But Blake was just grinning away. His cynicism was like a superpower; amazing how strong you became when you didn't give a shit. Wisher had won the physical fight but in the war of ideas, Blake couldn't lose.

'Go ahead. Prove me right. Let me die with a smile on my face.'

Whatever you say, Bill.

Wisher squeezed the trigger . . .

But it was his own body that jerked forward as a bullet slammed into it, deep into his body armour, knocking him off balance. Before he had time to think, Blake had kicked out at his knee and he was falling backwards, gulping river water, spluttering and stunned as the outboard engine roared back to life and the small boat sped away downstream.

Twenty-eight

'Thirty-two dead, last count. Are you happy now?'

Kincaid glared at Morgan from his position in front of the monitor wall, the position he'd taken up permanently when word broke that the Moldovan attack was unfolding ahead of schedule: a crisis that was solely down to John Morgan, making executive decisions without regard for the chain of command. Again. When it dawned on him what had occurred, Kincaid had launched a tirade of invective that had lasted some minutes, only subsiding once the firefight had kicked off along the Transnistrian forest road.

They'd followed the action via audio, patchy satellite hook-up and a couple of Moldovan army headcams. Reception had been hit-and-miss but there was no mistaking the scale of the clash between Florescu's men and the soldiers: lots of shooting, explosions and chaos, with fatalities on both sides. An international incident, in short, which would have repercussions over the coming months and years as the inevitable inquiry was set up and the buck passed around, with the CIA desperately working to keep its involvement out of the limelight.

It was presently two a.m. in Transnistria, two hours after the clash between Moldovan forces and Florescu's retinue; in Langley it was seven p.m., but felt much later. At least it did to Morgan.

He hadn't directly been responsible for any loss of life,

of course. He hadn't directly ordered anything, in fact. He'd merely made certain information available to his friend the ambassador. But he'd known where that information might lead. He'd known the possible consequences. He had blood on his hands, no matter if he could legitimately argue the opposite case under scrutiny.

'This was supposed to be a police operation. Instead it's a massacre. Good job, John. Good fucking job.'

Kincaid's voice projected, no chance that any of Morgan's colleagues would mistake the weight of scorn it bore. Peavey returned from the washroom, cellphone to his ear, snake tongue flicking, tasting the air as he took up his place at Kincaid's side. Morgan summoned what little confidence he had left. He wasn't going to let Kincaid's swagger embarrass him. Not this time.

'Florescu was a legitimate target. We had clear evidence linking him to— '

'Arkady Florescu is dead. You got any HEU so far?'

Kincaid knew very well that no highly enriched uranium had been found among Florescu's stock of weapons and contraband. His eyes bored out from under his dark brows like sticks jabbing at a frozen lake, cracks spreading where they struck.

'It's a large base. A lot of hiding places. We've only just started looking.'

'So there's hope then. That's good to know.'

A brittle smile – and it occurred to Morgan that he might have misread his boss. There was something just a shade off-key about Kincaid's tone; the sarcasm, so often surgical, seemed broad, flippant, almost. Morgan's heart skipped a beat: could it be that he actually had Kincaid worried? Could it be that the conspiracy between Florescu and Kincaid was real?

He chanced his arm.

'He must have had advance warning.'

'What?' Kincaid wasn't looking at the monitors now. He was focused solely on Morgan. Nervous glances flicked up from the lower echelons, data analysts at their workstations, struggling to direct their eyes away from the locking horns, the row threatening to explode.

All except for Jeanette, his fleeting comrade-in-arms. She was following the argument from behind her monitor screen, her expression at once grave and excited. Morgan felt the attention, rode it. His stock couldn't be any lower right now. The only card he had left to play was what he knew of the truth, might as well throw it out there.

'The plan was to encircle Florescu's HQ at 0600. That's still four hours away. The Moldovans were six hours early, but still they almost missed the boat. Therefore, Florescu knew about the planned manoeuvre, far enough in advance to almost slip the net.'

'What are you saying?'

'Well, I didn't tell him.' Morgan paused, then let the sentence roll to its inevitable conclusion:

'Did you?'

The words hung for a moment, tension sung – then Kincaid seemed to relax. He stepped over to Morgan, offered him a pat on the shoulder. The mask of nonchalance was really quite perfect, Morgan reflected. But as Kincaid leaned close, he spoke quietly, his words aimed at Morgan's ears only.

'Lock your doors, John. Bolt your windows.'

'I don't think I follow . . .'

Morgan wanted to pull away, but Kincaid had a hold of his shoulder. Closer still, the deputy director's voice was just a whisper, the words emitted quickly, in the rush of one breath.

'You'll never be safe from me.'

Kincaid straightened, smiled. It was as if he hadn't spoken at all, and yet Morgan had heard him clearly. Nausea washed through him, bile rose and was swallowed back. He kept his eyes down, aware that he couldn't hide the fear in them.

'Sir?' It was Jeanette, demanding Kincaid's attention, a welcome respite for Morgan. The deputy director took a step away. Morgan glanced up and saw Peavey was watching him, somehow more hawkish than shifty in the low light.

Jeanette's voice was audible over the room's computer hum as she addressed Kincaid.

'We're getting testimonies from some of Florescu's men. They claim they're working for us.'

Both Morgan and Peavey turned towards the new conversation. Kincaid was frowning:

'That seems unlikely.'

'They say there was an American with them. CIA.'

Morgan placed the look on Jeanette's face that he'd seen moments earlier, that odd mix of conflicting emotions. It was her conscience, getting the better of her ambition. Kincaid was all sober concern, stood beside her. Morgan eyed Peavey: the aide was rigid as a waxwork, listening in.

'Have they got a name?'

'They're working on it.'

Kincaid nodded, then beckoned to Morgan.

'My office, John. Right now.'

Peavey closed the door behind them. Kincaid sat down behind his desk, taking his time before he spoke. Morgan waited patiently. He felt re-energised, clear-headed.

'They're going to come up with Bill Blake's name.'

Morgan raised his guard: was Kincaid getting ready to negotiate? The veteran agent spoke calmly, thoughtfully.

'This is an unexpected development. I confess that I don't fully understand your agenda here, Lawrence. But if there's anything you want to tell me, now would be the time.'

Kincaid nodded soberly.

'I'm expecting you to take the fall for this, John.'

Morgan was blank for a moment. The statement literally made no sense to him.

'Why would I want to do that?'

'What you want doesn't come into this. It's purely about power. Mine versus yours. I have more. Therefore you do what I tell you to.'

Kincaid's gaze was unwavering. Morgan felt himself turn red as anger like he'd never known surged within him, its hormonal force so overwhelming it brought actual tears to his eyes.

'You don't talk to me like that. Not ever. You give me respect.'

His voice was trembling, he couldn't control it. A sign of weakness, he knew it, knew that Kincaid could read it, too. The deputy director remained composed as he continued:

'Eleven Moldovan soldiers are dead. On your orders, not mine.'

'I gave no orders!'

Morgan could hardly think straight. He saw himself from outside, a red-faced, spluttering old man. He hated himself.

'Eleven dead. Their government will want an explanation.'

Kincaid beckoned Peavey:

'Get me the Moldovan ambassador on the phone.'

Cold eyes savoured the cruel moment.

'He's a friend of yours I believe? Take a seat. I want you to hear this.'

Morgan sat. He was overmatched, outplayed, pinned to the mat. Peavey made the call, Kincaid picked it up on his desk phone. Over the next ten minutes he listened in glum silence as Kincaid destroyed him.

Ambassador, you have my condolences. I had no idea what John was planning. That's right, there was one of our agents at the scene. He worked under John on the Massoud Ahmed case. We're waiting for him to call in but I'm sure he was acting under orders. I realise there's no sign of any enriched uranium. Of course we'll be looking into it. We'll put our best people on it. We're as confused and angry as you. We're still piecing it together. It's my guess that John got frustrated, sir, it can be painful to see your efforts go unrewarded. I wouldn't like to presume that he intended for Florescu to run into your ambush like that. You're right, it would be out of character. John's a good man …

What was he supposed to say? He had no proof of the link between Blake and Kincaid. The chain of command went through him. It was his own lack of authority that had allowed it to be undermined. The Moldovan intervention had been his bid to strike back at that collusion and at the conspiracy he suspected – he damn well knew – was dictating policy at the heart of the CIA. But it had failed, spectacularly, miserably.

Of course he could still call Andrei off his own back and try to explain how he had been manipulated by Kincaid, but that would only make him look like a coward. The attack had been initiated through his intelligence. Lives had been lost, he had expected to take a measure of responsibility for that. But he had allowed Kincaid to dictate the terms.

He'd lost an ally in Andrei, for certain, and his reputation looked set to end in tatters. Kincaid would back him up if the incident went to an inquiry, of course; indeed he could already anticipate the twisted pleasure Kincaid would take in vouching for John's character while making damn sure he was hung out to dry.

A thought occurred to Morgan, a dim flicker of something other than utter gloom. Perhaps he could take them all down with him. He could proclaim his suspicions from the rooftops, unleash an almighty shit storm in the hope that some of it would stick. But would he believed? Not just on the basis of his word alone. He needed evidence, and he had none. There was Blake, at large in the field, presumably with the weapons-grade uranium somehow in his possession – if it had even been there in the first place. There were so many games within games going on, Morgan was starting to wonder whether the initial evidence trail that led to Florescu had somehow been fabricated. And even if the authorities could prise Blake out of whatever bolt-hole he managed to slither into, he would never take Morgan's side against Kincaid. He'd plant the blame back on Morgan without a second thought.

Another mission failure for the CIA, then, with Morgan as the architect and chief can-carrier. Thirty-two lives lost, eleven of them unequivocal good guys, one of them a definite bad guy who would have been considerably more useful alive than dead. Fuck it.

Peavey, headset on, spoke up from his own workstation, addressing Kincaid discreetly:

'Sir, you've got a call on the secure line.'

Kincaid nodded to Peavey, covered the telephone mouthpiece and shot Morgan a cursory glance.

'You can go.'

Morgan jerked to his feet like a marionette, exited Kincaid's office with the same wobbly steps. Hope might have given him some backbone but right now he had none. Glancing back through the smoked glass door he saw Kincaid engaged in animated conversation on the phone; Peavey at the adjacent desk was staring back through the glass at Morgan with something that might have been pity in his eyes.

Morgan thought of his two sons, the younger just graduated magna cum laude from Harvard Law, the elder already making his mark as an architect. He thought of his wife, a respected justice of the peace, busy laying plans for a well-funded and philanthropic future, unaware of the crisis that was soon to befall her beloved husband. Then he thought of the revolver in his desk drawer.

In some dark corner of his mind, it was starting to feel like the path of least resistance.

Twenty-nine

<surveillance audiofile #334219: auto-transcribe>
- Bill. Good to hear from you.
<voice ident: Kincaid, Lawrence> <abb:LK>
- It's over between us. This is my last call.
<voice ident: Blake, Bill> <abb:BB>
- What the fuck. Are you drunk. <LK>
- High on life, buddy. This is my last call. I don't need you any more. <BB>
- Where are you. <LK>
- I don't care about whatever game you're playing. I don't care about the agency. You all can just carry on doing what you do, going round in fucking circles. I've got what I need. <BB>
- Do you mean the contraband. <LK>
- The HEU. It's safe and sound. Thanks for asking. <BB>
<pause:6secs>
- I know it's been stressful out there. I've pushed you to the brink, I realise that. But we need to have a conversation. National security is at stake.<LK>
- What the fuck do you care. <BB>
<pause:5secs>
- What do you think this is about. <LK>
- It doesn't matter what I think. I'm going off the grid. I'm out of here. <BB>
- Bill, please, listen. This isn't about you or me. It isn't

about National Security, you're right. It's bigger than that. <LK>

  - I know. <BB>

  - What do you know. <LK>

  <pause:3secs>

  - What do you know. <LK>

  - They're after you. <BB>

  - Who's after me. <LK>

  - They're after me, and that means they're after you. <BB>

  - Who is. <LK>

  - You wouldn't believe me if I told you. <BB>

  - Try me. <LK>

  - Some other time. <BB>

  - What the fuck. Are you trying to play me. <LK>

  - Knowledge is power, right. Sayonara, boss. <BB>

  - You think you can fuck with me. I'll fucking destroy you. I'll hunt you down. There's no hole deep and dark enough. I'll bring pain like you've never known. <LK>

  <line#1 disconnect>

  - Fuck. <LK>

  <line#2 disconnect>

  <end audiofile>

Thirty

The bullet that knocked Wisher from the boat was Moldovan, the soldier who fired it an infantryman patrolling the southern edge of the forest, under orders to watch for stragglers from the ambush on Florescu's convoy. Telescopic sights had revealed what looked like an execution taking place, possibly of a local man. The soldier's aim and intent had both been true. But Blake had slipped through Wisher's fingers as a result.

The young agent surfaced, spitting out water. The bullet impact had hurt – a lot – but the range was long; at worst he might have cracked a rib. There was no time to take stock, though: the rifleman would no doubt be heading over to inspect his kill.

The fisherman bayoneted by Blake lay face down among the reeds, a dark mass floating just a few yards away. Wisher waded over, pulling out his handgun, its silencer still attached. It would work perfectly well underwater, at least for one round. He took hold of the corpse by the neck, shot through it from underneath, aiming for the same spot where the bullet had struck his Kevlar jacket. Now there would be a body for the patrol to find, one that should at least pass a cursory inspection.

Wisher slid low into the water, ski-mask pulled over his head, and backed away from the scene. Night was starting to leach from the sky, but the gloom was still deep. He'd be hard to spot, even with image intensification.

By the time the Moldovan soldiers found the fisher-man, Wisher had crept out of the marsh and was crawling on his belly to the foliage at the edge of the wood. By the time they had inspected the body and called it in, he was running back through the dark trunks and low branches toward where Maja lay. She was his priority now. Bill Blake was an empty, angry space, a void that he turned his back on.

It took several minutes to locate Maja, and when he did, for one dreadful moment he feared the worst. She'd found a hiding place between two thick roots, pulled loose soil and forest detritus over herself. Wisher had handled a dead body just minutes earlier; seeing Maja lift herself painfully from her shallow grave, he was aware how close to the end of life his comrade had come.

He lifted her out of the dirt, held her close. He was shat-tered and soaked, bruised and beaten. He wished he had some spare vitality to pass on to her. As it was he held her too long, until he realised he was actually trying to draw strength from her. He set her down gently. Her eyes were wide, watching him. He hoped she'd have the instinct not to ask about Blake, to just know he'd slipped the net.

Surrender to the Moldovans wasn't an option. He knew her well enough to know that she would not coun-tenance emerging from under the radar. But they needed an exit route. He fished out his cellphone; Maja shook her head.

'Public network . . . they can trace the call.'

'Don't care.'

He called Galloway. Three rings then he hung up, called again. Three rings, hang up. The headcams were gone, the tablet offline. This was the only signal coming to Galloway from his agents in the field. He had better damn well pick it up.

Three rings again, and the call was answered.

'It's Wisher. Maja's hurt. How close can you get to us?'

Near silence for a few moments. Wisher thought he heard hushed voices; hard to tell as a breeze was rustling leaves around him. Then Galloway's rasp broke through the white noise:

'Tevis will text you the GPS. It's seven miles away. Can you make it?'

'We'll make it. Just be there.'

Wisher hung up. Straight away his phone beeped, the coordinates for the rendezvous. He glanced at the screen, then plugged his phone into the control pack of the haptic belt. At least he wouldn't have to map-read.

Maja's eyes were closed, but she had been listening.

'How far?'

'Not so far.'

Wisher broke open an energy bar, handed her a piece. She shook her head.

'Don't argue. Just eat.'

She smiled wearily.

'Not right now.'

'If you want to come with me, drink something, eat something. I'm not carrying a fucking corpse.'

Maja closed her eyes, nodded.

'Bring it to me. Can hardly make my brain work.'

Wisher sat down beside her. For the next few minutes he fed her small pieces of apple-cinnamon soldier fuel, washed down with sips from his canteen, in between taking his own bites. It was like feeding an infant, it occurred to him, or someone very old. Still there was food, even at the beginning and end of life. It *was* life in some ways. It was that basic.

They managed three bars between them. When they had finished, the sky was visibly grey through the mesh of leaves and branches. Less than an hour till sunrise. Maja was thankfully less ashen. Nourishment had eased some of the stress from her face. She still seemed drawn, but there was an almost serene quality to her presence now. She closed her eyes.

He jabbed her in the ribs with his fingertips, hard. She gasped, jolted back to alertness.

'Fuck!'

'Don't go to sleep on me.'

He knew there was fear in his eyes, fear for her. He made sure she saw the emotion. She looked vaguely ashamed.

'Sorry.'

He didn't check the dressing on her injury. If the wound had begun to heal, he didn't want to risk reopening it; if the cauterisation hadn't worked, he couldn't fix it. Instead, he started shedding weight wherever he could. Jacket, mask, body armour, all were discarded. In training he'd regularly carried sixty pounds, including weapon and body armour. Maja weighed twice that. He undressed down to vest, trousers, boots, then started kitting up again with the bare essentials: handgun, water canteen, cellphone, haptic belt. The assault rifle weighed ten pounds. It was staying behind.

Next he went to work on Maja, taking off her various packs and pouches, even her boots and jacket. It was cold, but not critically so. She seemed properly awake now; he'd noticed her taking a couple of caffeine tablets, washed down with the last of their water. Good girl. She'd lost a lot of blood, but at least she'd remembered she was a fighter.

He unwrapped a foil survival blanket and draped it over her. She held it tight around her neck, cape-like, as he knelt down beside her and hauled her over his shoulders in a fireman's lift. She did what she could to balance her weight across him. When he stood, it felt okay. Heavy, but bearable. He could do this.

As they walked, they talked. Stupid stuff, word games, first memories, favourite meals. They both understood the deal: he had to keep walking, she had to stay awake. It was exhausting, but he could feel heat radiating up and out of the engine of his torso, warming and sustaining the pallid form of Maja folded over and around him, and that was something good.

Their route had been plotted to keep them in the woods, their best chance of remaining undetected. Wisher's free hand held the pistol, more as a deterrent than with any intention of using it.

By the third mile he was seriously struggling. His back muscles were on fire, his spine painfully compressed. The rib he'd hoped was only bruised throbbed like a bass line of some ghastly industrial dance track, shrieking out every time he inhaled. He fought to keep his breathing level, not wanting to reveal the extent of his discomfort to his passenger.

Wisher's pain wasn't the only bad news; it wasn't even the headline. Red had been slowly spreading across his white vest, on the side of the garment where Maja's legs folded round him. She wouldn't be able to see the new blood, evidence that her thigh wound had substantially reopened. The fabric was becoming sodden, clinging to his skin. He wanted to hurry, but he simply couldn't. His only hope of even reaching safety was in sticking to the rhythm he had found, letting the repetition and monotony blur the relentless increase in his fatigue.

He spoke again, his words coming out somewhat in gasps as he sought to drive his attention away from his failing strength.

'Can I tell you something?'

She was high on his shoulders, her face close to his when she lifted her head.

'Sure.'

'When you killed the hunter, I didn't like it. Not at all.'

She unstuck her eyes, squinted at him. Her voice was weak, the words slow and breathy:

'That's because . . . you're a pussy.'

She was trying to be funny, but she meant it too. As his feet thudded down and the impacts juddered through his bones, and Maja's weight bore down on him, Wisher couldn't bring himself to play along.

'You didn't just kill him. You enjoyed it.'

He was judging her, which she would hate. But what the hell. He was too tired to be sophisticated. He just needed to be himself. She didn't reply at first. He shot her a sideways look and saw that she was still conscious, she was picking her words.

'He stopped being human . . . when he tried to rape me. He was just prey. He deserved it.'

'Doesn't mean you have to enjoy it.'

Again, she paused. The noises of their progress rose to Wisher's attention: the footsteps and fabric rustles, his own heaving breath, Maja's weak exhalations, two heart-beats in the mix also. The noises of the surrounding woodland barely made an impression. Nothing around them but nature, empty of people, filled with life. Wisher looked down at his boots, willed them forwards. Maja spoke up, each phrase delivered with effort:

'It was like a warm bath. Like pissing. Pure satisfaction. Relief from tension. I don't deny it. I see the life ebb from his eyes. I know my face . . . is the last thing he ever sees. Filling his eyes, like the sky. I look down into his eyes and . . . I can see everyone who ever hurt me. And when they look up . . . they see me up here. Everywhere, like the sky.'

Wisher craned his neck to regard his burden, his lover, the killer slung over his shoulders. Her eyes were closed.

'Maja?'

She spoke without opening them.

'This is why we shouldn't . . . get together. You make me talk shit.'

She was too weak to lift her own weight or bend towards him. Instead she ran her slender fingers over the bare skin of his upper arm. Her soft touch brushed past his elbow, tingled the hair of his forearms. Over the protrusions of his wrist, her fingers spread to line up with his own digits, holding the Makarov pistol. It was at the edge of her reach; Wisher lifted his hand, bringing the gun to his chest, Maja's hand along with it.

Again, he felt the extraordinary rush of emotion that this woman brought out in him. So much strength, so much need.

'Maja?'

'Hmm?'

'When we get out of here – do you want to get married?'

'Sure. Who to?'

Her comic timing was perfect. Wisher grinned; his endurance was ebbing, but his spirit was renewed.

And so the day bore on. The sky above the trees was a wall of cloud, threatening rain, starting to spit by the time Wisher reached the edge the forest, nudged by the haptic belt towards the rendezvous point. He had barely looked up for the last mile. Pure determination had worked the levers of his legs, raised and lowered the leaden tonnage of his feet. All he heard was the beat of blood in his ears; the slender woman draped over his shoulder had become a granite boulder, a millstone grinding bone knuckles into their sockets . . .

And then the weight was gone, lifted from him. He hadn't even heard footsteps; now there was a man either side of him, taking Maja from him, laying her down on the grass. He dropped to his knees, keeled over backwards. A moment earlier, the ground had been his enemy, pushing back at every step he took. Suddenly, it was transformed into a soft and inviting friend. Horizontal had never felt so good.

'It's okay. You're safe.'

That was Jago. He didn't know the other man, early thirties, shaved head, sunglasses. Wisher tried to lift his head. The view around was blurred, consciousness ebbing now he'd reached his goal. He saw two trucks in the distance; Galloway's silver hair as he approached. Maja lay still a few feet to one side. She looked beautiful, free from pain.

'She needs a doctor. Lost a lot of blood.'

'We'll take care of it.'

That was the shaven-headed man. His tone was compassionate enough. Wisher slumped back, looked up at the shapeless mass of the sky, the rain drops falling towards him out of the grey. Someone spoke:

'Get some sleep, soldier.'

Good idea, he thought, and closed his eyes.

Thirty-one

'She's in a side panel. A hidden compartment.'

Wisher wanted to know where Maja was, so Galloway told him. Now Wisher demands to see the body, but Galloway says no. She's been wrapped in plastic. It's over and done with.

The lad has been out cold for two hours and the team is back on the road. The primary target – Arkady Florescu – has been eliminated, but the fallout has been chaotic – tragic – and the most deadly asset in the whole game, the weapons-grade nuclear material, is still unaccounted for.

They are driving towards Kiev, en route to Poland. There's a new safe house there, good for a couple of weeks at least. More than any of them, Wisher needs rest, to recuperate. But he can't control his anger:

'Stop the truck. Stop the fucking truck!'

Jago is watching in the rear-view mirror. Galloway nods to him and he pulls over, though not without pulling a frown, a rare display of emotion from the taciturn operative. The priority is to reach the safe house. Wisher can be sedated by a tranquilliser dart if required. There is certainly no need for a shouting match.

But Galloway is in the grip of emotion too, something he will acknowledge privately to Jago at a later date, when this round of the game has been played out and the fallen are in the ground. Right now, beneath the granite hood of his skull, Galloway's mental machinery is making decisions based on feelings, rather than his knowledge of the Consortium and its machinations.

Emotion. It's why the truck stops, it's why Galloway stands at the roadside, in plain view of the vehicles speeding past, trading verbal blows with his newest recruit. They shout until their throats are raw; Galloway fears he may spit blood and betray the fact of his illness, and so quietens. But inside he is still seething.

Wisher's extraction went against his own protocols and has left his small force vulnerable to detection. But he couldn't lose this particular young man to his fate – to the Consortium, in effect. He couldn't let them have that victory. That's why he shouts; his desperate need to protect, overriding the rational part of his mind.

Tom Wisher has known loss, first of his father, then his mother's slow descent. Now, with the death of Maja, his guts have been ripped out once more. But unlike many who have loved and lost, Wisher can put a name to the dark force that has dealt him this latest dreadful blow. Bill Blake. His was the blade that cut Maja, intending to delay her comrade, not realising he had also struck deep at his secret nemesis. Confrontation with Blake is Tom Wisher's destiny.

Galloway has read the transcript of a phone conversation between Blake and Kincaid, recorded just hours earlier, courtesy of Galloway's mole within the Clandestine Service. Blake appears to be in a heightened state: the discovery that Wisher is alive has tipped him from the typical spy mindset of controlled suspicion into something more like full-blown paranoia. As a result he has not disclosed the news of Wisher's return to Kincaid. This is a stroke of good fortune.

Kincaid will be furious, and desperate to bring Blake to heel. But Galloway has engineered a situation that will keep Kincaid busy at CIA Headquarters while he makes his own move.

The roadside shouting match is over. Wisher is leaving,

limping down the highway, away from the truck. It's madness – what will he do, hitch a ride? The young agent is burnt out and needs to be rested from the fray, but only the pursuit of Blake will occupy his wounded soul.

Galloway's own timetable is tight, ferociously tight, and that tirelessly scheming part of his mind wonders if even this rift between them can be turned to his advantage. He weighs the odds, then calls after Wisher, his voice rising over the din of vehicles speeding down the freeway.

'Blake has the uranium. We think he's working with Florescu's son Stefan. He's going to try to sell it, probably through the organised crime network in Odessa. Start there.'

Wisher does not turn – but he hears the words.

Galloway has been hatching a plan to retrieve the uranium. Now there is another move in play that can act as a smoke-screen for his scheme: the blunt instrument that is the grieving Tom Wisher, so earnest, so keen to find moral purpose, but instead a servant to the most amoral master of all.

Revenge.

Thirty-two

Stuart thought Rachel was losing it. He'd told her to her face during a heated exchange the previous night. Rachel's response was, losing *what*, precisely? Her sanity? Hardly: he knew she wasn't making this shit up. Her focus? Definitely not: she'd never worked as hard, never been so organised. Her perspective, then? Possibly. But she had seen what she had seen.

Then there was that reply to a blog post of hers. It had been sent a few days after Tom's supposed death, carefully worded so that the first letter of each sentence spelled out the word 'Rendlesham' – the Suffolk forest where they rambled as children, also the main part of Tom's online ID. Damn it if that wasn't a pretty strong indication that her brother was still alive and in hiding, despite the official line. And damn it if she wasn't going to dig for all she was worth until she could prove it.

After her close encounter with Tom's CIA colleague, Rachel had rejoined the anti-establishment protests with renewed energy, traumatised by the seeming rendition of her brother, incensed by the subsequent efforts to deceive and manipulate her perception of events. Her gut told her that everything she had ever thought about the so-called intelligence community was true, and as the protests spread, it seemed that the population at large might be agreeing with her at last.

But the ripples of civil disobedience that had risen up

in the wake of the Peshawar incident soon subsided, killed by consensus. People didn't want change in the end. More precisely, they wanted it less than they wanted protection from the wolves at the door, even if the wolves in question were being manufactured to order.

She knew that Stuart was on the same page as her regarding the way hidden forces shaped society for their own gain. As a jobbing physicist he knew full well the power of corporations when it came to investing in scientific research, and how vulnerable the major industries, food production, medicine and defence, were to the whims of said investors. The further you went up the food chain, the harder it became to find anyone resembling a good guy, particularly when it came to pharmaceuticals. Altruism was a virtual impossibility when profit was the only way to grow business.

Moreover, he'd been to Antarctica with his colleagues in the geophysical imaging department. He'd seen the incontrovertible evidence for global warming at firsthand, sipping vodka in the whiteout with as hardened a group of pessimists as you could ever encounter. But still he wouldn't buy into Rachel's conspiracy theories.

The way Stuart argued it, either there was hope, or there was not. Which side of that particular fence one stood on was pretty much an act of will. Hope told him that that there was more chaos than order in the problems faced by humanity. There was no big plan; there was just the daily battle to put food on the table and a roof over one's head, writ large across the billions of people crowding the planet. There was more than enough energy to go around, falling on to earth from the sun; technology would find a way to harness it. There was hope.

Rachel was less optimistic. There was a phrase that she'd come across during her undergraduate studies, referring to Liverpool in the wake of the riots of 1981: 'managed decline.' That was the concept at the heart of Rachel's own particular conspiracy theory. She believed it because it was rational, it was a conclusion she could imagine herself reaching given full possession of the facts about human civilisation, and the geopolitical power to do something about it.

What if there were a secret group of rich and powerful individuals who believed that society as it stood was beyond saving and were orchestrating its slow collapse for their own personal gain? Was it possible that the world's crises, the various battles over territory and resources, clashes of faith and ideology, even certain seemingly 'natural' disasters such as disease outbreaks, were being managed and possibly even initiated from behind the scenes?

Human civilisation was vast and chaotic, but there were clear hotspots. It would be easy to sow dissent, ferment unease, stoke the fires of radicalism, all the while steering certain groups – nations, faiths, militias – towards the trigger point, *beyond which open conflict and violent action were inescapable.* How the CIA fitted into the picture wasn't entirely clear – the conspiracy's interests would transcend those of any particular nation state, America included. But at the very least there would be moles within the Agency, reporting back to their secret paymasters.

In the days since Tom's disappearance, Rachel's bedroom wall had become covered with photos, computer printouts and newspaper cuttings, all linked to the near-detonation of the nuclear device in Peshawar. Her brother had been responsible for averting the blast, she believed, only to stand accused of trying to cause it. The incident had done much to further the cause of the military-industrial complex – with increased military spending in the region, for starters – but if there *was* a conspiracy, its aims would have been advanced more quickly if the blast had occurred. So, score one for the good guys – but who exactly were the good guys?

Someone had snatched Tom from the Suffolk countryside, someone who wasn't the police, who wasn't the CIA, who wasn't an agent of the weapons companies. Who? Did they want to rescue him, or eradicate him?

Stuart joined her in staring at the wall with its mass of words and images. That was when he told her she was losing it – and she was gripped by the fear that maybe she was.

She told herself she was out of her depth. She drank wine and nestled in his arms, listening to Fleet Foxes and planning a camping holiday. Cornwall maybe, or Wales: no Wi-Fi was Stuart's only requirement.

Then Transnistria happened and Rachel's quest for peace of mind was officially abandoned. As the first coverage hit the net she felt in her bones that it could be connected to the near-miss in Peshawar. It seemed possible that Soviet uranium had found its way to Pakistan via the Black Sea borders and the troubled states in the vicinity. Subsequent reports confirmed her suspicions: the target, Arkady Florescu, was suspected of supplying the bomb-making materials to Massoud Ahmed.

Moldovan forces and American intelligence had worked together to mount a surgical strike on the heart of the global criminal network and stem the flow of nuclear materials to rogue states and terrorist groups. At least that's how section chief John Morgan put it during his televised statement to the world's media. Rachel had seen him speak to the press before;

his picture pinned to her wall alongside those of other senior CIA employees. His confidence seemed unusually low on this occasion. Perhaps it was just tiredness, but his habitual gravitas had been replaced by a more gloomy, beaten quality, particularly once he started fielding questions from the floor.

Yes, he was disappointed and saddened by the number of fatalities. His sympathies were with the families of the Moldovan soldiers killed in the field. He hoped that it would not tarnish the bond of friendship between their nation and America. He went further, stating for the record that he would be seeking compensation from agency funds for the deceased. As a joint mission between Moldova and the USA it seemed only proper that joint responsibility should be taken for the loss of life.

Then someone asked about the contraband uranium – how large was the stockpile, was there any risk – and Morgan froze up. The questioning intensified: had there in fact been any nuclear materials within Florescu's base? Was the supposed quest for HEU a cover for an unlawful act of aggression against a controversial businessman who couldn't be touched via legitimate channels?

Rachel started paying closer attention. It seemed the government was headed for another 'missing weapons of mass destruction' scenario like Iraq in the wake of the 2003 American invasion. On the television screen, Morgan set his notes down.

'Let me be clear. This was not an act of war, or even military aggression. It was a police operation with tactical support.'

The CIA official's mood had changed. He stood straighter, the lights were on behind his eyes. Rachel leaned towards the TV. The live broadcast continued:

'In the wake of the Peshawar incident we had clear

intelligence linking Arkady Florescu to the contraband uranium used in the nuclear device. I passed this information on to the Moldovan government, and it was agreed that a search-and-retrieve operation was both morally justified and legally defensible. The operation was planned in total secrecy and at short notice, and yet Florescu received advance warning. The armed clash that has made the headlines was a direct result of that intelligence leak and the confusion it engendered.'

The members of the press, who had been entirely silent during Morgan's speech, burst into noisy life, demanding clarification. Morgan raised his hands for silence, a magisterial gesture that brought swift compliance. The hacks could feel it in their pencils: something big was coming.

'I joined the Central Intelligence Agency twenty-seven years ago with the conviction that I was signing up to fight for world peace and global security, through covert means, yes, but with moral purpose. I have since come to believe there are forces within our own agency, possibly within the American government itself, that are working to a different agenda. I believe there are individuals who looked down on last night's violence and the bloodshed on the banks of the Dneister and smiled. It is my intention that these individuals should be brought to justice.'

As the camera flashed and the journalists clamoured, one thought shot to prominence in Rachel's weary, enervated brain.

He *knows*.

Thirty-three

Finding John Morgan's home address was surprisingly straightforward. Getting Stuart to put the cost of the plane tickets on his credit card required more effort, but eventually he was persuaded. Within twenty-four hours of watching the tumultuous press conference, Rachel and Stuart were on the sidewalk close to Morgan's suburban residence in the Potomac Hills, a short commute from CIA headquarters in Langley, Virginia.

They weren't alone. The upmarket cul-de-sac was lined with press cars and outside-broadcast units. There were literally several hundred journalists present, along with an opportunistic hot-dog vendor and a score of irate fellow residents. Never before had Rachel seen so many simultaneous phone calls being made, reports to editors mixing with complaints to the authorities and police officers calling for backup. The ether must have been boiling.

The house itself was guarded by half-a-dozen secret-service types who formed a line along the edge of the lawn. Once she had pushed her way through the throng of reporters, Rachel found her way blocked by the out-thrust palm of a man in black:

'Stand back, miss.'

He must have been six foot two, with close-cropped hair and an utterly joyless countenance. Stuart put a hand on Rachel's shoulder, ready to steer her in the direction of the nearest coffee shop for a cappuccino and a serious rethink. But Rachel persisted.

'I need to speak with Mister Morgan.'

'That's not going to happen.'

'Tell him I'm Tom Wisher's sister. I'm Rachel Wisher.'

The bodyguard frowned. Though Tom's name had not been in the mainstream news, Rachel suspected there were few in the intelligence community who would not recognise it.

'Please. Tell him.'

Rachel had her passport as proof of ID; the bodyguard's colleagues had tablet computers with access to the CIA database. Within minutes her identity had been established, and she and Stuart were being ushered inside the Morgan residence. The interior was tastefully decorated, spacious but not ostentatious. There was evidence of siege preparations: multipacks of mineral water on the kitchen counter, cases of Pinot Noir stacked more discreetly in one corner. A middle-aged woman, Morgan's wife, smiled tightly as Rachel was ushered past her and through into the back study.

The security guard handed her over to Morgan's son Alec, a studious twenty-three-year-old who shook her hand solemnly and explained that he was acting as temporary counsel for his father. She introduced Stuart as her boyfriend, then realised from the fleeting pleasure that skipped across his face that she'd never called him that before.

Alec led them through into the study, where John Morgan himself sat in an easy chair, turned to face the door. A television flickered silently on the desk behind him. Morgan nodded to his son, who took Stuart back into the main living room, leaving Rachel and Morgan alone.

'Sorry about the chaos.'

'That's a big statement. Can I quote you on that?' Rachel realised Morgan was referring to his domestic arrangements, but she couldn't resist pushing it. The veteran agent smiled, unoffended. In person he seemed warmer than on TV, and considerably less stressed, too.

'I know you're a journalist. I won't do an interview for you, if that's what you're expecting. But you're Tom's sister, and that gets you my ear. I'm so sorry about what happened.'

There was no doubting Morgan's sincerity. Tom had never mentioned his work colleagues by name, but Rachel intuited that the relationship with Morgan was significant. The continuing quest for a father figure, no doubt. God knows, she'd spent enough of her own young life looking for one.

Morgan fitted the bill: his age, his kind manner, the quiet dignity, all these factors were combining without Rachel's conscious knowledge, turning a key. She pressed on, not exactly sure where she was headed.

'That's my question to you, Mister Morgan. That's what I'm trying to find out. What did happen?'

'I wish I knew for sure, Rachel. I really do.'

He reached across the table and took hold of her hand. Incredibly, she let him. The turbulent emotions of her last few weeks were rising up and ready to spill over. Her eyes were starting to glaze with tears, but it wasn't sadness exactly. It was relief. She was going to trust this stranger with her secrets.

'Are we safe here? I mean, can we talk? Is anyone listening in?'

'Not to my knowledge, though I'll be honest with you, I'm not sure what that's worth nowadays.'

He shot her a look, concerned but keen also, sensing the presence of things unsaid. Rachel drew a shuddering breath, and, unbidden, it all came out. The whole story. The communications from Peshawar, the rendezvous in Suffolk, the rendition, the interrogation. The body in the morgue, that she was sure was not her brother. She cried while she spoke: she hadn't realised how much she'd been bottling up, how much she'd needed to talk.

Morgan steepled his fingers as he listened. Rachel glanced at him, and saw his eyes were gleaming.

'What do you think?'

'I think you did the right thing, coming here. I'm going to take the fight to these people. I need all the ammunition I can get.'

'Ammunition?' Suddenly, Rachel was uneasy.

'Just a turn of phrase. This game is all about who knows what, and about whom. Your information gives me an advantage over our common adversary, an avenue to apply pressure.'

'And that adversary is?'

'The people who wanted to create a nuclear incident. The same people who sabotaged the Transnistria mission.'

'Who are these people?'

'We're still working on that.'

We? She'd thought Morgan was out on a limb, hell, she *knew* he was. And yet here he was, retreating behind the first-person plural. She felt the ground falling away, and clutched at straws:

'Have you heard whether Tom is still alive? Do you know anything about that?'

'Based on what you've told me, I can believe that Tom

Wisher wanted to stop a nuclear incident, not start one. And he succeeded. I can believe that he might still be alive. It certainly fits with what you saw.'

His manner had become professional: he was still avuncular, but she could picture an autocue just behind her head that he was discreetly reading from. For her part, she was becoming pushy, losing her cool:

'So what, you think he's still a spy?'

'Your guess is as good as mine on that one.'

'So where is he? And who's he working for?'

'That's something we'd both like to know.'

The reply was glib, the smile false. Rachel's heart, so full of hope just moments earlier, was starting to blacken. Whatever revelations she might have hoped to receive, it was clear they were not going to be forthcoming. She had showed hers, he hadn't showed his. And why the hell would he? Knowledge was power, after all. She now knew what his wife looked like, and the colour of the wallpaper in his study. But as for the enlightenment she'd flown the best part of four thousand miles in search of: jack shit.

Anger narrowed her vision to a tunnel. Good guy or bad guy, in the end, it didn't matter. Morgan was one of *them*.

The farewell was a formal handshake. Rachel could hardly meet Morgan's eyes as she left the room. Stuart was in the kitchen, chatting with Alec. He glanced round, picked up her mood, and made his goodbyes swiftly.

They didn't speak until they were clear of the crush of reporters surrounding Morgan's house. A few tried to interview her; others shot her jealous looks, presuming she had a scoop. Fortunately there were cabs at the end of the street, cruising in search of business. Rachel hailed one, asked the driver to take them to Washington Dulles International airport.

Soon they were ensconced in the back seat. She knew her mood was a black cloud, but she didn't care to adjust it. She just let it hang there, sour and heavy like a stomach ache.

'Alec's a good guy. Smart, too.'

Rachel made no comment. Stuart scratched his beard, pondering the best way to proceed with his attempts at conversation.

'So what now?'

She stared out through the window. In the distance, a passenger plane was rising into the sky.

'Back to Cambridge. Back to the drawing board.'

Rachel was regretting her confession, Morgan knew. It saddened him to have gained then lost her trust, but that wasn't his prime concern right now. Certainly, she wasn't someone he could share his own secrets with. That was why he hadn't mentioned the reports coming in from Transnistria, about an earlier attempt on Florescu's life, before the gun battle in the forest, with Blake as a secondary target.

Moldova was not behind this assassination run, nor was the CIA. Nor indeed the conspiracy that Kincaid was part of, who had sought Florescu's allegiance, not his death. Someone or something else, then – the same covert force that had staged the death of Tom Wisher?

Then there was the file that had been delivered, anonymously, to the law firm where his son Alec was interned. An actual paper printout in an envelope, addressed to him in confidence.

A sticky note attached to the document read: 'The tip of the iceberg.' The document itself was the transcript of a phone conversation between Laurence Kincaid and Bill Blake, the call that Kincaid had taken directly after dismissing Morgan from his office the previous day. An audio file of the call had been supplied on a data stick. Proof positive that Kincaid and Blake were conspiring to supply HEU to the world's terror network.

Someone out there was batting for the good guys, and now it seemed they'd recruited Tom Wisher to their cause.

The tip of the iceberg.

Morgan looked out through his half-opened office door and saw his wife passing by. She glanced in and offered a smile. She was ready to take a step back from her career; he'd thought he was, too, but it turned out he still had a job to do.

It was time to take out the trash.

Thirty-four

The German said he was looking for someone, a man called Blake, and showed Lem a photograph. Lem had been approached by strange men before, foreigners speaking broken Russian. He was healthy-looking compared to the average Odessa street kid. He made an effort to wash now and again, so he smelt okay too. Not that it would last, if the rest of his gang was anything to go by.

He'd only been on the street for a year; after his mother died, he been moved to the state orphanage. Then he'd met Dominika and everything had changed. She was thirteen, a year older than him and six inches taller. She was painfully thin, even back then, but her eyes were beautiful, grey-green and perfectly symmetrical. Her eyes had called him before her voice. She was sat on the edge of the Potemkin stairs, taking a break from begging. She shared her bottle of street-brewed rakia with him. The sweet and skin-crawlingly potent spirit that made him cough. She told him they shared everything on the street.

Her gang lived in a disused lock-up at the edge of one of the city's many grim housing estates. Five others, with ages ranging from eleven to fifteen; six children sharing three mattresses, together in a dark and fetid concrete box. Lem should have been repelled, by the darkness, the rank odour, the signs of drug use. And yet for the first time in months he was being offered something that filled the empty space inside his heart: a family.

The German – his name was Schiele – said he wasn't a policeman, he was a private detective. The man he was looking for was a crook, working for the black market. That was the connection he wanted to make through Lem: a pimp, a dealer, someone who could lead him deeper into the Ukrainian underworld.

Lem knew straight away that Schiele wasn't a cop: for a start, he wouldn't be talking to a street kid, he'd be shouting, probably swinging his boot at the same time. Cops had no time for Lem and his kind. They knew not to pity these youngsters, who had chosen the freedom and degradation of the feral life over the boredom and brutality of state-run accommodation.

So the German wasn't a cop, he wasn't a kerb-crawler, he wasn't a social worker, he wasn't a missionary type, either. Lem didn't know what the German was. Just a regular guy, he supposed.

Lem looked in the general direction of the photograph and shook his head. He was on a mission to buy flu medicine so Dominika could cook up a batch of baltushka and he was a few hryvnia short. He told the man he was hungry and held out his hand for money. The man grinned, and said he was hungry too.

The waitress hesitated when she saw Lem, but the German said the boy was with him and insisted their order was taken. Lem would rather have been round the back of the café, foraging, but he was focused on the money he still needed. This German was good for it, he was sure, he just needed to play along for a while.

And he did need to eat, too. It had been twenty-four hours probably. Baltushka with a side order of glue to sniff kept the gnawing at bay, filled you with giggles and floating dreams. But once you went out on the street and the air started to clear your head, your various organs started to make themselves heard: bowels, belly, brain too, if you weren't careful.

The waitress set the bread-basket down with a scowl. But the German smiled at her like a friend, and she couldn't help but smile back. She was young, he was good-looking and his foreign accent was kind of sexy. She told him the borscht wouldn't be long. He asked for plenty of sour cream on top and she blushed a little.

Lem started working his way through a sweet roll. He knew to take small bites at first, to ease his stomach back towards functioning. The bread was fresh from the oven, still warm; the smell from it rose into his solvent-raw nostrils and he had to choke back a sob. It smelled like childhood, like feather pillows, like a mother's love. Chew before you swallow, he told himself.

'You shooting up?' asked the German. Lem shrugged. The answer was pretty obvious, given the track marks that showed every time the sleeves of his hoodie rode up.

'I see you at night,' the German continued. 'You're like rabbits, coming out of your holes when it gets dark. I saw one kid come out of the ground, literally, from under a manhole. There must be hundreds of you.'

'Thousands,' Lem corrected him, proudly.

'In my country, we wouldn't let you live like you do,' he said. 'We'd look after you.'

Lem smirked, kept his head down. Maybe this guy was a missionary after all.

'You don't believe me?' The German was frowning now. Lem tried to explain:

'No one makes us live on the streets. They come round sometimes, cops and social workers, trying to round us up. But we're good at hiding and they get bored.'

'You don't want to live like normal people?'

'Normal people have to work at shitty jobs. We are free. That's why they hate us. They think we laugh at them.'

'Do you?'

'Sometimes,' admitted Lem, feeling strangely ashamed.

The borscht arrived, beetroot stew with beef and vegetables, wine-dark and lusciously fragrant. Lem flinched at the strange sensation in his mouth, then realised it was watering. As he tucked in, alternating greasy chunks of meat with lumps of gravy-soaked bread, the German asked him what he knew about the criminal network he shared the night with.

There were the pimps, but baltushka kids like Lem and Dominika who showed their tracks were known to be disease ridden and wouldn't fetch much of a price. Besides, there were plenty of fresh girls coming in from the villages every week who actually *wanted* to be whores.

There were dealers, but they tended to focus on the beach and the tourist areas where Odessa's middle-class youth clustered. Street children cooked their own drugs. Decongestants that contained ephedrine could be combined with vinegar and potassium permanganate to produce baltushka, which made the cold and the smell and the sadness disappear.

There were rumours about organ traders, on the look out for body parts to sell to transplant surgeons in Europe and India. The urban legend described a big man in a black suit, who drove a Bukhanka van – a Russian make, known by its 'loaf of bread' shape – and always wore sunglasses, even after dark. They nicknamed him Nozhnitsovich – 'Mister Scissors'. He was their bogeyman. Lem shuddered at the thought.

Of course, the cops were the biggest crooks of all. If the German was serious about making contact with organised crime, he should get himself a police cap and truncheon, the mafiosi would be stepping forward to shake his hand!

The German laughed, a proper big happy noise, like maybe he hadn't laughed for a while. Lem chuckled too, then spluttered as the borscht caught in his throat. The cough took hold of him, and now the German wasn't smiling any more. He was reaching across the table to Lem, who was starting to turn red as he retched.

Spew splattered over the tabletop. Lem choked, spat out lumps of phlegm. This wasn't beetroot, it looked more like blood. It *was* blood. And the room was spinning, the tabletop racing towards him . . .

The doctor told Lem he had TB – tuberculosis – and that he was HIV positive. He could have guessed the latter – there were leaflets and notices everywhere about the risks of sharing needles. TB was an immediate problem: they'd want to keep him in hospital for months, it had happened to other kids he knew, and he couldn't stand the thought. His gang was his family, his life.

Already he was risking exclusion: he'd been sent to get flu meds and he'd been gone for far too long. The others would be bitching and scratching at their scabs, starting to get desperate. But worse than being over-due, he'd taken food from a stranger. He'd eaten his fill instead of taking what he could get and sharing it with the others. Loyalty was everything within his group. If they found out what he'd been up to, he'd be punished.

The German was with him, sat at the foot of the treat-ment couch. He seemed concerned, of course, but bemused as well, like he couldn't really get a handle on

Lem's situation. When the doctor had left the room, he offered to help:

'I have money. Not so much, but enough. And I have contacts, too. I can find you space at a private hospital. They can treat the TB and help with the drugs too. This doesn't have to be the end.'

'HIV is the end.' Lem was merely being factual. But the German shook his head furiously:

'There are all sorts of treatments now. People in the States are beating all the predictions.'

Lem wasn't really listening. He needed to get back to Dominika. The German knew it. He stopped talking, crouched by Lem at the head of the couch.

'I just want to help.'

Lem nodded. He didn't doubt that the German meant it.

'I need ten hryvnia. If you want to help. That's what I need.'

The muscles in his would-be protector's face tightened. Lem understood then that the German was hurting, and trying to fix the hurt with kindness, but it wasn't working.

The German took out his wallet, and fished out a bill. The poet Franko on the front, Lviv Opera on the back. A twenty.

'Good luck, kid.'

He turned his back. Lem shrugged on his hoodie and slipped out of the treatment room.

It was dark by the time he got back to the lock-up. The bitter fumes of the baltushka bake seeped out through the entrance, a hole prised open in the corner of the metal shutter. They'd started without him. He crouched down; the hole was blocked by a mattress. He pushed against the obstruction but it didn't budge. Someone must be sitting against it.

'It's me, it's Lem. I've got the medicine!'

'Fuck off, Lem.' Dominika's voice, unmistakeable. They must have heard about the ambulance, the hospital. One of their number might even have seen him, being stretchered from the café.

Lem banged on the shutter for ten minutes, but only drew escalating curses from inside, from Dominika at first, then from the others. In the end he gave up. Despair squeezed a few tears out of him, but in his heart he knew he had broken the rules, and he had to pay the price.

He took his twenty down to the beach, hoping to score something to keep him up for the night. But as he progressed into the wealthier districts, he felt himself becoming increasingly conspicuous, drawing cruel looks from the partygoers who were heading out to the beach-side bars and clubs.

In the end he steered into a pharmacists instead, bought a pack of caffeine tablets and a cola drink, then caught a tram back to the edge of his estate. He walked the last stretch, relieved to be back on familiar territory. He'd already washed down a handful of pills and was starting to feel shaky. The litter-strewn street was deserted; he sat down on the kerb and took a few deep breaths to steady himself.

That was when he saw the van. It wasn't a Bukhanka, it was a Volkswagen Transporter, well maintained compared to many parked on the street. And it was black. It had pulled to a stop across and down from where he sat. The windscreen was tinted; through it Lem could see that the driver was wearing shades.

Mister Scissors!

The side door scraped open and a second man climbed

out. Lem was already running, fast along the pavement. He turned down the nearest alley, heart pumping—

Paw-like hands snatched hold of his arm, a plastic builder's sack was slipped over his head. They'd anticipated his escape route and now they had him. Lem writhed and howled like the trapped animal he was. The bear-handed man swung him like a doll into the alley wall, knocking him half senseless.

Lem's breath caught in his throat and he started coughing again. Spasms racked his body as he was lifted up and carried back towards the street. They wouldn't care if he choked to death. They didn't even want him alive. He imagined scissor blades sinking into his chest, cutting through his ribs, puncturing his frantic heart . . .

'Leave the boy alone.'

Lem couldn't see, but he knew the voice, the foreign accent. He kept up his resistance, but now he could hear a struggle unfolding in the alleyway, the grunts and thuds of a fist fight.

Lem's captor dropped him to the floor. The boy pulled the sack from over his head and scrambled to his feet. Looking back down the alleyway, he saw his rescuer in action, taking on three hardened Odessa criminals – and *winning*.

Fists flying. Blood droplets spinning through the air. Breath blasting like steam in the street light. Maybe it was the caffeine, or baltushka still coursing through Lem's veins, but he could have sworn the German actually *blurred* when he moved.

One man was down already, clutching at his guts. The second, the one who'd had hold of Lem until moments ago, was trying to pin the German while Mister Scissors cut him open. But Lem's guardian angel was too fast, too skilled. He broke Bear-hands' grip, then he broke his leg at the knee, using the thug's own weight against him. Mister Scissors – if that's who he really was – mistimed his dagger strike and stumbled forward, off-balance.

The German was on him in a moment. His fist slammed into the crook's face, snapping his shades in half and revealing the squinting pig eyes underneath.

Then he was riding on the pig's back, forcing him down on to the flagstones, pinning him with a knee while he bent an arm round his back, drawing a gasp of pain from his captive.

'Florescu. You know the name?'

The German's voice was a low growl, so different from the kind man who had rushed Lem to the hospital that afternoon. His long coat caught the breeze, lifting like a cape as he bent Mister Scissors' arm up higher, twisted it at the wrist. The crook groaned in pain.

'Please . . . no more . . .'

'I want to know where his men are, understand? They're somewhere in this city. I want you to show me.'

Savage purpose emanated from the German. Lem understood then that he was here to kill the man in the photograph. That was what had brought him to Odessa. He wasn't a cop, or a kerb-crawler or a missionary type. He was a soldier, and he was at war.

The lad took a step forward. The German saw the movement and glanced round. His eyes were wolf dark as he spoke:

'Go.'

Lem ran from the alley, back into the labyrinth of the city.

Dominika took him back in, thank heaven. The meal he hadn't shared with them was soon forgotten – he'd thrown it back up, after all – and the change from the twenty meant they could stay in their den through the chilly weekend.

And what a story he had to tell! The German was already more than a man in Lem's mind: he was a spirit, a ninja, the superhero who made Mister Scissors beg for mercy.

As the months pulled through autumn into winter, his dreams were filled with memories of that night. Again and again, he imagined the German breaking Mister Scissors' mirror shades clean in two, his fist trailing ripples as it glided through the air, like the prow of a boat through the water.

And when the end came for Lem, curled and shivering in a dark corner of Dominika's latest hole, it was the smell of fresh, warm bread that guided him to the light.

Thirty-five

'Drive.'

Wisher sat up front in the VW van with the creep he had just rescued Lem from. He didn't want to have to babysit this piece-of-shit people-trafficker, or whatever he was. But the man had recognised Florescu's name and sworn he could take Wisher to someone who worked for the Romanian, who drank at a bar across town. It was where they were headed now. Wisher didn't know the city's back-streets well enough to find his own way, especially not at night. And he had no more time to waste.

He'd been in Odessa three days. His Russian was good enough to communicate with the locals, but he stood out like a sore thumb outside the tourist districts. Plus the local police were in the habit of making life difficult for foreign nationals, checking passports and asking for bribes if they weren't forthcoming. Wisher had been stopped once already and didn't want it to happen again.

The young agent had his trusty Makarov pistol wedged under the driver's ribcage. He'd grown stupidly fond of the gun over the past few days, perhaps because it was his only tangible link to Maja. It had been on his hotel pillow each night, a memento mori wrought in dark metal. Wisher had pretty much hardened himself against grief: the emptiness he felt inside wasn't that unfamiliar, and he coped with it as he had always done, through action. Find Blake. Kill Blake. Do no pass 'Go'. Do not collect two hundred bucks.

It was a damn shame about Lem, though. He'd seemed like a smart kid, but the street ran too deep within him. It made Wisher sick to his stomach, to see track marks on the arms of someone so young. And it brought fresh heartache, even to his own numbed sensibilities, to observe the lad's quiet acceptance of his wretched fate. He'd saved him this time; he wouldn't be there next time the boy fell victim to his addiction, or to one of the countless lowlifes circulating in Odessa's back-streets.

Wisher glanced into the back of the van. Street light through the windscreen illuminated rolls of plastic sheeting, a tool bundle, half-a-dozen cooler boxes. He pushed the pistol deeper into his captive's side, prompting a grunt.

'What's your name?'

'Gregor.' The voice was low and smoker-gruff.

'And what the fuck do you do, Gregor?'

Gregor glanced towards Wisher. His grin revealed gnarly, nicotine-stained teeth.

'I sell ice-cream. What about you?'

Gregor turned his attention back to the road ahead. Wisher replied grimly:

'Me too.'

It was all too much: the long night, the abjection, this endless crawl through the city's underbelly. Right at that moment, the young agent wanted nothing more than to run headlong out of the shadows and to find his way to some kind of daylight. But not yet, not yet.

The bar was called 'Zvezda' – the Star – but it was far from bright. Parts of Odessa's old town were literally crumbling and this district was no exception. A sole street light flickered as the wind picked up and the black van drew in to the kerb. Phone cables strung high across the tarmac flicked like skipping ropes. A roof tile fell from up above to the pavement and shattered.

'A guy called Olek was in there last night,' said Gregor, shifting uncomfortably in his seat. 'A regular. I heard him talking. He said he was in the convoy with Florescu when the soldiers came. Only just made it out, from what he was saying.'

Wisher nodded. He was quiet. Grim. Gregor's attention was fixed on the gun barrel jabbing into his ribs.

'Is that all you want?' Gregor's question was cautious. He could feel the build-up of tension in his captor's frame. Wisher's head was swimming. He couldn't bring himself to look at the man sat next to him. But he could feel each breath the lowlife took, his torso expanding against the Makarov's silencer as he filled up with air. Wisher asked him softly:

'If I pull the trigger, will it save lives?'

'Not mine.' The comment was utterly deadpan, but Gregor was becoming increasingly fearful, not a mental state he was accustomed to.

'Do you take children and kill them? Is that what you do?'

Gregor swallowed, hard. Wisher was utterly still. Neither spoke for a few moments. Wisher stared out at the one failing street light, the whipping cables above it. A scrap of newspaper spiralled through his view, caught by a gust. He followed the movement with his eyes, shifting focus – and found Gregor's reflection in the windscreen, flickering with the light outside.

This dreadful man, this ugly soul, was rendered ghostly and transparent. Pig eyes sunk deep in their sockets; pallid fleshy features quivering slightly. His whole attention was focused on the pistol that Wisher was pushing into his ribs.

In the reflection, Wisher could see Gregor reaching out towards the gun, slow and steady, like he was trying to catch a butterfly. He jabbed the weapon forward and Gregor recoiled, up against the driver's door now, no room left to manoeuvre.

'I can change.' The voice was quiet, breathy. Desperate. Gregor could tell that Wisher was on a knife-edge.

'I want to change. To be a better man. Give me the chance to change.'

It struck Wisher that this low man would know what it looked like, to beg for mercy. He would have seen it and heard it many times from his victims. He could probably mimic it, while remaining unmoved inside. Maybe if Wisher could look into Gregor's eyes, he might be able to tell if there was any truth to his pleas. But they were sunk deep into the man's skull, they were like raisins, dark and shrivelled in the flickering reflection.

Wisher eased back slightly on his gun hand. He was an assassin, not an executioner.

Gregor fumbled for the handle, cracked the driver's door open. He shuffled backwards across his seat, away from the handgun and the rigid arm behind it. Then he slipped out into the night and was gone.

Wisher entered the Star and looked around. It was a dingy space, its décor decades old. The theme was the Soviet space programme: there were faded pictures of cosmonauts on the wall, a naïve oil painting of the Sputnik satellite above the bar. Three customers, a couple at a table and a burly man at the counter, staring at an empty shot glass. The couple were locked in some sort of grinding, low-voiced disagreement. The barman glowered, taking an instant dislike to the new arrival. Wisher approached him:

'I'm looking for Olek.'

The big man at the counter – Florescu's one-time lackey – lifted his head at the name. He was broad like an ox, but he was profoundly drunk too, his movements sluggish.

'Who wants to know?'

'A friend.'

'Go fuck yourself.'

Olek hadn't even bothered to look round. Wisher persisted:

'Can I buy you a drink?'

Olek shrugged, but he shifted his weight on his barstool, and Wisher sensed he was preparing for violence. The barman filled up Olek's glass, set down a second one. Wisher put the mugshot of Blake on the counter where Olek could see it.

'You recognise this man?'

Olek sipped his vodka, stared at the picture for a few seconds.

'CIA.' The letters were sounded with a thick accent. Wisher nodded.

'That's right.'

Olek peered at him from under his bony brow, his mind emerging from the fog of alcohol, aggression starting to push through.

'Are you fucking CIA?'

Olek was going dark. Wisher cut to the chase, keeping it clear and simple.

'He's with Stefan Florescu and some of his father's crew. They have uranium, to make atom bombs. They want to sell it to terrorists. I need to find them. I need to stop them.'

Olek's eyes were losing focus. Wisher couldn't tell if it was simply the booze, or whether his Russian wasn't up to the task of explaining the situation at hand. He elaborated:

'Atom bomb, you understand? Nuclear weapon. Thousands die. Thousands get sick with cancer. Like Hiroshima, you know? Like Chernobyl— '

Olek slammed his glass down on the table hard. Wisher's hand tightened on the gun in his jacket pocket. The big man spoke, the words falling heavily from him.

'My family – are from Kiev. My cousin worked at Chernobyl. He died there.'

'So you understand.' Hope was growing for Wisher: had he really got through to Olek? The Ukrainian continued, eyes drifting into the distance.

'It gets into the water, into the food. Children are born all twisted up. It never ends.'

Wisher made eye contact with Olek, held it.

'Tell me where to find them. I'll do the rest.'

'I waved him through.'

'What?' Olek's mind was starting to wander:

'At the gate. Stefan. His van was nearly scraping the ground. Arkady said to leave the uranium and he was right. He had honour. Guns and blades and fists. This is how men fight. Not with sickness in our food and our blood . . .'

Wisher took hold of Olek's shoulders, forcing him back to the here and now:

'Tell me where to find them!'

Olek grimaced,

'A man called Romanik. He owns a garage, down by the port. Goes way back with Florescu. I heard they were there.'

'Thank you.' Wisher breathed a sigh of relief. He had the information he needed. Olek refilled his glass; Wisher had not yet emptied his. The big man sent Wisher a bleary look.

'You have children?'

Wisher shook his head.

'Don't bother. Life is shit. But vodka . . . vodka is good.' He raised his glass, toasted:

'To vodka.'

Wisher touched his glass to Olek's, then swigged back the shot. The spirit seared his throat – it was his first alcohol in weeks – but the afterglow spread quickly through his chest, warm and comforting.

Behind them, the door crashed open – and Gregor barged in, now wielding a sawn-off shotgun, his face twisted into a snarl.

'Hey, motherfucker!'

He spat out the word in rough English; his gun spat out its load with glass-rattling ferocity. Wisher was already heading towards the floorboards, tucked into a roll. As he spun upright, his gun was in his hand. The Makarov pistol was sweet at this range. A hole popped open between Gregor's eyes, red like a Hindu bindi. The crook slumped backwards; Wisher skated over to him, handgun in a double grip, ready for another shot. But there was no doubt that he was dead.

Wisher turned back to the bar. Olek was slumped forward, a meaty hole ripped in his back. The barman stood slowly from behind the counter, saw that Wisher was still armed, and froze on the spot. Wisher glared at him.

'You know Romanik's garage?'

The barman nodded slowly.

'Tell me where.'

It was long past midnight by the time Wisher reached the garage, following the address scrawled on a beer mat by the barman at the Star. He had caught a taxi for most of the distance, but walked the last half a mile, ducking between buildings. He was tired, but the darkness worked to his advantage in terms of making his approach. He had to seize the moment.

In fact, the garage was easy to find. There were lights on, occasional vehicles drove out from behind its tall doors. Wisher had his pistol and the shotgun, plus a handful of rounds fished from Gregor's pockets. It wasn't much of an arsenal.

There was a boarded-up parade of shops across the street from the garage. Wisher forced his way in through a back door, climbed a rickety flight of stairs up into the first-floor store rooms. He took up a surveillance position by a broken window that looked out on to the main street and the garage across the way. All he had to do now was wait.

As the night wore on, he reflected on Olek's drunken remarks about the impact of Chernobyl. Even a thug could grasp the threat posed by nuclear terrorism. Hell-bent on revenge, Wisher had lost sight of the bigger picture: containing the threat posed by the contraband HEU. Whatever his intentions regarding Blake, stopping a black-market deal on the uranium *had* to be part of the plan.

Across the street, lights were switching off. A last truck departed and the garage's tall doors were pulled closed. All was quiet. Even racketeers crawled to bed at some point.

Wisher didn't intend to sleep, but it crept up on him. When he jolted back to consciousness, dawn was breaking. He lurched upright to the window, looked down on to the street, and saw the rear of a black saloon car disappearing into the dark of the garage.

'Damn!'

Wisher was down the detritus-strewn stairwell in moments. By the time he reached the street, the garage's tall doors had been closed once more. Wisher darted across the tarmac and into an alley down one side of the garage, overgrown with brambles and buddleia.

Light glowed from a small window, too small to climb through. Wisher peered through the grimy pane. A scrawny young man walked past, heading into the back of the building. At his side was a stocky type, presumably a bodyguard. Following close behind them was Bill Blake.

Wisher gasped. It might have been the involuntary sound he made or some accompanying movement, but Blake's attention was drawn in his direction. The traitor turned towards the dark window, saw the pale face framed within it – and grinned.

Then he was gone, following his new allies into the dark recesses of the auto-shop. Wisher ran round to the back of the building, but found it securely locked up. Returning to the front, he tried forcing the tall doors, but they were locked shut.

Thank God the Makarov was silenced. It took two rounds to shoot through the bolt. Slipping inside, Wisher crouched low behind the parked car, edged forward into the building's back rooms.

No sign of Blake. No sign of the others. Just a network of cluttered storage rooms. Wisher kicked boxes out of the way, barged open a locked door on to another interior filled with dust and darkness. Where the hell had they gone?

Voices sounded out in the main repair shop. Footsteps. The day-shift mechanics arriving. And Wisher had left the bolt buckled and hanging by its screws . . .

He ducked out of sight inside the storeroom he'd forced his way into. A shadow stretched across the doorway as a man made his way cautiously along the corridor, his raised arm holding a tyre iron. The mechanic was no match for Wisher. An elbow strike brought him down, and he was swiftly disarmed. He didn't even catch sight of his attacker.

Wisher managed to leave the garage unobserved. He spent the rest of the day at his vantage point across the road, hoping against hope that Blake or one of his accomplices would emerge. Instead, there was a clear response to his break-in earlier that morning. A lookout took up position by the front door, with a second henchman on a roaming patrol around the adjoining streets. Traffic in and out of the garage was reduced. It was unlikely to be left unguarded at night.

Blake could have left through a rear exit, or in the trunk of one of the repair cars. It certainly didn't seem likely he was still in the building. The trail had gone cold.

As evening drew in, so Wisher's patience ran out. Cold and huddled in the empty building, he did the one thing he swore he wouldn't do, back when he was shouting curses on the hard shoulder of the Kiev highway. He called Galloway.

'The number you have dialled is no longer available.'

Wisher switched off his phone, unexpectedly angry. He'd told the man to fuck off, after all. But somehow he'd imagined that Galloway had his back.

How wrong he was.

Thirty-six

Blake had never pushed himself as hard. He was nearly fifty, carrying a few spare pounds, and his musculature had lost whatever elasticity it may once have possessed. In the wake of his lucky escape from Wisher, he literally hobbled from the fisherman's stolen boat to the rendez-vous with Stefan.

Florescu Junior was waiting with a Turk called Guney, who was young like him but had considerably more composure.

He won't be second fiddle for long, thought Blake to himself as he snorted up a line of cocaine and felt his aches recede. Probably he should have slept, but the relief of making it back from the war zone brought its own high, plus he had the extraordinary revelation of Tom Wisher's existence to process.

It was almost like a dream, in fact. How the fuck had that happened? How, who, and why?

Of the three questions, the first was the least import-ant. Even he'd been suspicious of the body on the slab, back in England. As for the database biometrics, well, they'd been hacked. Simple as that. It had been done seamlessly, but it wasn't like he hadn't done similar tink-ering himself. It angered him but it didn't baffle him.

As to why, again, though he didn't like where his thoughts led him, the logic behind them was a familiar part of his world. Dead men can move under the radar.

For a spy, or an assassin, being wiped off the grid was a massive advantage.

So there you had it: Tom Wisher had been snatched out of the frame built for him by Blake, in order to continue his work as an agent, out of sight of the authorities and his enemies. The question remained: who the fuck was he working for?

This was the point at which Blake's exhausted mind started to fray. He prided himself in his cynicism. He was not inclined to trust anyone; he operated by gauging the balance of self-interest between himself and the people he dealt with. Case in point: Kincaid. From what he knew of the deputy director's agenda, it made no sense for Kincaid to be working against him. But who else knew about Florescu and Transnistria? Was John Morgan secretly running black ops under the radar? Blake couldn't see it.

Supposing he had become a liability to Kincaid? It was the option that made most sense to Blake. He'd been planning getting out of the game and Kincaid could have anticipated this. And certainly he knew too much about his paymaster's dirty work. Hell, he'd done most of it for him. But Tom Wisher acting as an asset for Kincaid? It simply didn't stack up.

Stefan passed a bottle over from the front passenger seat to where Blake sprawled, across the leather rear seats of a sleek saloon car. Blake swallowed a mouthful of the clear liquid and nearly choked: whatever spirit it was had a hell of a lot more proof points than was medically advisable. Yet as the burn spread outwards from his throat, it seemed to bring a wave of enlightenment with it. He glanced at his colleagues, two young crooks heading towards the top of their game, with a uniquely valuable asset to dispose of. If they were smart enough, they would understand that he was crucial to their plans.

He didn't need to be greedy: twenty per cent of the sale would buy him safe passage to a future without Kincaid and the spy game. Blake wanted to rediscover the wilderness, the mountains of his youth. Not literally, in America: no way he'd be able to stay under the radar stateside. Instead, he'd been thinking about Russia's Kamchatka peninsula: the terrain was famously challenging, but there were still plenty of bears to shoot. Just himself and a rifle, under the stars. That was the dream, once he'd closed a sale on the uranium – and tied up a few loose ends.

Blake lay back on the leather, folding himself at the knee to fit. His weird epiphany came back to him. Kundalini, the life force, resonating in his aching bones. He'd survived everything that fate had thrown at him, bombs, bullets, a dead man's gun in his face. Somebody up there liked him.

That was when he called Kincaid and told him where to shove it. He knew he was intoxicated, but he just didn't care. He'd taken too many punches for the man, he couldn't just slip away without flipping him the bird by way of a farewell. Plus he had the sweetest secret – the resurrection of Tom Wisher – to wave under Kincaid's nose. He felt like a schoolboy, all but snorting with laughter at the 'kick me' sign on his teacher's back. He felt good.

Next day, not so good. He woke from heavy sleep into a world of pain. Surface cuts and bruises; deep tissue strains and tears; exhaustion; plus a multilayered drug-and-drink hangover. He showered and put on a front before facing his new colleagues; they were young, he didn't want to seem old, even if he couldn't help moving like he was made out of wood.

Coffee and breakfast got him through the first meeting at Guney's comfortable townhouse headquarters in

Odessa. Plans were made to store the contraband with a local mobster called Romanik, while setting up the right deal for its sale. It wasn't until he could get Stefan alone and access his cocaine stash that Blake started to feel anything resembling functional again.

Still, he got away with it. Over the next couple of days he was able to lick his wounds and regain a measure of charm. But he was running on a permanent coke high, and he was starting to get edgy. Who the fuck was Wisher working for? What did they want? The questions ate away at him.

The city's whores provided ample distraction for Stefan, but Guney was starting to get restless. He knew Blake had contacts among the radical Islamic factions and wanted him to start reaching out. Blake urged caution: the uranium was safely stored, it made sense for them to take their time and find the right customer. Guney wasn't convinced, however. He was confident trafficking drugs and girls, guns even, but, like the late Florescu, he was uncomfortable with handling stolen property that could draw the eyes of the world to his door.

Blake sent out a few feelers on to the black market, hoping to appease the young Turk. But his real priority was Tom Wisher. He needed to get a firm handle on his former protégé. It seemed there were deep, dark waters running beneath even Blake's own murky level of subterfuge. Wisher was the key to finding out more – and Blake knew just how to turn him.

On his third morning in Odessa, Blake saw Wisher's face at the side window of Romanik's garage, as he arrived for an early morning meet with Stefan and Guney. The lad had seemed forlorn, like a puppy on a rainy day. Blake grinned again as he recalled the sight.

He relished the thought that his exit from the garage

would baffle Wisher. It gave him a buzz that his nemesis was so tantalisingly close on his heels. Certainly they needed to meet, but when they did, it would be on his terms. And for that, the timing was perfect.

It was cold outside Odessa Station, and Blake was jittery under his great coat. He didn't like being out in the open; the crowds made him feel twitchy. His skin was itching where his shoulder holster bunched up the fabric of his shirt. He kept catching motion in his peripheral vision and glancing towards it, then forcing his gaze back towards the station entrance. He didn't want to draw attention to himself, but he was struggling to stay calm.

Drugs were his Achilles' heel. When he was clean, he could see the problem clearly. When he was amped, the insight receded, though it never completely disappeared. Odessa was a crossing point for trafficking routes from Afghanistan and north Africa, and supply was plentiful. No way he could clean up his act until he was out of the city. Hopefully he'd be finished there soon.

And then he saw her. Rachel Wisher. She was walking from the main doors towards the taxi rank, accompanied by a tall, scruffy academic type. Stuart, Blake remembered the name from the surveillance files.

He'd contacted her by posing as her brother online. Since Tom Wisher was now officially dead, the numbers and email addresses associated with his file – including Rachel's – were no longer under scrutiny. But Blake had judged that she would have kept checking for messages. He'd had her SIM card and laptop drive copied while he was interviewing her in Cambridge, then run diagnostics on the various contact details he'd gathered. In particular, he'd been drawn to the decade-old cellphone found in Rachel's bag, alongside her up-to-the-minute media phone. He'd guessed, rightly, that this was the siblings' secret line of communication.

He'd kept the fake texts and emails short, implying that Tom Wisher was alive, in hiding, broke and desperate, and only Rachel could help him. And it had done the trick. Right back at their first encounter, when he'd been so attracted to her, he'd had the strong feeling she was holding something back from him. And he'd been proven right. She knew her brother was alive. She'd been waiting for him to contact her. And now she'd come running at his call.

Blake didn't want to be seen yet. He eyed the couple from a distance, drinking in the lean curve of Rachel's hips, the elegant arch of her eyebrows, the arrogant lift of her chin when she turned. He felt an ache in his groin, desire mixed with a measure of something else, some higher quality. Could it be magic? The pop-song refrain ran through his head as he lifted his cellphone to call her with the precise directions for their imminent rendezvous.

Perhaps drugs weren't his Achilles' heel after all.

Thirty-seven

Stuart loved the ground. He loved rocks and soil and clay and the layers they formed. There was something incontrovertible about the earth's crust. The history of the world was written there, hundreds of millions of years compressed by unimaginable forces to a few tens of kilometres of minerals. The origins of humanity could be excavated from just the top few metres. It never ceased to amaze him.

His first degree had been geology, but his physics was strong too, and he brought the two disciplines together at PhD level. His field of expertise was geophysical imaging, using technology to explore the subterranean realm. He'd done some research on Odessa as an undergraduate, crunching data from an ongoing project to map the city's famous network of catacombs. At the time, the online student banter from the city had focused as much on the constant street hassles as the scientific work in progress, with grim reports of begging, theft and police corruption. So it was with some misgivings that Stuart had agreed to accompany Rachel to the city.

In fact, his first impressions were more favourable than he had expected. Odessa seemed to have cleaned up its act somewhat: certainly, there were no obvious vagrants or junkies begging on the station concourse, nor in the streets immediately outside. Nothing else about the visit was remotely reassuring, however. Not the thought of getting involved in some kind of spy war. Not the two-thousand-mile wild goose chase to the benighted edge of Eastern Europe. And certainly not the gaping hole that this short-notice journey had left in his already fragile finances.

At twenty-nine years old, Stuart had had a few girl-friends, and even thought he was in love a couple of times. But he had never experienced anything like the passion he shared with Rachel. Part of what drew him to her was her drive, an inner fire that he knew he lacked. He could see how he might appeal to her as a calm and rational counterweight to that intensity. She set him alight; he kept her grounded. It was a hell of a combination, one worth fighting for. That said, the current situation was pushing his boundaries, and not in a good way.

Rachel received a text on her phone just as Stuart was following her into the back of a taxi. No doubt her brother had them under surveillance. He'd contacted Rachel via his Skype ID, text only, no voice or video. He said he was in Ukraine, in hiding, afraid for his life. She was his only hope.

The secretive nature of the contact made Stuart uneasy, but he knew Rachel was desperate for a new lead after the disappointment of the visit to John Morgan. She *wanted* to believe in this conspiracy nonsense. And while it might seem suspicious that Tom Wisher didn't reveal himself more fully, what motive would an imposter have for luring them to Odessa?

At least, that was Rachel's line of reasoning. Stuart would have been happy not to find out the hard way.

He asked the driver to wait while Rachel jotted down the GPS coordinates for a meeting point outside the city centre, then looked up the location on her phone. She showed the map-view to the driver, who craned his neck to look them over. He asked in accented English:

'Catacombs?'

Rachel frowned but Stuart interjected:

'Yeah. We like to explore.'

The driver shrugged. He obviously didn't think they looked the part.

The Odessa catacombs wound and coiled for an incredible 2500 kilometres beneath the city and its outskirts, and that distance was just an estimate. It was the largest tunnel network of its kind in the world, and almost entirely man-made. The city had been built out of limestone carved from under its foundations, a process that continued to the present day.

During the second world war partisans had used the catacombs to stage their resistance against invading Romanian and German forces. Relics from that struggle were still occasionally discovered by the urban explorers and daring teenagers who now frequented the tunnels. In 2007 the desiccated corpse of a young woman had been discovered, some two years after she wandered off during a drunken party underground. Her body had been perfectly mummified by the cold, dry air.

The city council was on a mission to seal off unauthorised entrances to the catacombs, but with hundreds to find, it was a near impossible task. Meanwhile huge sections remained unmapped and unvisited by the public. Stuart had heard rumours that organised crime had its own subterranean transport routes through the labyrinth. It made sense that the renegade Tom Wisher might have squirrelled himself away down there, literally under the radar.

The taxi dropped them beside a stretch of waste ground at the city limits. There were no other vehicles;

the nearest houses were fifty metres along the road, back towards the city centre. The land around was sparsely wooded, with crumbling farm buildings close by and tilled fields to the north. It was a bleak spot.

Stuart checked he had a cellphone signal before paying the driver. As the car drove away, a man stepped into view from the entrance to a derelict barn.

Rachel was holding Stuart's hand; she squeezed it hard as she nodded in the direction of the figure.

'Shit. It's the CIA.'

The man – Bill Blake – beckoned them. Hesitantly, they headed over. Stuart had glimpsed him before, through a couple of layers of glass doors at the police station in Cambridge. Back then he'd appeared very slick, very American, well fed and sharp-suited, despite the wound dressing on his cheek. The individual who greeted them now was dressed in scuffed jeans and combat jacket. His eyes were dark-rimmed and darting, his chin bearded. The wound on his cheek looked like it had been reopened; fresh abrasions and bruises had joined it.

Rachel strutted towards Blake with her anger front and centre.

'What the fuck is this?'

Stuart had cautioned Rachel about being confrontational in the past. Right now it didn't seem like the smart way to play the situation. Stuart was taller than Blake, but the closest he'd been to a fist fight since kindergarten was a heated argument over evolution with a drunken creationist at college.

The CIA man didn't rise to Rachel's attitude. He seemed anxious, but excited, too.

'Tom's alive, Rachel. I've met with him. He wants to see you.'

'Last time I saw you we were standing over his corpse.'

'Ah, but you're a smart cookie. You knew something was up, even back then. You suspected. Tell me I'm wrong.'

Rachel's tone remained steely. If Blake intimidated her at all, she wasn't showing it.

'So where is he?'

'He can't risk being seen. But he sent me here. He wants me to take you to him.'

Blake shot Stuart an uncomfortable look.

'Just you.'

Stuart felt a jolt of anxiety – was Blake trying to split them up? Rachel glared at the spy:

'Last time I spoke to Tom, he told me not to trust anyone. I'm pretty damn sure he was referring to you.'

Blake nodded, eyes flicking, checking the exits. Force of habit, Stuart imagined.

'I understand that. I'd be worried too. But . . . what's going down here is bigger than me, or Tom. It's a conspiracy like you wouldn't believe. No one can be trusted. No one's safe.'

Stuart watched Rachel's eyes light up. This kind of spiel was rocket fuel to her. He looked back at Blake, saw the zeal in his eyes, too. The American continued, all earnest urgency:

'You don't need to hear this from me. You need to hear it from Tom.'

Rachel kept her expression stony, but she was sold, Stuart knew her well enough by now. He stepped up, doing his best to make his physical presence felt.

'I'm coming with her, wherever she goes.'

'Stuart, this isn't about you . . .' Exasperation in her voice, disappointment that her boyfriend was interfering. Stuart chopped the air with his hand:

'That's not up for negotiation.'

It was just a gesture, but Rachel actually flinched. She wasn't used to Stuart asserting himself. She shot him a look that was bordering on wounded, and he had to hold back an apology. Instead he addressed the enervated Blake:

'He's underground, right?'

The agent shot him a sideways look.

'You know about the catacombs?'

'I've studied them.' No point in false modesty.

Blake grinned.

'Hell of a hiding place. Come and see.'

The rear wall of the barn was visibly subsiding, its rows of bricks slumped in the middle – like rock strata, thought Stuart, as he peered into the gloom. The cause of the subsidence was a deep gash in the floor, its sides tumbled with dirt and stones: a cave-in entrance to the catacombs below.

Blake handed Stuart a flashlight.

'This is my back-up light. You might need to give it a bit of encouragement.'

Stuart switched it on, shook it, tapped it on the side. The bulb flickered reluctantly into life. Blake was already at the side of the cave-in, shining his own, brighter torch into the darkness below, lighting the way for Rachel as she descended. Blake beckoned:

'This way, Stu.'

Stuart stood at the lip of the hole. A rope ran down into it, fastened to a rusting plough in the barn, taut now under Rachel's weight. She glanced up at him, her eyes silver like a fox's, then skidded down the last few feet of tumbled earth until she was out of sight.

'Stu?'

Blake's eyes twinkled. Maybe once upon a time he had been a secret agent; right now he was a fairground hustler, ushering another unsuspecting punter through the curtain and on to the ghost train.

Stuart felt a rush of fear like he'd never known. Reason told him not to leave daylight behind. But Rachel was down there, waiting. He took hold of the rope, flashlight beam waving as he made his way down into the shadows below.

'It's about three hundred yards,' said Blake, as he brought up the rear. His voice was subdued; somehow the catacombs demanded it. The tunnel walls were pale, square-cut, jagged where the stone had been hewn away one block at a time. The air was bone dry and bracingly cold.

Stuart led the way, stepping carefully over the rutted floor. From time to time he ran his hand over the rugged surface beside him. The limestone was pale and glistening, the petrified remains of countless billions of sea creatures, compressed into white stone. He visualised its formation, flecks falling through dark water to the ocean floor. Sections of the catacomb were carved out of sandstone: he'd seen photos, tunnel walls seamed with a rich caramel swirl of pale and dark browns. He hoped he'd get the chance to explore further, when the meeting with Rachel's brother was over. This really was a unique environment. He'd heard there were bears, too.

Ahead, the walls narrowed as their tunnel merged with another. Stuart flattened himself to pass through the gap, then reached back to guide Rachel through. Her hand was warm and incredibly comforting. She smiled at him:

'You okay?'

'Never better.'

The way ahead forked; Blake shone his beam up at the roof, where a scratched arrow marked the favoured passage.

'Smugglers' route. A lot of history down here.'

Stuart nodded, interested despite himself. Who knew how many criminals had crept through this labyrinth over the decades, transporting contraband from the docks to the fringes of the city. Silks and spices in the 1800s; phones and DVDs, nowadays. But always the black market persisted.

They pressed on in the direction indicated, gaining a few yards on Blake. Rachel kept hold of Stuart's hand; she whispered to him:

'Why would Tom hide this far in? Why not wait by the tunnel mouth?'

Stuart realised she was scared. He'd been so busy soaking up the details of the tunnel system, he'd allowed his mind to wander from the real purpose of their expedition. And she had a point too. Wouldn't it have been easier for Tom to come to them?

'What do you want to do?'

There wasn't time for Rachel to answer. Blake caught up with them, steered them through an archway and into a store-room type space containing a few boxes, a mattress on the floor. There were voices coming from a connecting room, speaking Russian.

'What is this place? Where's Tom?' Rachel glared at Blake. The agent's face was devoid of emotion.

'It's the end of the line.'

Blake reached inside his jacket and Stuart's instincts took over. He grabbed hold of Blake's arm, pushed at him with the advantage of height. Blake staggered but didn't fall. Stuart felt himself being levered; Blake's foot hooked round the back of his knee and spoiled his balance, forcing him to stumble back. Blake's hand was free now, and holding a gun.

The shot was deafening. Stuart hardly felt the bullet hit, but in the next moment he was falling, instantly inert, his beloved ground rushing up to meet him.

Thirty-eight

Wisher frowned at the sound of breathing on the line.

'Rachel?'

'It's Bill. Let's meet up.'

The words, and the familiar rasp of Blake's voice, turned Wisher's spine to ice. Night was drawing in outside, smoke from the lookout cigarette glowed like ectoplasm in the light spilling from the garage doors. Wisher had spent the day waiting for a sign of his adversary. Now Blake was calling him from the old phone, his private line to his sister.

Wisher kept his emotions in check, braced himself for bad news. Whatever reason Blake was on this number, he knew damn well it was going to burn him like hell.

The meeting place was a bar in the old town. Blake's choice: a public venue, protection from any planned assault by Wisher. At ten o'clock, the evening trade was roaring. Wisher had to push through the crowd clustered at the bar to locate Blake, who was seated at a corner table.

The young agent made no effort to hide the Makarov from Blake. He withdrew it from his pocket and sat down with his back to the room, the handgun now in his lap. Blake wiped at his nose, rubbed the sides. With his free hand he pushed a glass of beer across the table.

'Drink it.'

Wisher kept his eyes on Blake. His former handler was stubble-chinned and leaner than Wisher had ever seen him. He looked older too. The past few weeks had taken a toll on them both.

'What's in it?'

'Enough ketamine to knock out a horse. Drink.'

Wisher probed under the table until the silencer muzzle made contact with Blake's leg.

'I've got another suggestion. You take me to Rachel or I'll blow your kneecap clean off.'

Wisher had never been more serious, but his threat had little impact. Blake's face twisted into a contemptuous snarl.

'You think you can threaten me, you fucking amateur? Your sister's alone, she's in pain, and if you don't drink this glass of piss-poor continental beer, right now, she'll die. Is that clear?'

'Prove it. Let me see her or speak to her— '

'Look into my fucking eyes, Tom. That's all the proof you'll get.'

A dozen retorts whirled through Wisher's mind but nothing he could think of seemed worth saying in the face of Blake's intensity. There was a madness in his former mentor. A dark force had awoken in him. He was taut like a trigger-wire, ready to explode.

Wisher picked his words carefully. All that mattered now was reaching his sister.

'You don't have to involve Rachel. Just tell me what you want.'

'When you wake up, you'll find out.'

Blake had him, and he knew it. Wisher took hold of the beer glass. He glowered, about to speak, but Blake beat him to it:

'Please, don't threaten me again. It's embarrassing.'

Fuck you, Bill.

Wisher downed the beer quickly. His mind was

spinning, like he was falling off a cliff. What if it wasn't ketamine? What if it was something stronger, something lethal? As Wisher drank, Blake relaxed somewhat, from scary down to plain old maniac.

'So. How you been keeping?'

It took a few minutes for the drug to start working. Wisher surrendered his handgun at the table, but Blake kept him waiting there all the same, until he started to feel woozy. He had to help him to his feet, support him as they staggered out together, just another drunk tourist and his less indulgent friend.

Outside, empty threats started to spill from Wisher's slurring mouth. Even in his intoxicated state, it was humiliating, but he couldn't seem to stop himself. More than anything, he wanted to cry. Unconsciousness loomed, like a black hand clamped over his face, sparing him that indignity at least.

He surfaced briefly in the back of a taxi. City neon streaked past outside the window. He lay in the back of the car, his head in Blake's lap, Blake's hand resting on his arm. The older man glanced down at him. He spoke softly, like a father to a drowsy child.

'Go back to sleep.'

Wisher went back under. He couldn't help it.

When he awoke, he was underground. He pushed up through a mighty hangover, thirst clutching at his throat. The room swam and settled. Rough-hewn stone walls, no door in the entranceway; he could see through into the corridor beyond, more rough stone. Light spilled in from somewhere out of sight, the only source.

He was sat on the ground, shivering cold. His hands were cuffed behind his back, around a post he couldn't see. Across from him was his sister. She was tied up also, to a wooden ceiling support. Her clothes were scuffed and dirty and there was a bruise developing on the side of her face. She looked scared, of course; but overriding that, she looked furious.

Tom fought to speak through the lifting haze of the sedative:

'Rachel . . . why . . .'

'Messages through rendlesham91 and the old phone. You said they were secure.'

She glared at him accusingly. Wisher shook his head, despair flooding in. Was it his fault she was here?

'They must have cracked them after we tried to meet. They would have gone through your bag, your laptop . . .'

'What about the message on my blog? You spelled out 'rendlesham'. What was that supposed to mean?'

Of course. It could have implied that he wanted her to get in touch. He could see that now.

'I shouldn't have sent it. I just wanted to let you know . . .'

'What?'

'That I was alive. I thought you'd want to know.'

He couldn't believe how pathetic he sounded, how weak. Rachel's facade was cracking too; tears were welling, even though she kept her face rigid.

'I came looking for you.'

'Well, you found me.'

She was his only close relative. He hadn't seen her in the flesh for almost a year, apart from a fleeting wave, at a distance of a hundred yards. And now here they were, trapped in a nightmare, yet bickering like children.

Thirst scoured his throat. His pulse beat in his brow, pulling his whole face tight around its centre. He was still in a drug haze, not thinking straight. He couldn't help either of them in this state.

Wisher closed his eyes. He imagined a grid that stretched into the distance, infinite space, infinite structure. He sent his thoughts out into the pockets of the grid. They began to separate out and find their natural order. An obvious question came forward:

'Where are we?'

'Catacombs. Under the city. I don't know where exactly.'

Of course. The tunnel network ran throughout the city, there must have been an entrance leading from inside the garage. That was how Blake had managed to leave the building unseen, while Wisher had kept the street under surveillance like a prize fool.

Rachel's lower lip was trembling:

'Stuart's dead. Blake shot him. Right in front of me.'

Seeing the shock and pain in Rachel's eyes brought back to Wisher his own horror at the meaningless loss of life, the injustice of it all. And it was his fault. He had sought out the cutting edge. He'd chosen the life of the spy, fully aware of the dangers it posed. He'd thought he could keep Rachel out of harm's way; he'd failed miserably. What could he say now?

'I'm sorry.'

'Gee, that really helps.' Bitter sarcasm. He deserved it too. He held her gaze, soaked up her contempt as best as he could.

'It's all I've got, Rach. For now. But this isn't over.'

Killing Stuart was sloppy. He wasn't in the game. He didn't need to die. Covering tracks was hard work, expensive too. The fact that Blake had gone and done it anyway could imply that he was losing his grip. Or it could mean he was planning on dropping off the radar himself and didn't care what kind of mess he left behind – in which case he was even more dangerous.

Each passing moment brought increased clarity to Wisher's thoughts. The numbness was leaving his senses. He could feel the wooden post behind him, similar to that which Rachel was bound to. He dug his fingers into the rough grain. The desiccated surface splintered easily. A first tear rolled down Rachel's cheek.

'Why is this happening? What does he want? What did you *do*, Tom?'

'I need your shoe buckle.'

She just stared blankly at him.

'Your shoe. Kick it over to me. Don't miss.'

It took her a moment longer to grasp his change of tack, then she snapped alert. Her brother hadn't given up. He had a plan. There was still hope.

She pushed at her heel, worked the shoe loose. At full stretch her toes were just a yard or so from Wisher's. She flicked her foot and the shoe skidded over to him. He swept it closer with his own feet.

'Can you get free?' asked Rachel.

'I can try.'

Shuffling upwards on the beam was agony but somehow Wisher managed it, his muscles taut and trembling by the end. He moved the shoe until it was behind the post then slid back down. It was a so-called 'monk shoe' with a single, substantial buckle and strap. Now he had the buckle in his cuffed hands. He worked the strap loose, enough for him to manoeuvre the metal to the grain. Wood flaked and fell away as he started to scrape. He could feel the fragments on his fingertips.

'Is it working?'

He nodded.

'I think so.'

But the post was thick, six inches square. He would need hours to finish the job – time he wasn't going to be given.

Footsteps approached. There was the sound of a tool bag being set down. Blake appeared in the entranceway, fluorescent lantern in hand, with one of Stefan's men behind him, a burly guard armed with a holstered handgun. Wisher squinted in the light as Blake held it up. The scene was laid bare: a rickety table and chair to the back of the room, a few stacked boxes, two prisoners. Rachel tried to tuck her leg up, to hide the missing shoe. Blake just smiled.

'Good thinking, Tom.'

He set the lantern down and strolled behind Wisher. He found the shoe, took it from his captive's hand. Then he knelt in front of Rachel, mock-chivalrous, and held the shoe out:

'I think this is yours.'

Rachel kicked him right in the face, with her shoeless heel.

It was a wild effort, but the blow hit home, Wisher could tell by the recoil. He caught Rachel's eyes and she smiled, trying to reconnect with him, to get back on the same side, the punchy little girl from the garden of their childhood, *show me kick-boxing!*

Wisher wanted to return the sentiment, but he knew what was coming next.

Blake got to his feet. He nodded to the man accompanying him, who carried through the tool bag, then took up a lookout position by the entrance. Blake took a bottle of water from the bag, the sort with a push-and-pull cap. He opened it with his teeth, held the bottle up to Rachel's lips. She clamped her mouth shut, twisted her face away. Blake shot Wisher a look.

'Tell her.'

'It's just water, Rach. You might as well drink.'

He knew the protocol. Rachel glanced at him, and he couldn't keep the misery from his face. Blake pushed the bottle forward again, this time Rachel sipped from it. He turned to Wisher:

'Tom?'

'Please.'

The water was like spring rain, like a mountain stream as it ran down his throat. It was a measure of hope, as Blake intended it to be. In some deep part of his brain, away from his cold prison and the dreadful situation, Wisher regrouped, took stock of his meagre resources, and braced himself.

'This is routine spook stuff. Tom has wandered off mission and you can help me get him back on track.'

Blake was talking to Rachel now, his voice conversational as he laid out tools on the work table, which he had pulled forward into the lantern light.

'Specifically, I need to know who he's working for now.'

'I don't know. I don't know who he's working for.' Could Rachel really not see where Blake was heading?

'I realise that. Tom is the one who knows. But he doesn't want to tell me, so . . . I need to put pressure on him.'

Blake picked up a pair of secateurs, the sort you might use for pruning roses. He flicked off the safety catch, tested the sprung blades. Wisher saw from Rachel's stricken face that reality had dawned. She was about to be tortured.

'But first, a confession of my own. I've got a bit of a thing for you, did you know that?'

The gift of water. The relaxed tone. It was all part of the technique. Destabilise the subject. Increase the fear.

'In fact I'm planning on having sex with you at some point during the next twenty-four hours. I'd prefer it if you were still alive, of course. But it's not a deal breaker.'

Blake was maximising his own pleasure too, which was a weakness, but nothing Wisher could get a handle on.

'Just tell him, Tom. Tell him what he wants to know!'

Rachel looked to her brother. Wisher held her terrified gaze. It was an act of microscopic courage, really. But there was nothing else he could do for her, except to be there, to not look away.

'Tell him!'

Blake went behind the post, to where Rachel's hands were cuffed. Wisher arched up, jolted back and forth, growled like an animal, strained until the metal of his cuffs drew blood.

Behind Rachel, the secateurs squeezed shut.

Pain burst like a flashbulb, silent and blinding. It felt to Rachel like the tip of her finger was glowing white hot. Like ET.

Blake set the bloody stub on to the tabletop so Rachel could see it. It was upright, with the nail facing her.

'I've started on the far left. I'm going to work my way across, just down to the first knuckle. I'll skip the thumbs on this pass.'

Rachel put everything she had into her voice. All the pain, fear, anger, outrage. All of her mind and body. She launched the words from herself like cannonballs, pushed them like boulders, down the slope to where her brother writhed in his own personal hell.

'TELL. HIM.'

She genuinely expected her brother to start talking.

273

There would be a quiet confession, with Blake as the patient priest, nodding, taking notes, perhaps. The hand-cuffs would be unlocked. She would be given a white robe to wear, she and Tom would walk hand-in-hand into the sunlight, where Stuart would be waiting.

Instead, her brother, her dear brother, shook his head. How could those heavy, rolling words of hers missed him?

'I can't. It's all that's keeping us alive. As soon as I talk, we're both dead.'

Blake the monster, the bringer of pain, offered a rueful shrug:

'He has a point.'

Rachel could feel the blood pumping from her severed finger. She could smell its iron tang. Blake crossed the room, hunkered down next to his other captive.

'But you've got a breaking point, too, Tom. Everyone does, buddy.'

Rachel couldn't take her eyes off her brother. He was the same, he couldn't look away from her. His eyes pleaded for understanding, for forgiveness. Hers were filled with anger, at him and his world, his secrets, the living hell he had drawn her into.

Blake was behind her again. She struggled, even though it was pointless. The secateurs snipped. They were rusty; there was just the slightest squeak of the spring as they closed, then the flashbulb went off again.

She kept staring at Tom. Until now, the bond between them, forged by childhood grief, had been her fixed point in the universe. Sometimes she thought of it as a mighty structure of bolts and girders; sometimes as a living thing, sinewy but flexible, like the hand of a giant. But she had been wrong. What had seemed invulnerable had just been shattered, like glass in slow motion, its million pieces now spinning away into nothingness.

Rachel was a thinker. She always had been, obsessively so. It had been a flaw when it came to finding happiness in her everyday life, but right now, it was a power. It was wings.

As Blake went to work on her, she left hope behind and took to the skies. She could see Tom down there. He was shouting, cursing, tied up in a hole in the ground. She didn't pay attention. He was nothing to her.

Thirty-nine

Maybe it was the circumstances, but Dale Peavey seemed even more sweaty than usual. He was sat across the table from Morgan in a particularly gloomy Langley backroom. The ceiling was low, the lighting diffuse, the atmosphere calculated to be oppressive. Peavey would know that, of course, but it wouldn't stop it having its effect.

Morgan had come prepared. He took a fresh handkerchief from his pocket and handed it over. Peavey smiled nervously, dabbed at his brow. Morgan indicated the printout in front of him, the transcript that had been mysteriously delivered to his son's office. The missing link between Blake, Kincaid and the missing uranium.

'Did you know about this conversation?'

'I don't know what to say, sir.'

'I'd go with either "yes" or "no".'

'Sir . . . I report to Deputy Director Kincaid, not you.'

Morgan couldn't imagine that loyalty was an attribute prized by Peavey. The assistant was killing time, trying to calculate the most advantageous route through this crisis.

'Kincaid is under investigation and suspected of corruption. This transcript is at the core of our evidence. And so I ask you again, did you know about this conversation?'

'Really, I'm not sure . . .'

'We have witnesses who put you in the room at the exact time the conversation occurred. I'm one of them.'

Tip of the iceberg, Morgan thought to himself. He doubted that Kincaid discussed strategy with his assistant, but for sure he would vent his spleen, if nothing else. The question now was twofold: firstly, how much did Peavey know; secondly, how much would he be prepared to spill to save his own skin?

'If I did overhear the conversation, I would only have heard the deputy director's side of it, obviously.'

'Here's my understanding of this transcript. Bill Blake has possession of the uranium that the Moldovan force was seeking. He was sent to Transnistria by the deputy director for this purpose. The order was given after my announcement of the Moldovan mission. Therefore it was the deputy director's intention to make sure the HEU remained in circulation on the black market. Feel free to stop me at any point.'

'What do you want from me, sir? Do you want me to point the finger? Do you want me to admit that the deputy director was . . . was . . .'

'Was what?'

'Well, I don't know. Bad, or something?'

Don't make this about Kincaid. Make it about Peavey.

'What I want, Dale, is for you to think about your own situation.'

'I'm doing that, sir. Believe me.'

This, at least, sounded like the truth to Morgan.

'You see, Dale, I'm wondering how far back this goes. I'm thinking about Peshawar, about the atom bomb that never was, and I'm wondering if this uranium connection goes back that far. I'm wondering if this isn't a game that's being playing out over years, not months.'

'I don't know how you'd go about proving that, sir.'

Either by accident or design, Peavey had hit upon the nub of Morgan's problem. He could use the

Blake-Kincaid recording to kick up a stink but it wasn't enough to nail the coffin lid down. He needed more. He needed more evidence.

A team of analysts were currently scouring the intranet, but all they had found so far were clean-swept corners and tidy cupboards. Kincaid's house was in order, probably thanks to Peavey's efforts. But the data must have existed at some point. Secret communication was the essence of any conspiracy. He could only hope that Peavey had been smart enough to have covered his own backside.

Softly, softly, catchee monkey.

'I'm not asking you to fall on your sword, Dale. I'm asking you to help me make sense of all this.'

'I have no intention of falling on my sword. I don't even have a sword.'

Kincaid's lackey was starting to babble. Sweat was beading his forehead, gathering above his eyebrows; pungent body odour forced its way past an overdose of Nautica Blue aftershave. Morgan pressed on, keeping it friendly but injecting a level of urgency.

'I need data on Kincaid. Anything that can show he was working against Agency directives. Emails, phone logs, audio files, surveillance clips. I don't care about the source.'

'I would care about the source. I would care about that.'

'What I mean is, I wouldn't care to identify the source. Or to look further into how they acquired their data. I just need to know what they know.'

'Well, obviously you do.'

The reply was flippant, irritable. Peavey was squirming in his seat, pallid, wretched, clearly desperate for the inquisition to be over. Morgan let the moment draw out.

When he spoke, it was with as much paternal warmth as he could muster.

'What do *you* need, Dale?'

Peavey drew in a nervous breath.

'I need a frequency scanner and a junction detector.'

Both devices were used to detect the presence of hidden surveillance devices. Morgan tried to reassure his nervous interviewee.

'I can assure you this room is free from bugs— '

'Frequency scanner. Junction detector.'

'Yes. Of course.'

It took Peavey twenty minutes to inspect the room and satisfy himself that walls and door were audio secure. Morgan couldn't fault the man's attention to detail. Pity he was such a creep.

When it was done, and the door was closed, they both sat down once more at the table. Peavey spoke softly, but clearly.

'I can give you Kincaid. But I stop at Amaro.'

'Who's Amaro?'

'I won't repeat myself. Are you interested?'

Morgan drew a breath. *Amaro?*

Of course, it couldn't just be Kincaid behind this conspiracy. He was the tip of the iceberg. Peavey knew enough to point Morgan towards deeper waters, but why mention it at all?

To fuck with him, that was why. Peavey was passing on the pain. He might be backed into a corner, but he didn't want to spill the beans without letting Morgan know how little his efforts meant in the bigger scheme of things. The implication was that Kincaid, who loomed so large in Morgan's mind, was just a small fish. It was a profoundly disturbing notion.

Morgan knew he ought to dig further. If he was really the paragon of truth and justice he was puffing himself up to be, he should demand to know everything. He had colleagues who weren't afraid to use enhanced interrogation techniques, even within the legitimate CIA framework. Maybe he could get more out of Peavey if he squeezed him.

Or maybe he'd get nothing at all. And if Peavey did point the way to a whole new layer of subterfuge, was Morgan really up to that investigation? He was on the cusp of retirement, goddammit. He'd experienced more turbulence in the last two weeks of his career than in the preceding thirty. He had a family. He had a wine cellar. Bottom line: he was scared to look further.

'I'll take Kincaid.'

The actor Lee Van Cleef famously once said,

'Being born with a pair of beady eyes was the best thing that ever happened to me.'

Dale Peavey could relate to the quote. He was barely five foot five tall, with awkward looks and oily skin. At thirty-one years old, he still got asked for his ID in bars. People saw him, heard him speak, and thought they knew him. The real Peavey could remain invisible.

Peavey had been a liar all his life. It was his defence mechanism, his bear growl, his lizard frill. As a sickly seven year old, he'd mastered the art of turning his enemies against each other. By the time he reached college, he was weaving vast fabrications in order to get the simplest things. Deceit had become his modus operandi.

He didn't tend to hold on to relationships. He told himself this was because he was a man of importance, always moving forward, leaving friends and lovers behind. He cast himself as a figure of pathos, misunderstood, rather than a liar, despised.

The thing was, Peavey liked humanity. He loved the natural qualities he saw in others, beauty, charm, strength of character. As someone entirely self-constructed, he looked up to genuine souls, even as he took advantage of them. He believed he was a good person at heart. Accessing this innate virtue was just somewhat more complicated for him than it was for others.

He'd gone into the financial sector after college, and done well at it, amassing his first million after twelve months, and his first ten million within the following year. But he was lonely. He knew he wanted to do good, to be a 'hero' of some kind, but he couldn't connect that fantasy to the real world.

When he had first been approached by Galloway, it was like a light-bulb had been turned on. Here was someone built like him, who understood how good came nestled within bad, truth within deception. Galloway had initially come in search of financial investment, but he found much more. He'd found the ultimate infiltration unit.

Together they'd planned his entry into the agency, precisely targeting Kincaid's office. Galloway's dance with the current deputy director had been going on since 9/11, when Kincaid had begun his rise, sponsored by the secretive organisation Galloway had made it his life's work to bring down.

This was the Consortium, about which Peavey knew little. Galloway was reluctant to talk about his adversaries. After all, secrets were the main weapons in the shadow war he was waging. Peavey imagined a chess game in which the individual pieces were also playing chess, using chessmen they shared the board with. Surreal, like an

Escher print or a Dali painting. Chess through the looking glass.

Peavey was a pawn, positioned to take down Kincaid with a sneaky diagonal move. But it was also his role to induct a new rook onto the board: John Morgan, idle on the home rank, unaware that he would soon find himself catapulted into the heart of the battlefield. At least that was Galloway's prediction – and he was rarely wrong.

Peavey put his foot down. It was forty miles to Chesapeake Bay Bridge, from where he would be jumping to his supposed death. A staged suicide, necessary theatrics to wipe him from the grid. Plausible too, given the crisis unfolding at Langley, even if Kincaid wouldn't buy it for a moment. That was why Peavey had agreed to undergo an immediate facial reconstruction procedure once he was back in Galloway's fold. They'd never find a better beady-eyed sneer, but he'd much rather get remodelled than rubbed out by a vengeful Lawrence Kincaid.

Besides, he'd read somewhere that plastic surgery could alleviate excessive sweating. He'd have to look into that.

Forty

Four bloody fingertips stood in a row; it looked like an intangible hand was pushing up through the table. Wisher stared at the stumps, at his slumped sister. She'd passed out, but Blake would have no problem bringing her round. Right now he was tending to her wounds, dabbing glue on to the bloody ends to stop the bleeding. A crude solution, but it would keep her alive, for now.

When he'd finished, Blake fished a wrap of coke from his pocket and sniffed up the contents. Then he walked over to join Wisher.

'Had enough yet?'

'I always had a hunch you were a fuck-up, Bill. But I never knew you were a such a coward.'

It was the only angle he could think of, to chisel at Blake's pride, his self-respect, provoke him to redirect his violence and spare his sister. But Blake wasn't biting.

'Am I? I'm one of the bad guys, remember? I'm selling nuclear weapons to terrorists. Thousands could die. Hell, it could be hundreds of thousands. If you'd had any guts you could have shot me in that bar. It could have been you, sitting where I am, twisting me until I broke. And I would have broken. I'm a burned-out old man. You could have had me, if you'd grasped the nettle.'

Wisher held Blake's eyes, but inside he was starting to crumble. Self-doubt was the enemy. He wasn't sure of anything. He didn't know why he was here, or what he should do.

Blake leaned in.

'What are *you* scared of, Tom? Loneliness? Failure? Seriously. I want to know.'

Wisher knew the answer to that question.

People like you, Bill, who have no conscience, and can do anything as a result.

'You're dead inside, Bill. You're just a shell. A hollow man.'

'Makes two of us.'

'I'm not dead yet.'

'No. Not yet. But soon.'

Blake's pupils were drug-dilated, close to full black. He was up close now, a whispering snake.

'I'll let Rachel live, Tom. That's a promise. It will be on my terms. I won't be kind to her. But she'll have a chance, at least, to learn my ways, maybe even get the better of me. What do you say?'

Wisher's mind had been darting, his senses on full alert, trying to formulate some kind of escape plan. But with Blake in the room, a guard on the door and himself still bound tight to the beam, he was desperately short of options. He'd tried to tell himself that his best hope lay in drawing out Blake's process while hoping for an act of fate to offer him the opportunity to strike back. He'd been wrong. Rachel had screamed and bled, and he had watched, and nothing had changed.

'Who are you working for, Tom? Who took you undercover? Who set you on my tail?'

Wisher was prepared to talk. Not because he'd surrendered, or been persuaded, but because he understood now that he had to take the pain upon himself, whatever the cost. Not Rachel. Him. It should be his pain, not hers.

He couldn't know whether Rachel would live, despite Blake's promise. He could only control his own actions, the path that he chose next. It was certainly the case that after he told Blake what he knew, Blake would kill him. At last, he was ready for that.

Then a face appeared in the doorway. Two young men, one of them Stefan Florescu – the family resemblance was unmistakeable. Wisher noticed the quick glance that took in the torture scene. If the barbarity on display troubled Stefan or his accomplice – a Turk – they didn't show it.

'We need to talk, Blake.'

Russian, which Wisher understood well enough. Blake got to his feet. His irritation was obvious, but he didn't act up. Wisher's senses were on fire. This was the opportunity he'd prayed would come. His captors were distracted. He had to make it count.

Blake pushed past the hoodlum standing guard at the entrance to the room and headed out of sight into the corridor in the company of the two young criminals. Wisher couldn't follow their conversation, but it was brief and ended with a gunshot.

The thug standing guard drew his handgun and pointed it down the corridor. Blake's voice barked, authoritative:

'Watch them!'

The guard's gun wavered, his loyalty divided. Footsteps could be heard, Blake and the others heading away down the tunnel. With sudden energy, Wisher jolted back against the post he was tied to. He was rewarded with a definite crack, a yielding of the bone-dry timber. He lurched forward again, entirely focused on his efforts.

Suddenly, things went black. The world rushed away, then rushed back in a swirl of dancing specks. The guard's pistol butt, smacked into his forehead, was the cause.

Wisher blinked and shook his head, to little effect. There was a limit to how quickly the brain could recover from such a well-placed blow. Through watering eyes he saw the guard was hunkered down next to Rachel. She was conscious again, probably due to the gunshot. Her skin was bone white; her focus was tight on the man in front of her.

'Set me free. I'll do anything you want.'

That's it Rach, thought Wisher. *Work any angle you can find.*

'I don't need to set you free.'

That was the guard, setting his gun down so his hands could start exploring. Rachel's eyes met Tom's; she could see his muscles straining, tendons proud of the skin, his body pulling against the rotten wood he was tethered to.

She started to writhe, to recoil from the guard's touch: a diversionary tactic. She cried out, getting louder.

'No, please, no!'

Wisher gave it everything, jolting back and forth, the sounds of his grunts and the creaking timber covered by Rachel's screams and the blood pounding in the guard's ears. The thick beam splintered, he could feel the grain give way.

The final snap was loud as a handclap. The guard looked round; Wisher lurched forward, head first, slamming into the big man's gut, voiding his lungs. The man sprawled, gasping. Wisher tucked up small, got his cuffed hands round to his front. The gun was right there on the floor. Then it was in his hands. Then it was against the guard's head.

Wisher grabbed a discarded jacket and wrapped it round his gun hand to muffle the sound. He looked away as he pulled the trigger. When it was done, he looked to his sister. She'd been watching him. She'd registered his distaste at the termination of the guard who had been happy to rape her. She glowered, Maja-cold.

No one had come running at the first gunshot. Wisher fired again to break open Rachel's cuffs, again doing his best to muffle the sound, then passed her the gun. That was when he saw her finger stumps. Her hand looked like a cartoon hand, globs of glue rounding off her digit ends. That was rape too, rape of form, robbery of flesh. It was her left hand and she was right-handed, but still clumsy with the gun, worryingly so.

'You okay with that?'

'Yes.'

Wisher spread his own cuff chain against the wooden pillar. Rachel pressed the barrel up against it, they both looked away as she fired. Metal flecks and splinters flicked harmlessly from the blast. The bullet was safely buried in the beam. They were free.

'Rachel.'

'Don't talk to me.'

'They're selling weapons-grade uranium. I have to try to stop them. I have to stop Blake.'

No reaction. She wouldn't even look at him.

'This is my fault. I know that.'

He took hold of her by the shoulders, tight, so she couldn't pull away. Their eyes met, and he spoke again:

'I can't undo what's been done to you. But if I – if we – can stop these people then at least it means something. The fact that we endured means lives can be saved.'

She remained cold, but at least she was looking at him.

'I won't forgive you.'

'I understand.'

Rachel handed back the pistol. Wisher checked the magazine. There was a place in the room where neither of them would look: the tabletop with its grisly mementos.

Four fingertips on the table. Four bullets left in the handgun. Not a lot of ammunition to save the world.

He lifted the lantern, peered out into the tunnel. No one in sight, just white stone walls leading into darkness. There was blood spilt on the floor, the gunshot they had heard moments earlier. Something big must be going down. He spoke without turning:

'Follow me. Not too close.'

Forty yards brought them to a fork in the tunnel. Wisher raised the lantern, Rachel pointed out a trail of blood spots.

'That way.'

This stretch quickly became cluttered with boxes of old car parts. Wisher realised they must be underneath the garage, close to the exit point. He could pick out raised voices, not far in the distance. Round the next corner, the tunnel opened out. The uranium was there, crates positioned at intervals of a few yards along both walls. Stairs headed up towards a cellar door, its cracks and edges radiant with daylight.

He crept up underneath the hatch, listening. A deal was going down for the sale of the uranium, meaning Blake and his cronies could come down the stairs at any moment. Wisher beckoned Rachel to follow him further down the corridor. Thirty yards away was another exit, with a rusted, little-used ladder. Wisher tried the hatch; it barely moved. Better perhaps to take their chances at the garage exit.

That is, until an explosion in the building above smashed down through the cellar door, lighting up the tunnel with flame.

Forty-one

When Stefan said what he'd done, Blake shot him. It was an angry gesture, and also fairly ill-advised considering that Guney and the guard were close by, but Blake was in a heightened state. Rachel's blood was on his hands, the smell of her sweat and hair lingered in his nostrils. His scorched nasal membranes, dulled by drugs, should have been numb to any subtle odour. And yet that girl's presence cut through. It was like magic, what they had. Shame about the fingers.

He'd shot Stefan in the arm, storming up to him along the catacomb tunnel from where his two captives were being held.

No point in killing him, but the lesson was important. He had explained at exhaustive length that caution was the key when dealing with the uranium sale. The objective here was financial, not geopolitical, and time was required to ferret out the right deal.

But Stefan had decided to show 'initiative'. He'd put out his own feelers on the black market and made contact with a South African businessman, in Odessa to sell minerals to Ukraine's refining industries, who'd offered to take the entire cache off his hands for fifty million rand, a price that Stefan seemed to regard as something of a coup.

Never mind the schoolboy error on the price – it worked out at six million US dollars, a fraction of the market value – Blake was certain that Odessa would be on the radar of the intelligence services after Transnistria. Every spy and their dog was currently looking for the missing HEU; Stefan had just waved a giant flag announcing its location.

Guney had a gun on him, and so did the guard along the corridor, at the door to the room holding Wisher and his sister. Stefan joined them, wincing with pain as he tugged free the pistol tucked in his belt. He looked woozy from the injury and dumb enough to take a pop at Blake out of spite. Blake just brazened it out. Was he wrong? No. Was Stefan an utter fool? Yes. The right deal could make them multimillionaires. This deal of Stefan's was *not* the right deal.

The guard hadn't been picked for his brains, but Guney was sharp enough to see sense. Blake had a hand grenade in his pocket to back up his side of the argument, but it wasn't needed. He'd been reckless to react so violently to Stefan, but in the end it had worked in his favour. The balance of power was with him now.

Blake pulled off his belt and passed it to the lad to use as a tourniquet. The South African was due shortly, hence Stefan's interruption. A few forceful words persuaded Guney and the guard that the garage was quite possibly under police surveillance. He and Stefan could sort out their differences after the situation at hand had been dealt with. The sale needed to be called off and the contraband moved out of the catacombs to a new hiding place.

Above ground, Blake took charge, with Stefan's reluctant blessing. A trusted medic was called and quickly on hand to tend to the young Florescu's flesh wound while Blake organised the remaining men. He shook hands with Romanik, the garage owner, a grizzled veteran who was happy to sit in his glass-fronted office and sip vodka while Blake organised a sweep of the nearby buildings. No surveillance nests were discovered, and Blake relaxed a little. There remained the South African to placate, but he felt confident he could wing it. And if not, he had a dozen guns at his shoulder.

With a few minutes still to kill, he had a shave in the garage washroom. Without stubble he looked and felt younger. He was certainly enjoying his new-found authority among the Odessa mob. His cynicism suited a position behind the throne, but now he had stepped up, there was an undeniable nobility in command.

The call came in that the South African's arrival was imminent and Blake headed out front. Stefan walked up to his side, seething but scared, too. Blake offered a handshake and Stefan accepted. The lad was used to being bullied. He'd done well to break free of his father, but he wasn't alpha material and Blake reckoned he was starting to accept it. The gesture was noted by the guards close by, and by Guney too, who nodded toward Blake, acknowledging him as the current pack leader.

A sleek black van appeared at the end of the road, a recent model with a robust back axle. The South African was clearly expecting to collect his contraband uranium. He was going to be disappointed.

The garage doors were pulled wide. Blake stepped up to the front of the group; he was starting to feel jittery, coming down from his latest high, but he was the boss and he needed to act the part. The armed men fanned out behind him. The welcoming committee was set.

The black van reversed up to the tall doors. The driver disembarked, a lean black man with the poise of a trained fighter. His shoulder holster was in plain view over his shirt, his attention zeroed in on Blake. The passenger door swung open and a stocky man with cropped grey hair climbed down, carrying a briefcase. He turned to face Blake—

And a whole bunch of puzzle pieces fell into place. In an instant, Blake knew who had been masterminding the resistance to the machinations of Kincaid. He knew who had targeted and eliminated Florescu despite Kincaid's efforts to protect the Romanian. More than anything, he understood why Wisher had been rescued and recruited. It all made perfect sense.

He wondered whether Wisher himself knew the whole truth. He doubted it. Certainly he'd believed this particular face from the past had been long buried. Not that his old acquaintance had much of a face left. Reconstructive surgery had left him barely recognisable. But Blake had spent two months as his colleague in the build-up to Desert Storm, and they'd left an impression.

Perhaps parts of the story were true, about him being captured and tortured. But his execution had clearly been an elaborately staged sham. Blake had no clue who had arranged that initial deception, or why, exactly. He didn't even know what the man's name was now, though he knew what it used to be. One thing was for certain: this pretender was his enemy.

Blake wanted to pull his gun, but he knew the black man would beat him to it. He had a veritable firing squad lined up behind him but again, ordering them to shoot would cost him his life. He was pinned.

And so he played along, pretending the man was from South Africa and looking to buy some HEU. He said what he had intended, that the deal was off, the money was nowhere near enough, that he risked the wrath of the Odessa mob with such an insulting offer. He gave it his best shot, but the speech was unconvincing. He didn't believe it himself, and it showed.

The man responded, talking past Blake, addressing Stefan and his crew. He spoke plainly, oozing natural authority, and Blake knew his brief sojourn as a Ukrainian mobster was at an end. The wild wave of violence and intrigue he had ridden since Peshawar had hit the rocks. He'd burned his bridges with Kincaid; he'd dared to dream of leaving the game.

The briefcase was snapped open, the cash revealed. Glancing round at Stefan, Guney and the others, Blake knew they'd accept the offer, and he'd be left with nothing.

But he still had that fire inside, burning bright and raw as it ever had. All he needed now was the right moment to set it free.

Galloway has not been this exposed for years. Indeed, his success so far has hinged upon his policy of complete invisibility. And yet here he stands, in front of a dozen guns, with only Jago at his side. Blake is there, and has recognised him, which is unfortunate, but unavoidable. This is the end game.

There is no sign of Tom Wisher or his sister. The messages between Rachel, Blake and Tom have been tracked: he prays he is not too late. During the past twenty-four hours Tevis has been driving through the surrounding streets with scanning kit slung under his vehicle, building up an accurate map of the catacomb tunnels in the vicinity. Stuart would have been impressed.

Galloway has brought the agreed sum, fifty million in South African rand, a small amount compared to the stakes. Blake wanted much, much more but knows now that he isn't going to get it. His eyes are starting to dart, rat-in-trap style.

Galloway sets out his stall for Stefan. The contraband uranium is tainted after Peshawar, too hot to handle. Florescu senior knew it, tried to leave it behind. Their dream of netting a fortune is just that, a fantasy, sold to them by Bill Blake. But there's no shame in taking the money on the table. It's just business. And they won't get a better offer.

Guney, Stefan's sharper colleague, wants to know why Galloway wants to buy the HEU, if it's so worthless. He says his factory can reprocess it for civilian use and make a tidy profit in the process. Everybody wins.

Blake is shifting his weight, one hand in his pocket. He's getting ready to move. Galloway picks up the nervous energy, so does Jago at his side. As soon as the grenade drops, the sleek agent is in motion, rolling to snatch it, to throw it away from his commanding officer.

The blast detonates in the back of the garage, kicking up debris. The armed mobsters are startled but not sure where to aim their guns, given that the outsiders are the ones who just saved their lives.

As the smoke clears an engine roars. Blake has commandeered a car from the repair shop. The vehicle surges past Galloway, rams into the gap between the black van and the tall doors. It barely fits, its tyres squeal and smoke as Blake floors the gas pedal. The car grinds through the gap, scraping paint from the black van as it barges its way out on to the road.

Stefan's men open fire, riddling the trunk with bullet holes, shattering the rear window. But already the car is revving away down the road outside. Has Blake slipped the net?

More gunshots. Glass smashes. Tyres screech on the tarmac. A metal crash. Galloway runs to the door and sees Blake's getaway car just a few yards away, in the centre of the street, upside down. The windscreen has been knocked in and there is someone else in the car, fighting him.

Tom Wisher.

Forty-two

Shoulder slam, desperate force. The cellar hatch lurched upwards, tipping boxes on the concrete above, and Wisher climbed up into the basement of the empty building where he'd kept watch, the day before.

Rachel was left behind as he raced toward street level, instinct and an explosion telling him that now was the time to face Blake, now was the window. It had to be now.

He sprinted up the basement stairs. Cracked door glass showed daylight behind. He led with his shoulder again, meeting scant resistance from wood and glass. He was outside.

The tall garage doors were right in front of him, the black van rocking as a silver-grey sedan gouged an exit past it. Blake was at the wheel. Gunfire sprayed from inside the garage.

But the car had scraped free, and it was getting away. Wisher had a gun, four bullets. He fired his rounds, puncturing the windscreen. Blake ducked low, avoiding the shots, steering by guesswork, on a trajectory toward Wisher.

The young agent threw down his gun and ran at the car. He jumped, slid over the hood. The windscreen caved and he was inside, on top of his adversary. Blake had his foot jammed down, steering wheel turned hard. The vehicle spun, then rolled.

Amid the moments of whirling disorientation, both

men fought for an angle. As gravity pulled Blake from his seat, he was reaching for his gun. Upside down, Wisher grabbed for his wrist.

The gun discharged into the dashboard, leaving the electrics exposed and sparking. The two were writhing on the upturned car's ceiling, with hardly space to move, knees and elbows jutting and jostling, like twins sharing a womb. Blake had the gun but Wisher was on top. That was the balance between them.

Their faces were close, teeth bared. Wisher was stubble-chinned, grimy from the catacombs; Blake was clean-shaven but grey-skinned and bloodshot from drugs. They strained, testing each other's strength, seeking a weakness. Blake spoke in gasps:

'I've got to . . . hand it to you . . . you're one . . . tough son of a bitch—'

Blake fired again. The bullet punched through the floor of the car above them. Wisher redoubled his efforts. He needed to break the deadlock. He needed to break this bastard underneath him, who beat him and betrayed him, who killed his lover and mutilated his sister. He needed to win. Blake kept talking, distracting him:

'Want to know – a secret?'

A voice shouted in Russian from outside:

'Get out of the car! It's over.'

It was Stefan, playing at being the leader again. A quick glance showed other figures around the vehicle, closing in. Still the two men inside the upturned car remained locked in combat. To give the slightest ground would be to lose everything. This fight was to the death.

Wisher smelt gasoline, saw liquid dripping from the bullet hole in the floor. A severed fuel line. Petrol was dripping on to Blake's back, but he seemed oblivious.

Wisher loosened his grip on Blake's wrist, just the slightest amount. Blake rose up, desperate to capitalise on any sign of vulnerability. Wisher slipped down as Blake turned him. Now they were facing each other. Blake had his back to the dashboard and was hoping to press home his advantage. But Wisher held firm, bracing his legs against the frame of the car.

Stefan was shouting, but they weren't listening. A bubble of quiet seemed to contain them. Blake's voice rasped:

'The man with the scarred face – you know who he is?'

What the hell was Blake on about? Wisher's mind raced, even as his exhausted limbs strained to keep his enemy at bay. Blake sensed Wisher's ignorance, pressed home his point:

'You know who he *really* is?'

Wisher frowned. He couldn't help it. Blake's lips peeled back in his trademark grin. He opened his mouth to speak:

'He's—'

Wisher heaved, pushing Blake back into the dashboard. A spark crackled from the broken wiring, and Blake's gasoline-soaked shirt burst into vivid, fiery life.

Blake's face contorted with animal fear. Wisher wriggled free of the vehicle, leaving Blake to flail, becoming like a flame himself as he waved and shuddered. The car was bound to explode. Stefan's men were already retreating, barely seen.

Wisher staggered, confused. He turned back towards the burning vehicle. A blow from behind brought him down. As he fell to the ground, he saw the sky was blue and clear of clouds. He closed his eyes, happy to disappear.

When Wisher woke up, hours had passed. He was in a hotel suite, somewhere upmarket. In bed, with the heavy, high-quality linen deliciously soft against his bare skin. Medical equipment had been rigged up, monitors and an IV drip.

He got up, wincing at his sore muscles. He was butt naked; he caught sight of himself in a long mirror and hardly recognised his body. He must have lost fifteen pounds and he was literally covered in bruises. His eyes were dull and sunken with tiredness. He looked like a zombie.

There were jeans and a T-shirt laid out for him. He emerged from his room to find an unfamiliar guard on duty in the corridor outside. A woman in her late thirties, dressed in a pantsuit like a politician but with the alertness of a soldier. *One of us*, he thought.

She offered a handshake.

'I'm Ramona. They're through there.' she said, pointing down the corridor. Wisher pushed through a panelled door into a comfortable lounge suite and found Rachel with Jago. They had been talking, but turned as he entered. He quipped:

'I didn't know you did small talk, Jago.'

'We weren't chatting.' Rachel shot him a look laced with anger and he tensed up. Things clearly weren't okay.

'Where's Galloway?'

'Busy.' Typical, less-is-more Jago.

'Just us then.'

There was a pot of coffee on the table. He poured himself a cup, sat down with them at the easy chairs. Cream too, the way he liked it. The coffee, at least, was hitting the spot.

Rachel's hand was wrapped in clean bandages. She cradled it close to her body as she spoke, her voice thick with contempt.

'So this is what you do now, is it? No law, no police, no courts. Just you and your pals, sticking it to the bad guys.'

'Is that such a bad thing?'

'I guess not. I mean, never mind the torture, obviously. Never mind who else dies in the process.'

And now Wisher was reddening, he couldn't help it.

'We didn't kill Stuart.'

'Blake was CIA, Tom.'

'We're not CIA.'

'So who the fuck are you?'

Wisher bit his tongue. He wanted to say more, but he didn't want to draw her in any deeper. Already, his new career had cost them both dearly. Why did she have to be so damn persistent?

Jago interjected, low and firm.

'Blake was a rogue agent. The situation has been managed.'

'Are you going to "manage" me too?'

Wisher rolled his eyes.

'Of course not.' He was hurting as much as her, didn't she understand that? Right now he needed a friend, not an argument. He reached across the table to her, but she lifted her hand away from his touch.

'You know I'm going to make as much noise as I can about this, right? I'm going straight to the police. I'm going to tell them Stuart was murdered. I'm telling them everything.'

'They won't find a body.' That was Jago, to the point as ever.

'It doesn't stop it being the truth.'

An uneasy silence fell. Wisher was irritated, his nerves and senses still raw, but he was trying to contain it.

'What else, Rachel?'

'I'll tell them you're still alive. You work for a man

called Galloway. You're like a secret organisation. Spies R Us. You hunt people down and kill them. You're not loyal to any country. You think you're above the law. Which makes you a criminal, right?'

She glared at her brother; he glared right back.

'No one will believe you, Rach.'

'Some of them will. Maybe just the freaks and weirdos at first. But others will start to listen. I'm telling the truth, after all, aren't I?'

It was a rhetorical question. Wisher slugged back his coffee. The caffeine seemed to buzz around his head like dancing flies. He got to his feet and threw the china cup. It smashed into the wall, splashing a dark stain. Rachel jolted at the impact, a bag of nerves herself. Wisher grabbed her by the shoulders, battling an overwhelming urge to shake some sense into her.

'We're on the same side! We're fighting the same fight!'

She shook herself free from his grasp and stood to face him, guarding her bandaged hand as she shouted:

'No we are not!'

The lines had been drawn. Wisher took a step back, his heart sinking. He'd lost her. She snatched up her jacket.

'I'm going now. Does anyone have a problem with that? Or are you going to "manage" me, or "retire" me or "cap" me or whatever the fuck you call it nowadays?'

'If we're so evil, why *aren't* you dead? Why haven't you been silenced? You're free to go, doesn't that prove anything?'

Rachel wasn't giving an inch.

'If your people wanted me dead, I'd be dead. They'd find a way to sell it to you.'

'No. I don't believe it.'

She sighed wearily. Dismissively.

'It serves you to do what you do. It always has.'

Sibling rivalry? Was that the heart of it? Rachel headed to the door. Wisher limped after her, drained by the squabbling.

'Rachel, please. Can't we talk about this?'

She held up her hand to block him – the hand with stumps for fingers. She held it there in front of his face, knowing it spoke louder than any words. Her face was stern beyond its years.

'When you're behind bars, brother of mine. Then we can talk.'

She stepped out into the corridor, and left. Jago spoke into the bead microphone on his earpiece wire.

'Let her through.'

He glanced over at Wisher, who had slumped into an armchair.

'We should move out. Galloway's waiting.'

Wisher ran his hand through his hair.

'Is it down to me? All this mess, the deaths, the torture. Rachel's fingers. Is it my fault?'

'No.'

There was no doubt in Jago's voice. Not a shade. Wisher was grateful for that. He shot his colleague a somewhat embarrassed look. Jago patted him on the shoulder, which was about as warm as he got.

'There isn't room for love in this life. That's just how it is.'

Wisher nodded. Jago, man of few words, continued.

'When Galloway brought you in, I thought he was making a mistake. But I understand now. A body isn't just brain and muscle. It needs a heart. It needs hope. That's what you bring.'

Wisher shrugged. Jago actually smiled, albeit briefly.

'We need to go. You can help pack up, if you're up to it.'

'Sure.' There would time to think once they were on the road. Right now, Wisher was happy to keep busy.

Forty-three

Kincaid looked at his watch. It was coming up to twenty-four hours since he had been detained. More than enough time for his lawyers to start knocking holes in the case against him. Designer viruses were already at work within the CIA mainframe, destroying and redirecting the data trail even as John Morgan's team tried to follow it. This was the digital age: let them try to make the mud stick without the files to back it up.

Thanks to Peavey, Morgan now possessed various recordings and transcripts of supposedly secure phone conversations between Kincaid and Blake. But even this 'smoking gun' evidence was surprisingly flimsy when the best legal minds money could buy started picking it apart. A lot of the actual dialogues were shorthand and laced with jargon, leaving room for interpretation as to their precise meaning; a lot of what remained could be pinned on Blake. That was the angle his team planned to work. Blake was the real bad guy, not Kincaid. Blake had played his naïve, upstanding boss for a fool while colluding with the late traitor Tom Wisher in a demented plot to spread nuclear terror throughout the world. It hurt Kincaid's pride to play the patsy, but it was the best-fit solution with his current predicament, especially given that Blake was currently in the vicinity of Odessa, precise location unknown. Assets had been activated in the region with orders to make sure he never made it back to the States – unless it was in a body bag.

In the meantime, Kincaid was being held at the D Street police facility in downtown Washington DC, having been confronted in his Langley office by three uniformed officers and a senior detective, at the behest of Morgan. In theory, he was being detained under the Patriot Law, having been accused of conspiring to commit acts of terrorism. In fact he had volunteered to accompany the officers, meaning a formal arrest had not yet been made. It was a bold move, carried out with some swagger by the deputy director. How it must have burned Morgan, to see Kincaid so utterly confident that he would be proved innocent of the charges against him.

An executive cell was how his jailers described it. Roughly ten feet square, clean linen on the bunk. TV. En suite toilet – fitted with surveillance cameras, of course, but still, somewhat civilised. And he wouldn't be here much longer, he reminded himself.

Morgan might be career CIA through and through, and yet he was soft at heart. He saw a basically good world with some bad people in it, which put him at a serious disadvantage when it came to the dirty work of espionage. Kincaid found it hard to believe he had cracked Peavey, until it dawned on him that his assistant might be behind the move to discredit him. This had forced a radical rethink of his situation.

It had seemed inconceivable at first to Kincaid that there could be agents working against him without his knowledge. He himself was a mole, the secret representative of a powerful allegiance of super-rich individuals who had taken it upon themselves to shape world events according to their own agenda. There was no corporation or nation state on earth that could match his hidden paymasters for power or ruthless ambition. Whoever was challenging them must be flying on a wing and a prayer.

There were six on the board. Six multibillionaires. Four had been born into money, though to their credit they had possessed the acumen to make their wealth grow, rather than squander it. Two had self-made fortunes. Amaro was rich too, but he was not on the board, not yet. He was connective tissue, like Kincaid, one of several people charged with implementing the board's directives. A middleman, though he would have you killed for calling him that.

Kincaid didn't like the word 'conspiracy'. It implied secrecy and defiance of the law, which was correct. But there was something old fashioned about the term, too. It reeked of cloaks and daggers, of scaffolds and gunpowder. Kincaid preferred the expression 'necessary evil'. It felt pragmatic and professional, which was more how he saw himself. The world was sick; he was the doctor. If there was pain, it meant the wound was healing. It was a good sign.

The twenty-four hours were at an end. It was time for the authorities to charge him, or release him. On cue, his lawyer showed up. Wade Collins, of Collins Hope Zuckerman, a great white among the shark-infested waters of the capitol. And all the bastard did was hand him a cellphone.

It was Amaro. The conversation did not last long. It turned out Peavey had been more thorough than anticipated. The evidence against Kincaid was substantial and Blake was off the grid – dead, if the latest word from Odessa was to be believed. In short, the trail still led back to Kincaid. He could be linked to the uranium sale in Safed Koh and the subsequent failed nuclear blast. His team could slow the legal process and mitigate the sentence, but its destination was unavoidable: prison. Kincaid would be compensated via the usual offshore channels. He would be truly rich for the first time in his life – but he would be in jail for some years.

Amaro offered a short apology, which Kincaid accepted, and the call was over. Collins added his commiserations, then left, and Kincaid was alone.

He sat down on his bunk. He still had influence, of course; he could arrange for a distraction to be staged uptown then get himself busted out of D Street before his case went to trial. But he would just be stepping into another prison, physically free but massively restricted in wealth and resources, and with the board's top assassins on his tail. No, he had a part to play here. The board had no desire to kill: it wanted to rule, to control. It needed Kincaid and his kind. And it would be grateful for his complicity during the coming weeks and months.

Thoughts gushed cold and clear within him, like a river through the heart of a mountain. He was not finished. Not by a long shot. This unexpected new direction would provide extraordinary opportunities. Since childhood he'd had a knack of bending the weak to his will. What better place to find weak men than in prison? His innate arrogance kicked into high gear. Within a few months, he would be running the place.

He lay back, checked his watch, then tucked his hands behind his head. Morgan would be getting the news around now. Fucking John Morgan, who had finally decided to grow a pair after a life of eating humble pie. Kudos to Morgan for finding the guts to stand up and be counted. He'd taken on Kincaid and he'd won the battle, if not the war. He'd earned a place at the high table. Let him see how he liked the view.

★ ★ ★

Morgan sat alone in his office, thinking. He hadn't slept, but he wasn't tired. Not since the news had come. David Morgan, aged twenty-six, architect, had been knocked from his bicycle last night. The young man had died in hospital soon after. Morgan and his wife had been at his side. An apparent hit and run; David's injuries were consistent with a vehicle impact. No witnesses.

When Morgan closed his eyes, he imagined his own hands on the wheel of that truck. He saw his son, ahead of him on the road, caught in the headlights. He felt the jolt through his seat as the thick tyres of his vehicle mounted the kerb; then another jolt, softer, as the juggernaut ran over the cyclist.

He had killed his own son.

When his eyes were open, he could put the facts together more rationally. It was Kincaid, punishing him, just as he had threatened to do. He had underestimated his superior's ruthlessness, overestimated his own altruism. If he had known the true cost of exposing the deputy director's corruption, he would not have proceeded.

He could certainly relate to Kincaid's disdain for the law. He'd had a crash course, if you like. Due process be damned. There was only one way to balance the books now, and that was man to man.

Morgan felt the hot flush of freedom. Right now, he truly didn't care if he lived or died. This wasn't to neglect his wife, or his surviving son. They would want what he wanted. Revenge.

This internal shift in Morgan's priorities didn't mean his personality was suddenly erased. He was still thoughtful and articulate. He was still organised. He showered and changed, packed an overnight bag, made sure he had the right plastic in his wallet. The funeral was scheduled for the following week, but it didn't seem appropriate to wait until then. The situation required immediate attention.

D Street would be his starting point; there might be an opportunity to strike while his former boss was being relocated to another holding facility or even – the thought made Morgan shudder – being released back on to the street pending a review of his case or some such legal bullshit. That particular outcome was not permissible. The revolver would do for now but he was thinking about more subtle weapons, too. Poison appealed, for some reason. The concept had metaphorical weight. Poison got inside you, muddied your senses, went about its business in secret, an unseen killer. Toxic, like Kincaid. Like the CIA and the whole goddamned spy game.

He found his wife in the kitchen, at the counter. She had made coffee, but hadn't touched her cup. Instead she was staring at a framed photograph of her two sons. One of them sat at the breakfast table across from her; the other was in transit from the morgue.

'I have to go away. Business.'

The euphemism was for the benefit of the field agent who stood on discreet guard duty by the screen door, on the orders of the director himself. Morgan knew this particular officer and trusted him. He was happy to have extra protection on the home front. Although he had said nothing to his colleagues about his conviction that Kincaid was behind his son's death, he still saw his other family members as being under threat. Who knew how much a pound of flesh weighed nowadays?

His wife didn't seem perturbed by his announcement. In fact she hardly looked up as she replied.

'Call me when you close the deal.'

She knew the truth. He had shared his suspicions with her, because he wanted her to know that David was not in any way responsible – and also that he was partly to blame. He couldn't expect her to stay with him on any other terms. He wouldn't presume to ask for her forgiveness now. But he needed something: acknowledgement, perhaps, that this could be their last goodbye.

'Gail . . .'

She did glance at him then, with twin black holes of grief and anger and indignity. He felt his soul shrivel up and fly away, like a scrap of polythene caught on a bonfire.

'Go. You've got work to do.'

Morgan nodded once, and left.

Forty-four

'I won't kill for you. I'll defend myself but I won't kill to order.'

'Why not?' asks Galloway. They are speaking on the phone. Wisher is in the back of the unit vehicle, heading towards the safe house in Poland. Galloway is elsewhere.

'Because it's wrong.'

It's a valid opinion. On another occasion, Galloway might want to argue the point. Killing a man who is about to detonate a nuclear bomb, for example, might be considered a good idea, if morally debatable. Even Tom Wisher seemed to think so, once upon a time.

The young agent continues:

'I want to work for you. I think I can make a difference. But not through murder. There are courts and prisons and lawyers. We are not the only people interested in justice.'

'We are the only ones who know who the real enemy is.'

Ethics aside, he doesn't want his newest asset to self-impose a limit on his capabilities. But Wisher is insistent.

'If you can use me, then use me. But those are my terms.'

The man called Galloway, the lion, the dying general, smiles. Not with irony, or scorn, or weariness. Not with effort, to ease the fears of those who look to him for guidance.

He smiles because he is proud.

The phone call ends and darkness descends. He takes a plastic evidence bag from his pocket. It contains four fingertips, collected from the labyrinth by Tevis. The flesh stumps are blackening now. He'll bin them soon – but not just yet.

Trigger Point

He steered clear of Rachel in the wake of the Odessa show-down. No point in picking at that particular scab, hardened many years ago. It pains him that she has set herself in opposition to his organisation, but that is a problem for the future.

He examines the finger stumps, reminding himself. Right now the world can wait. He has pressing business to attend to.

Forty-five

As the fire engulfed him, Blake's life rushed past, just like they always say it does. The career of the spy, the killings, the countries, fell away quickly from his mind's eye. Tom Wisher's face, filled with hatred, dissolved like a chalk drawing on the sidewalk, caught in the rain. Rachel's face replaced her brother's, frowning, judging, then swallowed by shadows.

His childhood loomed up with its playground victories and indignities. He ached for the crisp air and breathtaking vistas of the White Mountains, his private image of heaven. He wished he'd returned more often to the raw tranquillity of its crags and valleys. He wished he'd stayed there.

In a cave among the ragged peaks, the serpent Kundalini coiled tight around the knowledge that his father never, ever liked him. The cave reached far back into the mountain, its darkness drawing him in effortlessly, like a leaf on an unseen stream. Cold yet comforting, the void was bliss, and Blake was grateful.

Then he woke up. He couldn't see, and panic gripped him. He was in bed; he tried to sit up and found himself restrained. He fought for calm; the pounding of his heart receded. He could hear the sounds of hospital equipment: monitor beeps, fluid bubbles, the sigh of a ventilator. There was a tube down his throat. Footsteps padded closer, and the tube was withdrawn. He gasped. It hurt to widen his mouth. He couldn't imagine what kind of ruined state his body was in. Did he still have eyes? Why the fuck was he still alive?

A voice spoke, somewhere close by, and Blake understood why. Because of all the shit in his head, that was why.

'Been a while, Bill.'

They hadn't greeted each other, back in Odessa. Hardly surprising, what with the uranium and the hand-grenade, not to mention the guns and the torture. In fact, maybe that was the reason he had been kept alive. On reflection, torturing Tom Wisher and his sister had probably not been the smartest move. Who knew their father was still on the scene?

Blake's jaw could hardly move – probably not a whole lot of meat left on the bone. His voice emerged reluctantly, dry and rasping as it broke the crust of his face.

'Hello, Frank . . .'